Denise Robertson has worked extensively on television and radio and as a national journalist. Starting with *The Land of Lost Content* in 1984, which won the Constable Trophy for Fiction, she has published sixteen successful novels. Denise lives near Sunderland with her husband, one of her five sons and an assortment of dogs.

D1017735

Also by Denise Robertson

The Land of Lost Content
A Year of Winter
Blue Remembered Hills
The Land of Lost Content: The Belgate Trilogy
The Second Wife
None to Make you Cry
Remember the Moment
The Stars Burn Out
The Anxious Heart
The Beloved People
Strength for the Morning
Towards Jerusalem
A Relative Freedom
Act of Oblivion
Daybreak
Wait for the Day

ILLUSION

DENISE ROBERTSON

POCKET
B O O K S

LONDON · SYDNEY · NEW YORK · TOKYO · SINGAPORE · TORONTO

First published in Great Britain by Simon & Schuster UK Ltd, 1998
This edition first published by Pocket Books, 1999
An imprint of Simon & Schuster UK Ltd
A Viacom Company

1 3 5 7 9 10 8 6 4 2

Simon & Schuster UK Ltd
Africa House
64–78 Kingsway
London WC2B 6AH

Simon & Schuster Australia
Sydney

A CIP catalogue for this book is available from the British Library

ISBN 0-671-01035-2

Typeset by SX Composing DTP, Rayleigh, Essex
Printed and bound in Great Britain by Caledonian International
Book Manufacturing, Glasgow

ILLUSION

London, Saturday, 29 March 1997

The presenters were turning to one another, beaming euphorically as the last thirty seconds of the final programme ticked away. "Demob happy," someone whispered in Rachel's ear.

She glanced back to see Pat from Wardrobe. "Aren't we all?"

There were only seconds to go now, but as floor manager she was responsible for everything that happened and couldn't afford to relax until the last credit faded from the screen.

"So we'll be back with you in the autumn." The presenter raised a farewell hand to camera, there was the sound of a cork popping, and then champagne was foaming into glasses as the signature tune began and the credits rolled over a crowd composed of everyone who worked on the programme, all of them smiling and waving to camera and jigging in time to the music.

"Nine . . . eight . . . seven . . . six . . ." In Rachel's ear the count went down. "Three . . . two . . . one" "Thank you, everyone," she said, removing her headset. "That's it. We're clear."

People were appearing from behind the cameras with plates of food, presenters and researchers were clustering around the champagne, but the crew worked on, repositioning cameras and microphone booms, winding up the studio so that it was ready for whoever would take over.

When at last she could abandon duty Rachel moved over to join the others. "Freedom!" Dave, the lighting technician rolled his eyes in ecstasy. "Where are you off to next, Rach?"

Rachel shrugged. "Who knows? I'm seeing Nick the week after next. I'm hoping I'll get a break before he reassigns me. In the meantime I'm off to Paris this evening and then north for my sister's wedding. What about you?"

"Well, not Paris, that's for sure. Paris!" He feigned awe.

"It's for two days, Dave. Leigh's there, working. We'll only have Sunday — he's due back on Monday."

"Well . . ." Dave raised his glass. "It's been good working with you, Rachel. Here's hoping we do it again."

"I'd like that." They clinked glasses and moved off in different directions. It was always like this at the end of a series. So many goodbyes to say, so many awkward moments with people whose contracts would not be renewed . . . and too much false bonhomie from people who had bugged you for nine months and were now ready to kiss you on both cheeks and tell you you meant the world to them. She gritted her teeth, fixed her smiled and set out on the rounds. Best to get it over quickly and then make a dash for Heathrow.

Three hours later she was airborne. She lay back in her seat and looked out on packed cloud. Somewhere down below England was slipping away, the Channel was rocking gently. Soon she would be landing in Paris and Leigh would be waiting at the airport. She closed her eyes and thought about how good that would be.

They had been apart for almost a week. Leigh had gone off on Monday morning, less than enthusiastically it had to be said. "Who wants to be in Paris now, darling, when everything's happening here?"

"Here" was a Britain rocked by election fever, the Tories seemed to be disintegrating by the hour and Leigh was completing a documentary on the French National Front that had been commissioned a year ago, before the English political scene had hotted up. "Cheer up," she had soothed him. "It's only one more week and then you'll be back on the scene." But they both knew that the plum election jobs had been allocated weeks, if not months, before. He would be lucky to get the minor interviews and not be condemned to a long run of vox pops in tricky constituencies.

She made a vow to give him a wonderful weekend to cheer him up, and then thought ahead to the wedding and her trip home to Harrogate. Liz, her middle sister, had been licking her wounds after the break-up of a disastrous marriage when Hugh entered her life and, as far as the family could tell, he was the perfect husband-to-be. "Let her be happy." Rachel offered up a silent prayer and then smiled to herself. For someone who wasn't sure there was a God she did a fair amount of praying. Leigh called it superstition but whatever it was it was comforting.

She opened her eyes as a steward reached to lower her table so that he could set down a neatly packed tray. The male aircrew on Air France planes all had world-weary Sacha Distel faces, but they wore wedding rings and their eyes flicked disinterestedly over female passengers, unlike the Italians who seemed to be looking eternally for romance.

The French stewardesses were elegant, with lacquered faces and little touches of chic that set them apart. One had a knotted rope of pearls that streamed defiantly down her uniform jacket. Another had a tiny chiffon scarf knotted tightly at the base of her neck. They all looked wonderful.

Rachel tried not to be envious and turned her attention to the meal. The salmon terrine starter was eatable and Rachel crunched dutifully on the various foliage around it before pushing her tray aside, saving only the tiny coffee cup. Tonight they would dine somewhere special and then go back to the hotel and bed. She tried to suppress a smile that must surely be lascivious, but no one was watching so what did it matter?

Leigh was waiting just outside the arrivals lounge at Charles de Gaulle. "Rachel!" He was bending to kiss her, relieving her of her bags, taking her elbow. "God, am I glad to see you," he said, and she gave herself up to the luxury of being cherished.

They made love as soon as they reached the hotel. "You're sure you're not hungry?" he asked, but already he was reaching for her.

"What about you?" Her hands were already at his tie, the neck of his shirt, unbuttoning it and peeling it back so that she could kiss the so-desirable flesh.

And then he was kissing her, soft kisses at first, on her lips, her eyes, her neck. Fiercely on the mouth now, his tongue licking, pushing, joining with hers in that union so disgusting with anyone except the one you love.

"You're beautiful, Rachel," he said, when at last they were quiet, lying together on the padded coverlet, warm where their limbs touched, shivering slightly where they did not, listening to the sounds of Paris outside the window as evening fell. Unwilling to move because that would mean it was over and they wanted it to last.

2

Paris, Sunday, 30 March 1997

They lingered over breakfast, sitting cross-legged on the bed to eat dripping croissants and drink hot, sweet, pungent coffee. "What shall we do today?" Leigh licked butter from his fingers and looked at her expectantly.

"Not much," Rachel said. "A nice quiet day would suit me very well."

"Tough week?" He was sympathetic.

"The last week's always hectic. People get excitable, timings go, every hand-over to ITN's a cliffhanger. I felt such relief when the credits rolled yesterday. I can't describe it."

"Will you go back next series?" He was munching a *pain au chocolat* as he spoke.

"Probably. At the moment I feel once was enough but you know how bad memories fade and you only remember the good times. It was a good crew and the presenters were more bearable than most."

"Thank you!" he said. "I'm a presenter, remember?"

"Exactly," she said, and ducked as he reached out to slap her.

They had meant to get out early to make the most of the day but the shower was their downfall. He stepped in beside her, drawing her close, cupping his hands to decant small pools of water on to her soapy body. In the end he held her with one hand while reaching with the other to turn off the flow. "Not again," she said weakly, but it was more in astonishment than disapproval.

It was sunny when they emerged at last into the Paris street. "Nice," Leigh said, lifting his face. His dark hair was still damp and curling from the shower, his tanned face thin and vigorous in spite of the shadows beneath his eyes. I love him, Rachel thought exultantly. I really, really love him.

They walked along the Champs Elysées and then through the subway to the Arc de Triomphe. The creamy stone glowed pale apricot in the sunshine and they sat down on a stone bench.

"It's wonderful, isn't it?" Rachel said, contemplating the carved roof with its pattern of flowers and cherubs. "How ever many times I see it, I marvel."

"Napoleon's stamp is everywhere upon this city." Leigh was surveying the walls where the names of Napoleon's heroes and their battles were listed. Jaffa, Peschiera, Riveredo . . . Moreau and Lafayette and Bernadotte. They sat on until the stone struck chill into them and it was time to move on to a pavement café and warm themselves with coffee and Cognac.

down." She tried to sound animated about going home but, really, she would have liked to stay longer in Paris.

Tonight they would be in their own flat for the first time in a week, but she knew he would be preoccupied with letters and faxes and phone messages accumulated in their absence. And on Wednesday she was going north for her sister's wedding.

She could hear Leigh talking about the forthcoming interview but her mind had wandered to her sister, Liz, and the forthcoming ceremony.

"Le Pen was a Poujadist at first . . . in the 'fifty-six election. That was a dirty campaign but it got them two and a half million votes." There was a pause and then he spoke sharply. "Sorry if I'm boring you." When she looked up she saw that he was frowning, and she hastened to mend fences.

"No, I was just thinking about Le Pen, wondering if he'll co-operate. I know it means a lot to you."

"I'll survive." He was brushing his short brown hair with brisk strokes. "Four weeks and two days to polling day. Who in Britain gives a shit for nationalism in Europe?"

"I'll miss you next week," she said, hoping to divert him. He turned and smiled, the rueful smile that always melted her.

"I know, darling. I'd be there if I could, you know that. Tell the newly-weds to come and stay. I'll get to know them properly then. Fix it up for after the election and I'll make sure I'm free."

She was used to going home alone but it still hurt. She

thought of the questions, the raised eyebrows, worst of all the sympathy. Last time Vanessa had said, "Poor you . . . Still, if you will shack up with a household name what else do you expect?"

As if he had read her thoughts, Leigh crossed to the bed and took her in his arms. "I love you, you know that. It's this business, it's death to family life." A long kiss, and then he was gone.

When she had finished packing she took up her coat and handbag, and rang down to the concierge. Leigh had promised to sign the bill on his way out. Once a bell-boy had taken charge of the bags she was free to walk out into the streets.

Yesterday the prospect of a day to herself in Paris had not seemed intimidating. Now that it was here, seven hours seemed an eternity. You couldn't walk for seven hours, or window-shop. She walked for two blocks before sinking down at the nearest pavement table and ordering *café filtre*.

The tiny cup seemed to empty almost immediately. She thought about ordering another but if she drank coffee like this in the first few minutes of the day what would become of her? She took the bill from under the saucer and wandered inside to pay.

By the time she emerged into the sunshine she had half made up her mind to go to the Tuileries gardens but as she looked for a taxi she noticed a small art gallery across the way. She could browse there for half an hour, might even find inspiration. Her deadline was looming ever nearer and a little help would not come amiss.

There was a nude portrait on an easel in the centre of the tiny window, a stark picture of a naked woman staring uncompromisingly at those who dared to play voyeur. The signature in the top right-hand corner was that of Suzanne Valadon, the date 1931. Rachel had learned of Valadon, the mother of Maurice Utrillo, while she was studying for her degree. Valadon had been the model for many of the famous names of French art, and mistress of most of them. She had also been a greatly undervalued painter. Rachel tried the door but it was locked. A cab came into view and she hailed it.

At the Tuileries she paid off the cab and made her way to the ornamental pond. Everywhere the horse chestnuts were in blossom, pink and white, each tiny flower perfect, a little white orchid with pink stripes, clustered together in what she had always thought of as candle shapes. She had called horse chestnuts candle-trees when she was a child. Now she sat on a green metal chair and watched as the single blooms fluttered to the ground like flakes of snow.

"April in Paris, chestnuts in blossom." She had come to Paris for the first time when she was fourteen. They had stayed at the Hôtel Meurice because her father was a military man and fascinated with its war-time history. "This was the officers' mess for Allied HQ in the war," he had said in awed tones, and her mother's eyebrows had signalled that she should look suitably impressed. How happy they had been while she was growing up. At first the five of them, mother, father and three sisters, had moved around Europe because of her father's job, from barracks to barracks, but her mother had made each temporary home the safest place on earth. And then, when it was only her and her parents, all she could remember was laughter.

A sparrow was perching on a nearby chair, its hair-like inch-long claws clutching the green slats. "I've nothing for you," Rachel said ruefully. It cocked its head then flew away and she turned her attention to the water. Metal containers were anchored below the surface, supporting green water plants, and at one end of the pool a lonely statue stood in an amphitheatre filled with weeds. There was a clump of irises, too, unopened and tight, not yet ready to burst forth. They would probably be yellow if they grew by water. If only she could stay here for a month and see them bloom! For a while she was lost in contemplation of the month ahead. Where would her next job be? When she looked at her watch, an hour had gone by. It was going to be all right, after all.

She had lunch outside a café opposite the Paris Opéra. As she ate her omelette *fines herbes* and sipped wine, she marvelled at the splendour of the opera house, the gilded figures at the gate, and the eagles atop the green dome. Impossibly ornate, impossibly French. The windows of the upper storeys were shuttered, except for one draped with curtains. From behind them two children were peeping. Offspring of the châtelaine? Strange to think of children existing in that vast, echoing edifice.

She narrowed her eyes, imagining the early days of the Opéra, the great names of Paris with their wives on their arms ... or perhaps their mistresses. Nowadays the

Afterwards they took the Métro to Trocadero and emerged to see the Eiffel Tower before them, like something from a fairy-tale.

A black man was dancing on the terrace, to music emanating from a ghetto-blaster. His feet were swift and agile, making staccato rappings on the pavement. They stood watching admiringly for a time before moving on, down towards the bridge over the Seine, its ramparts lined with paintings offered as originals but looking suspiciously alike.

"Conveyor-belt art," Leigh said, tugging her onward when she would have lingered to look. "Where do you want to eat tonight?" he asked as they moved on. "I won't see much of you tomorrow so let's make tonight special."

Rachel would have been content to walk all day, hand in hand as now, but she knew he loved the intimacy of good restaurants, liked to use his plastic, eat and drink well.

"Montparnasse," she said. "Someone told me about a place where you get wonderful oysters. I've got the address in my bag at the hotel."

They slept for an hour or two when they got back, falling asleep almost immediately, face to face, feeling each other's breath like a benediction.

When they awoke it was dusk and they stood in the window, looking down on the street, seeing families returning from family gatherings, watching young lovers hurry to meetings, still checking their appearances as they went. When at last they turned from the window Rachel felt tranquil. Her stay in Paris had been brief, uneventful even, but it had been good.

They took the Métro to Montparnasse, rocketing high over Paris streets, sometimes through quarters that looked rough and uninviting but always interesting. Even this early in the year the pavements of Montparnasse were thronged with tourists, peering into buildings that seemed, almost without exception, to be given over to food.

One restaurant they passed was crowded but Leigh tugged at her sleeve. "Look," he said. A man was sitting at a restaurant table munching his way through a plate of *moules*. There was a white napkin tucked in at his neck and a frown of concentration on his face. But it was the chair opposite that had attracted Leigh's attention.

It was occupied by a terrier, sitting erect, watching every mouthful taken by its master but otherwise immobile.

"It's so good!" Rachel said.

"Obviously well trained." Leigh was already moving away but Rachel stayed put. There was something sad about the pair and she felt tears prick her eyes at the sight of the lonely diner and his faithful companion.

They moved on then, to La Coupole where the oysters were indeed luscious, the waiters glided between ornamental pillars and a Cuban band played to lend gaiety to the evening.

"Champagne, I think," Leigh said grandly. "I think my grateful employers can afford it."

They clinked glasses and gazed into one another's eyes. "Happy?" Leigh asked, and she nodded emphatically.

3

Paris, Monday, 31 March 1997

The familiar shapes of dressing-table, chair and linen box did not swim into focus as Rachel's eyes adjusted to daylight. Instead there was a blank wall, peach-coloured and dappled by sun filtering through curtains rippled by a breeze. Of course! She was in Paris, in an hotel room with a window that opened on to a narrow street. Last night Leigh had struggled to open it, declaring it unreasonably warm for the last day of March.

She felt him stir beside her. "What time is it?"

The travelling-clock on the bedside table showed seven fifteen. She turned on her side and kissed his ear where it peeped above the duvet. "Time to get up."

He snuggled further down. "Don't fool about. What time is it really?"

"Seven fifteen." There was stillness and then he was turning, reaching for her. She hesitated, wondering if there would be time, hating the idea that he might love her and leave her. Instantly, because once satisfied he was again the journalist and not the lover. But her hesitation was only momentary. His lips were warm and sleepy, his hands alive and questing. She gave herself up to the pleasure of it and tried not to think that their Parisian idyll was almost over.

Afterwards, she listened as he showered, heard the hum of his razor, watched as he moved purposefully around the bedroom. Against the white towel that swathed his hips, his body was an even tan.

"Wake up!" He was bending to kiss her as he strapped on his watch but she could tell that his thoughts were already elsewhere because his green-grey eyes were vacant, his brow furrowed.

"I am awake," she said. "I was thinking."

"What about?" He did not wait for an answer. "What are you going to do today?"

"Nothing much. Window-shop probably, until it's time to meet you at the airport."

Today he was hoping to interview the leader of the French National Front Jean le Pen. After that, they were free to go home.

"Are you sure you'll be finished in time to catch the flight?"

He grimaced. "I'll be finished! I can't wait to get this job edited and done with. God knows when it'll go out. 'Who gives a fig for France at the moment?' I said. But they never listen. So . . ." He was looking around the room to see if he had forgotten anything.

"Don't worry, I'll check around before I send the bags

it chose to do so. The plane was gaining speed, the ground falling away until puffs of cloud began to obscure her view.

"OK?" She saw that Leigh was looking at her and realised that her hands had tensed on the arm-rests.

"I was thinking about Le Pen." Below them, the cloud was now an Arctic waste, seeming as solid as pack ice. "He couldn't ever gain power, could he?"

"Not in our lifetime." Leigh patted her hand reassuringly. "Anyway, not to worry. We've problems of our own at home. It'll be a Labour landslide but how they'll fulfil everyone's expectations is another story." He unfastened his seat-belt and closed his eyes. "What time do you leave on Wednesday?"

"About lunch-time." She had hoped he would suggest something nice for tomorrow, a loving farewell before their separation, but he only grunted and settled down in his seat. "We'll do something nice when you get back," he said, closing his eyes. "Unless they need me for campaign coverage, of course."

Rachel struggled to see the humorous side of it, even pondered briefly whether or not she should jerk him awake with an ultimatum, but he was asleep now, his face softened by exhaustion, and she hadn't the heart to disturb him. Besides, she had always known how much his job meant to him.

I'll think about it tomorrow, she thought, and closed her own eyes for sleep.

4

"It's a suicide wish, of course. The whole bloody Tory party scrambling over one another to leap off the precipice!" Leigh was still wading through Sunday's papers, Monday's piled neatly beside him waiting their turn. "I mean, what can you say about Merchant?"

The newspapers were full of political indiscretions, almost exclusively Tory. The affair between Piers Merchant, member for the safe Tory seat of Beckenham, and a seventeen-year-old Soho club hostess was splashed across the tabloids, the chairman of the Scottish Conservative party had resigned because of "an indiscretion" and Neil Hamilton, who seemed to have been enmired in sleaze allegations for years was being urged to withdraw from the election.

"He's been a fool," Rachel said.

"Who?" Leigh had already moved on. "Oh, Merchant. Silly bugger. It's Hamilton who interests me, though.

What I'd give to have the real low-down on that!"

"We'll know when the Downey Report comes out," Rachel said, but Leigh's response was a hearty guffaw.

"God, I love you, Rachel. You really believe in the establishment, don't you? Wait for the inquiry then we'll have the truth! My darling, most inquiries bear as little relation to the truth as I do to Chou En-lai, because most people giving evidence to them lie through their teeth."

Rachel resented his patronising attitude but it wasn't worth trying to defeat his cynicism. It was best to leave him alone when he was in a mood like this.

"Well," Leigh was folding his papers and rising to his feet, "I'd better get going. We hope to go in to edit straight away if there's a suite available. I can't wait to be done with Le Pen and get my teeth into Major and Blair. If I get the chance, of course."

"You will." She tried to sound reassuring but news was a cut-throat area of the profession. Leigh would be in on the election only if someone, somewhere, liked his face. "What do you want to do about food while I'm away? I could freeze a casserole and do some pasta." She so often had to leave him to his own devices, it would be nice to be domesticated for a change.

"No need. To be honest, darling, I don't expect to do more than touch base while you're away. No reason to come home if you're not here." He was planting a kiss on the top of her head as he spoke. "I'll probably doss at the office and eat out most of the time."

"Not at Mario's, I hope." She shuddered, remembering seafood linguini that had rendered her prostrate with

vomiting last month. She had blamed the mussels but
Leigh had been sceptical.

"Not at Mario's, if it keeps you happy. I still say you
had gastric flu, though. I'll probably eat near the office."

She felt a sense of relief that there was no need to rush
around shopping and cooking. Her mother seemed to
enjoy caring for people around the clock but she had not
passed on the trait to her youngest daughter.

Rachel thought about her mother as she showered.
Maternal, certainly, strong, resourceful, always calm . . .
and yet completely in her father's shadow. No, Rachel
thought suddenly, as she blow-dried her hair. That's not
true. The Army had made the big decisions, where they
lived and for how long. And Daddy had decided things
like holidays and expeditions. But it was her Mum who
had coped, Mum who had made things tick.

Once had dressed she set about tidying her bedroom.
When at last it was to her satisfaction it was twelve
thirty. Outside, the sun was shining. She could go for a
walk in the park, get something for their evening meal on
the way back. She would make do with a bowl of soup in
the meantime, which would leave her free to house-clean
for at least two hours.

She encountered Jago on the landing. He was huddled
inside his sheepskin, which usually meant he was hung
over because the ancient coat was his comfort blanket.
Behind his wire spectacles his eyes were narrowed, as
though in pain. "How was Paris?" he asked, in martyred
tones. And then, without waiting for an answer, "It was
shitty here while you were gone. Nothing but rain and the

23

place like a morgue."

"Two drops of rain, then, and you only gave three parties?"

"God, you're mistrustful," he said bitterly. "And going out as well, before your feet have touched the ground! Some people."

"You can come in for some soup when I get back," she said, moving past him. "And I've got a pressie for you."

"Thanks but no thanks," he said. "Unless its vodka consommé. I could brighten up a bit for that. The lunch, I mean. I'll be glad of the pressie whatever it is, as long as it's expensive."

"Ungrateful boy," she said, carrying on down the stairs. "See you at one fifteen."

This morning she had read a meteorological report stating that last month had been the third warmest March in Britain since records began in 1659, and seated in the park she could believe it.

She sat on a bench for a while, feeling the sun on her face, listening to the far-off sounds of traffic on the road outside and children playing in the sanded section reserved for them. Her eyes snapped open as a child cried out. A group of mothers clustered together on a bench had scattered like startled birds at the sound of one of their offspring in trouble.

The child who had yelled was crying now, rubbing his eyes with tiny balled fists. The girl who went up to him looked, at first, too young to be his mother but the way they reacted to one another showed he was indeed her child. She was patient at first, trying to find out what was wrong, but as his sobs continued she grew increasingly frustrated. Finally she seized him by one arm, yanking him until his feet left the ground. Rachel looked at the other mothers, hoping one of them would intervene, but they sat placidly, obviously seeing nothing wrong in their friend's behaviour.

She's too young to have a child, Rachel thought. She felt her mouth purse in disapproval but she didn't move from her seat. Instead, as the still-yelling child was dragged back to the group of mothers, she tried to imagine what it must be like to be responsible for another human being . . . a small but already individual human being. It would be frightening. Thank God for the pill. Yesterday she had finished her cycle, any moment there would be the comforting bleed that meant she was safe. She got to her feet and turned for home.

She bought mince at the delicatessen-cum-butcher and a string of huge Spanish onions. She would cook the mince, then jazz it up in a lasagne. She pictured the scene. A nice bottle, the candles Liz had given her at Christmas, their favourite Eric Clapton on the stereo and a night together, their last for a week.

Jago was waiting on the landing when she got home, blond and rangy and looking less like a refugee from the night before. "Soup still on?" he asked hopefully.

"Come in," she said. "I don't suppose you've eaten since we left."

"*Au contraire*, cleversides. I had lunch at the Ivy with someone who just might keep me in work for the rest of my life."

"Who?" She was opening a tin of minestrone, slicing bread for the toaster, reaching for the butter dish.

"A bloke from the BBC. It'll probably come to nothing but he seemed to know what he was talking about. He wants me to do some session work but he's interested in my own music. He does drama-docs. It could be fruitful. We'll just have to wait and see."

They sat either side of the kitchen table to eat their soup. "What was Paris like?"

"Nice," she said. "Very nice. It's always lovely to get away but there's something about Paris."

"What did you do?" He reached for more toast.

"Ate and drank. And ate and drank. Walked in the Tuileries gardens. Slept."

"But not a lot. I know you two. Insatiable."

"I should be so lucky. We work too hard to be sex-mad — Well, Leigh does. And this was a working trip, remember."

"On expenses, then. Jammy buggers." He drained his mug and stood up. "It pains me to deprive you of my company but I've work to do. I'm glad you're back."

"Not for long. I'm going north, remember."

"Oh, the family gathering. Poor you. They're terrible things, family reunions. Skeletons out of cupboards, nookie behind the portcullis, all kinds of mayhem."

"Not in my family." She knew she sounded smug but it didn't matter. "We get on well. Always have done. The only fly in the ointment was Liz's first husband. Steve. He was a bastard. I don't think that's too strong a word. But this new man is wonderful . . . right for her. We all like him."

"Oh, well . . ." Jago paused in the doorway. "I'm glad someone has the perfect family background. My lot were more dysfunctional than the Windsors, and that's saying something."

"Get out," Rachel said amicably. "I won't have treason in here. I'll see you before I go, though."

"You might, if nothing better turns up. Only kidding, you know I adore you."

As he clattered down the stairs Rachel smiled to herself. He was fond of her, she knew that. And it was mutual. One day, hopefully, he would make a lasting relationship. He was out of sight before she remembered his underpants. She would have to give them to him tomorrow.

She put him out of her mind then and went back to work. Except that as she dusted and polished one sad little face kept intruding, the face of the boy with the child-mother. Mothers should be grown-up, as her mother had been. I've been lucky, Rachel thought. Very lucky indeed. She was like her mother in so many ways. Genes were wonderful things. At six o'clock she abandoned her duster and went to get ready for Leigh coming home.

She had showered and changed, put the lasagne in the oven, made up her face and was reaching for the matches to light the candles when his call came. "Sorry, darling, but they want me in Beckenham for vox pops. The Tories are meeting tomorrow to decide whether or not to sling out Merchant. If they do there'll have to be a new candidate. Imagine that now, at the eleventh hour."

"Will you be home before I leave?"

"Of course. I'm doing the interviews tonight . . . Conservative clubs, nightclubs, anywhere I can find the punters. I'll bring the film back as soon as I've finished. I should be home by three or four but go to bed. We'll talk tomorrow. I might even be able to see you off. I'll try."

But as she climbed into the lonely bed she knew he would not see her off. He would be swept into the whirlpool of election fervour that was engulfing the media. And she had better accept it because that was how it was going to be.

5

They woke to sunlight filtering through the curtains. Rachel had already been in bed when Leigh returned at two a.m. and they had both simply tumbled into sleep. Now Rachel hoped he would turn to her as he usually did, but it was not to be. "God, what a day ahead," he said, and reached to fumble for the bedside radio. John Major was rumoured to be making a speech and everyone was forecasting what it would contain. She turned on her side and put out a tentative hand. He did not flinch as she touched his chest but his only response was to lift his arm and slide it beneath her head.

She lay there for a while in the crook of his arm, wondering if she should point out that it would be six days before they were together again. In the end, listening to his intake of breath at this news item or that, she decided against it. He loved his work, lived for it almost. She had known that from the start, unfair to let it irritate her

29

now. She felt him grow tense as the eight o'clock pips sounded and roused herself. "Eggs all right?" she asked, and reached for her wrap.

"I love you," he said, as they parted on the landing. "Just let me get the next few weeks over . . ."

"I know!" She put up her face to be kissed, to interrupt what was threatening to be an apology that would be embarrassing for them both. "I'll get back as soon as I can on Monday. We could have a meal somewhere . . . or I can cook. I'll bring something back with me . . ."

"Hey!" It was his turn to interrupt. "Don't go domesticated on me. You're the girl who said she couldn't boil water, remember?" Long after they had embraced and parted she stood on the landing, listening to his departing footsteps, remembering the night they had decided to move in together.

"I can't cook!" She had said it because she was suddenly overcome with embarrassment and excitement and couldn't think of anything else to say.

"It doesn't matter. I make a mean Bolognese. That'll do for us. I love you, Rachel. I've never felt like this before. All I know is I want you there when I get home. And I never felt like that before."

"Me neither."

"Nor me," he corrected her jokingly. "Anyway, what do you say?"

It was later, long after her joyful acceptance, that they had laid down the ground rules. No joint bank account, no questions about work on either side, no statutory home-times, above all no children. "Not yet, anyway, Rachel.

Not while things are so fluid." She had never questioned that he would be faithful because she knew their love was unassailable and she had been more than happy then to wait for life to settle before they had children.

As far as she could see, however, his life as a freelance television journalist would never be less than fluid, never safer than a twelve-month contract. She picked up the milk from its metal basket on the landing and went back into the flat.

She was in the shower when the phone rang. For a second she hesitated. It was probably Phil about work and he would call back later. But the ringing continued until she snatched a towel and padded, dripping, into the bedroom.

"Rachel? It's me, Van." Vanessa was her eldest sister and not given to making phone calls.

"Hello, this is a surprise. Are you home yet?"

"I'm at Mum and Dad's, if that's what you mean. When are you leaving?"

"I thought I'd catch the twelve thirty. I should be home about five." She was doing it again, calling her parents' house home when her home was really here. "Is something wrong, Van? They haven't called it off, have they?" Liz was marrying the man she had lived with for a year. Impossible to believe it would fall through now but sometimes such things happened.

"It's not Liz. It's . . . Well, if you're sure you'll be here for tea." Vanessa sounded agitated. "I'll pick you up. Are you changing at York? Ring me and tell me what the connection is. I might bring Liz with me — I'll see."

"You sound strange, Van." In the mirror Rachel could see her reflection, brown hair plastered to her head after the shower, face bare of makeup, shoulders smooth above the tucked-in towel. In a bad light she could pass for Demi Moore. "In your dreams," she said aloud, and realised she had not been listening to her sister's reply.

". . . so it's better to wait until we're together. My money's running out . . . I'll—"

"Why are you ringing from a phone-box?" But it was too late. The line had gone dead and there was no point in ringing home when Vanessa was manifestly elsewhere. Nothing to do but make sure she caught the early train.

She was dressed and packed by eleven. Time to go downstairs and tell Jago she was off. But even as she opened the door he was there.

"Thank God I caught you. Milk, for the love of Allah, and I know you're off so if there's anything surplus in the fridge I'm never embarrassed by charity."

"Who will you scrounge from in my absence, Jago?" But already she was opening the fridge, checking what Leigh might need and what could be spared.

"Time for a coffee?" He was switching on the kettle as he spoke, assembling mugs and spooning instant into them.

"Don't tell me, you're out of coffee too."

"Lies! I've two sachets of Gold Blend. They came through the door with a leaflet. I only came up here to wish you farewell. Thanks for the appreciation! But enough of the recriminations. Paris did you good. You've got colour in your cheeks."

He left, loaded with most of the perishables from the fridge, his present and a promise to keep an eye on the flat. "I don't suppose Leigh will be home much," she said. "What with the election and everything."

"Poor you." For a moment, genuine sympathy gleamed behind Jago's wire rims but then he was hurling himself downstairs, reappearing to pick up her bags and carry them down to await the cab she had summoned for eleven thirty.

"I see you're taking work," he said, looking disapprovingly at her briefcase as he handed it into the car. "It's supposed to be a festive occasion, a wedding. Why flog yourself?"

"Because I like to eat, darling. You should try it sometime."

"Eating?"

"Work, Jago. We can't all be musicians." His shriek of outrage was lost as the cab drew away and she settled back on her seat. Only then did she remember Vanessa's phone-call. Why ring when they were due to meet tonight? And why be so vague? She contented herself with the thought that Vanessa had always been able to make mountains out of molehills. It was only when she had paid off the cab and was crossing the great bustling vestibule of King's Cross that she recalled the agitation in Vanessa's voice. Something was up.

When she travelled with Leigh they went first class. Today she bought a cheap ticket and was glad to find a half-empty train. She had packed a writing-pad. If she got a table to herself she could catch up on some letters that badly needed replies.

But as the train pulled out of King's Cross and London fell away she felt suddenly drowsy, and even coffee from the trolley-service failed to rouse her. She closed her eyes at last and thought about the family and the week ahead.

Her childhood had been spent in Europe, moving from place to place as her father's Army career had blossomed. He had ended up a full colonel although, in her mother's eyes at least, he had deserved to be a field marshal. Rachel had been the youngest of three — "My afterthought," her mother had lovingly called her. Vanessa was the eldest, forty-one this year, or was it forty-two? Liz was three years younger. And I am twenty-eight, Rachel thought, and shivered a little at the thought of life ticking away. Seven years to the half-way mark. If she was going to have children . . . She put the uncomfortable thought from her and looked from the window to see that they were rolling into Peterborough.

She had been thirteen when her father retired and they left Sennelager to come back to Britain. Liz had been teaching in London. Vanessa was already married to an accountant and the mother of a boy and girl. The house at Fenton Marske had been quiet and spacious, she had had a pony in the paddock alongside and attended a private school. After that she had gone to Brighton and obtained a degree in graphic art.

She had come into television by accident. Jenny, a friend from university, had gone as a runner to an independent company in Wardour Street. A year later, when Rachel was working for a magazine and bored with pictures that seemed the same from week to week, they had met for a drink. Jenny was a trainee floor manager by then and enthusiastic about her work. "There's a vacancy for a floor assistant," she said. "The money's crap but you'd enjoy it."

Just for a while, Rachel had thought. Until I decide what I want to do. But the job had gripped her. She had been a floor manager for six years and had twice been assistant director on a film set. She had done two series of *Let's Get Together*, her present show, working on six-monthly contracts, and would probably return for a third. After that, she wanted something different.

"No pension," Dad had said darkly, when she moved on to contract work. Her mother had smiled and said, "Plenty of time for that, Philip." A wave of love for her mother engulfed Rachel as she remembered. Always there, always comforting and now only a couple of hours away.

She had been in television for two years when she met Leigh, at a book launch. "So you're in telly too," he'd said, when they were introduced. Three months later she moved into his flat. That had been almost four years ago. How time flew!

She must have dozed then and when she opened her eyes they were in Doncaster. Next stop York and time to change trains.

When she reached Fenton Marske Vanessa was alone on the platform. One look at her hunched shoulders and furrowed brow confirmed Rachel's fears.

"Let me take one of those," Vanessa said, reaching a

well-manicured hand for one of her sister's bags. On her ring finger her solitaire diamond blazed above a platinum wedding band. Rachel had always disliked platinum, thinking it too clinical to be proof of love, but in the spring sunshine the diamond gleamed, making her realise how impressive it was. If she married she would have a ring. A plain gold wedding band.

"Thanks," she said, surrendering the smaller bag. "Thanks for meeting me, I could've got a cab."

"We need to talk." Vanessa was striding purposely towards the car-park.

"What's wrong?" Rachel asked. No point in beating about the bush when every line of her sister's body bespoke fury.

"When we get in the car. We don't want the world to know."

"Know what?" Rachel tried hard not to let irritation show but sometimes Vanessa could be exasperating. Years ago Liz had christened her the Drama Queen and she hadn't been far wrong.

"He's done it again," Vanessa said, when they were in the car, doors closed and seat-belts fastened.

"Who's done what again?" But even as she spoke Rachel knew what was coming.

"Daddy, of course. Flaming Daddy, who can't keep his hands to himself. Yes, you may well groan. When I think of Mummy . . . It's bad enough for us. I can't bear the thought of the children finding out. But to be married to such — such — a prat!"

She obviously wanted to use a much harsher epithet

and Rachel struggled with a crazy desire to laugh. "Tell me what's happened," she said instead. "He's still at home, isn't he?" How could they have a wedding without the father of the bride?

"Of course he's still at home!" Vanessa gained speed with a clashing of gears. "He's not likely to leave a place he treats like an hotel, where his every whim is catered for and he's fed like a king. He wouldn't still be there if I had my way . . . and it may come to that before we're finished."

"Who is it? The girlfriend, I mean."

"The Parkin woman. You know her — short blonde hair, lots of gold jewellery. Her husband's a surgeon."

"Dad plays golf with him!" Somehow that made it worse, a kind of double betrayal.

"He did. He'll be lucky not to get an iron cracked over his skull. Roger Parkin is suing for divorce — well, he's threatening it. If he does it'll make the papers. 'Rotarians in Love Battle'."

"They don't have headlines like that in Yorkshire," Rachel said, still trying to grasp the facts.

"Yes, I knew you'd be flippant." Vanessa spoke through clenched teeth. "Don't you realise what this means, Rachel? I'm quite sure Leigh could take it in his stride but some of us have less cosmopolitan partners. Trevor was livid last time . . . and I just squirm. Dad's sixty-four, for God's sake."

"Are you sure it's true?" The house was coming into view now, white and rambling and welcoming. Usually welcoming but today, as they climbed out of the car,

Rachel felt a sudden sense of foreboding. She had come home to be cosseted. Now it looked as though she would have to give more comfort than she received. "Does Liz know? I hope it doesn't spoil things."

"Of course she knows," Vanessa said. "The whole world knows."

The hall was full of the usual fragrances of flowers and polish, but this time there were glum faces. Rachel put down her bags and turned to Liz, who was leaning on the newel post of the stair. "How's the bride?"

"Bearing up." The words were lugubrious but the eyes were as sparkling as ever. She looks tired, Rachel thought. But happy, in spite of the upset.

"I've told Rachel," Vanessa said defiantly.

"Of course you have," Liz said, swinging down from the stair. "I shouldn't think you wasted a second, did you, sister dear?"

"She has a right to know," Vanessa said, and then they all turned as their mother appeared in the kitchen doorway.

"Darling, I didn't hear the car. Let me look at you . . . You look wonderful. So slim!"

"I've told her, Mummy." Vanessa's tone was defiant. "I'm sorry, but we can't pretend nothing has happened." Her voice trailed away as she saw her mother's lips purse and then set.

"You might have waited till she got into the house, Van. Come on, why are we all standing around in the hall? I've got the kettle on."

They turned towards the kitchen, all of them

uncomfortable, wishing that what was making them so would simply go away.

"That's what I mean," Vanessa said, her voice suddenly breaking. "Thinking of Rachel now, when even that must hurt you. You're a saint, Mum, or else a bloody fool!"

"Vanessa! That's enough!" Her mother's voice was a clarion call, and a second later Vanessa turned for the stairs and flung herself upwards.

"Let her go." Liz had gasped at the outburst and was already turning to follow her sister, but her mother's words stopped her. "I won't have everyone upset. Not when we're all together . . . and for such a happy occasion. Liz, you can take Vanessa a cup of tea in a moment. I expect she'll have calmed down by then."

"We have to talk sometime, Mummy," Liz said.

"I know, dear. And we will. Later on. But not when Rachel has hardly taken off her coat. Now, sit down, all of you. What was the journey like, darling? I did so hope Leigh would get away at the last moment but I see he couldn't make it."

They talked then, or rather gabbled, all grateful to make small-talk and postpone the time when something unpleasant must be confronted.

"Where's Dad?" Rachel whispered, when her mother had retreated into the pantry in search of the cake tin. "In the dog-house?"

"It's not funny, Rach. Not this time." Liz's freckled face was crumpled with unease. Rachel had always envied her sisters the colouring they had inherited from their mother, the golden brown hair and ruddy cheeks, cheerful in Liz, alluring in Vanessa, which had not been passed on to herself. "It's all round the county," Liz whispered. "I heard it from someone at work. She thought I ought to know for Mummy's sake."

She's so beautiful, Rachel thought, watching her mother as she sliced cherry cake. How can he be so foolish?

"I've put you and Liz together, in your old room," her mother said, when she came over to them. "Vanessa is in the guest room. She'll need the space when Trevor and the girls arrive. I've put the children in the sewing room. Hugh will go over the garage when he gets here."

Rachel smiled and accepted the piece of moist, cherry-laden cake, but something was nagging away at the back of her mind. Something that had happened in the hall, the moment when Liz gasped and the sun had suddenly sent a shaft across Vanessa's face. There had been dust motes swimming in the sunlight and something hanging in the air. A breathlessness! What Vanessa had said was shocking, certainly, words said in anger by daughter to mother, but there had been more. Her mother's words had not only been angry, they had been a warning.

She went up to her room, still puzzled, but when Liz joined her and they hung up their clothes together it ceased to niggle. They fought good-humouredly over hanging space and oohed and aahed over treasured possessions long forgotten, rediscovered now, safely stored in the wardrobe.

"Mum is a darling, isn't she?" Liz said, stroking a tattered Afghan waistcoat. "Anyone else would've chucked this but she keeps it for me."

They sat down on the bed together, suddenly sentimental. "Are you sure it's true?" Rachel asked.

"As far as I know. And Dad's keeping a low profile. Mum says he's got a meeting in Wetherby, but I wonder. He'd know Van would tell you as soon as you got here. She rang me before I left Manchester. Couldn't wait! I think she was almost disappointed that I knew already. Why is she being so vicious? She's usually uptight but this is something else."

"I know there was that teacher, while I was in Leicester . . ."

"And the groom at the riding stables and—Well, not to put too fine a point on it, my love, our beloved papa is what I think they call a serial adulterer."

"That sounds awful." Outside the light was fading and the mood in the bedroom was sombre.

"I'm not going to let it spoil my wedding," Liz said. "Woe betide Van if she wants to keep the post-mortem going right through the weekend."

"She's probably just stressed out with all her do-gooding and Inner Wheeling. She'll calm down."

"I hope so," Liz said, and sighed. "Before she does too much damage."

At the back of Rachel's mind the niggle reasserted itself. What had Vanessa said? Rachel closed her eyes momentarily, seeing sunlight and dust, Vanessa's face with the freckles standing out on the bridge of her nose, Liz's swift intake of breath . . . What had Vanessa said? And suddenly it came back *"That's what I mean . . .*

thinking of Rachel now, when even that must hurt you."
That's what she had said to make Liz gasp, to make her
mother's face harden. Rachel put out a hand and touched
her sister's arm. "Liz . . . just now, in the hall . . . when I
arrived, I mean. Van was going on at Mum and she said
thinking of me must hurt her. What did she mean?"

Liz was rising from the bed. "God knows, darling.
What does she ever mean? She just goes on, you know
what she's like. Don't try and make sense of it because you
won't be able to. Let's look at my dress instead. It's in that
plastic cover, there."

"She must have meant something," Rachel persisted.
"If I'd been going away I could understand it but I was
coming home."

"Hush!" Liz had risen to her feet and was unzipping
the dress from its cover. "Let's not waste time analysing
Van. What do you think of this for restrained chic? Will it
knock Hugh's eyes out or won't it?"

She was holding it against her, its warm apricot folds
making her face glow.

"You look lovely," Rachel said simply.

"As good as last time?" Suddenly Liz's eyes were moist.
"I was the perfect first-time bride, wasn't I? Yards of tulle
and green as grass. I thought we'd live happily ever after
and we lasted three years."

"This time will be different." Rachel moved to take
her sister in her arms. "Hugh is not like Steve. You'll be
blissfully happy for ever and ever and ever."

"Your turn next," Liz said, as they laid the dress back
in its tissue. "Has Leigh popped the question yet?"

"Not yet."

"He will. He's a fool if he doesn't. And you have heaps of time. I'm the one with the biological clock ticking to the witching hour. I want three children." Her voice quavered as she went on, "I only hope I can have them . . . Sometimes . . . well, you can't be sure."

"Three sounds a good number." Rachel was moving towards the door, her hand outstretched to the light switch. "It's dark in here, let's have the light on."

"No." Liz's voice was suddenly urgent. "Not yet. I want to tell you something. I don't know why but I do. I must tell someone."

They sat down together on the end of the bed. "Go on, then," Rachel said, but Liz stayed silent. "'Fess up," Rachel said, using a childhood phrase that somehow loosened Liz's tongue.

"It's crazy," she said slowly. "I've kept it to myself even at the beginning, when the pain of it was almost unbearable. Why do I want to tell someone now? And yet I simply must."

Rachel felt a shiver of apprehension overtake her but she kept her voice steady. "Tell away, then, and then let's go down and see what's for supper."

"I had an abortion, Rach. After Steve left me. When I realised he wasn't coming back. I've always regretted it. I thought I hated him, you see. And I thought I'd hate his baby. Afterwards, well, it was done and I had to make the best of it. I've told Hugh. He was lovely about it. Part of the past, he said. I don't know why I'm telling you now. But it's a relief to tell someone."

Rachel had put her arms around Liz and she could feel her sister's body shaking. "Don't let it upset you, Liz. You did it for the best . . . and it probably was for the best."

"Are you sure?" Liz's eyes were pleading.

"Very sure. I've thought this through before. Hasn't every woman? Sometimes the kindest thing all round is not to go ahead. And you were very mixed up then, broken-hearted. I think you did the right thing." She hugged Liz fiercely and then, as she let go, looked into her face. "Does Mum know?"

"She's had enough to bear without my burdening her. So you mustn't say a word."

"You know I won't." They clung together briefly and then Liz moved away. "Right, then, put on the light and then we'll get out of here. Do I look awful? Mascara is so treacherous."

"Rub under your right eye. That's better."

They went downstairs, both of them silent, but feeling close.

Again Rachel remembered the scene in the hall. *"Thinking of Rachel now, when even that must hurt you."* Had it been a meaningless remark as Liz had insisted? Or was she a problem to her parents?

But before she could answer her own questions her father appeared in the hall below them, handsome as ever, hair silver against the thin, tanned face.

"How are my girls?" he said, holding out his arms, smiling without a trace of embarrassment, leaving them with no alternative but to move meekly into his embrace and be soundly kissed for their pains.

6

Fenton Marske, Thursday, 3 April 1997

Rachel was awake at daybreak, her mind racing although she was mentally and physically exhausted and longing for sleep. She tried counting sheep, hours, unfinished tasks . . . even her favourite of rescuing refugees and drawing them into a safe haven. Nothing worked. All she could think about was Liz's confession about the abortion.

Why hadn't her sister told her before, when it had happened, when she could have helped? She had told Hugh before her own sister. Should she have told Hugh? *Would I tell Leigh?* That was the next question that popped unbidden into Rachel's mind, swiftly followed by the thought of her period. Where was it? It should have happened yesterday or the day before. She worried for a moment before she remembered that the pill was infallible . . . or almost infallible. There were other things, real things, about which to worry.

What would become of her parents' marriage? Would Leigh get what he wanted out of the election coverage? And if he didn't how would she make it up to him? What shape would their future together take? Did they *have* a future together? The questions tumbled around her head until, at last, as dawn infiltrated the bedroom, she fell into an uneasy sleep.

She woke to the guilty certainty that she was late. With so many tensions within the family she should be down there, helping her mother, acting as a buffer between Vanessa and her father.

She bathed and dressed as quickly as she could and arrived downstairs just as the others were sitting down to breakfast. She was about to say, "Where's Daddy?" but choked back the words just in time. Better not to ask.

She did her best to eat the full plate her mother placed before her but it was a struggle, and she could see that her sisters were equally uneasy. Last night, her father had employed his usual charm to diffuse the tension; now, in his absence, it hung heavy between them.

Perhaps we're all too grown-up now, Rachel thought. There had been affairs in the past, times when her mother had been red-eyed though smiling and her father unnaturally urbane, but they had been younger then. All that mattered was that the fabric of the family should stay intact. It could fray at the edges, even become threadbare, as long as it remained in place.

Now, though, I'm not sure I want her to stay . . . not if it makes her unhappy, Rachel thought. She looked at Vanessa, grimly forking kedgeree into her mouth and chewing as though on broken glass. Was Van thinking only of her mother? There was something vengeful in her attitude, as though she wanted her father to get what was coming to him. Even Liz, who had always been the softest of the three of them, had refused to meet her father's eye last night or respond to his sallies. And, despite her father's charm, his every movement had betrayed his desire to be anywhere else but here. What's happening to us? Rachel thought and was relieved when Sue, the family's cleaner of long standing, arrived, headscarf in place and as imperturbable as ever.

They all rushed to hug her and tell her she hadn't changed, and as usual she hid her pleasure at the sight of them behind a screen of indifference. "All right, that's enough. I'm glad you're pleased to see me. I'm glad to see you if you're not going to get in the way. There'll be a fair old body of work with you lot around." She glanced at her employer, standing now with her back to the Aga, the cooking done. "She's a saint, your mother, and that's a fact."

Had she said it deliberately? Whether or not, it put a considerable dampener on the atmosphere.

"I'm going upstairs," Vanessa said. "If anyone wants to discuss Saturday's arrangements, I'm in my room." It was a coded message and they all knew it.

Rachel saw her mother's brow cloud and felt a wave of sympathy. Were they interfering? Left to her own devices her mother would simply ride out the storm. Until the next time, Rachel thought, suddenly bewildered that she could love her father so much when he was such a — she sought a palatable word and could only come up with "philanderer".

They left the kitchen singly, making excuses as they went, excuses that held water for neither their mother nor Sue, if the set of her shoulders was to be believed. So even Sue knew about the affair with Esme Parkin, which meant it was common knowledge in the village.

"It's unforgivable," Vanessa said, when they were all in her room. Rachel perched uneasily on the window-seat, Liz on the side of the bed, while Vanessa held court in front of the dressing-table. "This time he's gone too far. Esme Parkin is thirty-four and he's sixty-four. It's obscene!"

"Film stars do it," Rachel said defensively. "Look at Clint Eastwood." She knew she was being flippant but didn't understand her own motives.

"Don't be silly!" Vanessa's voice was chilling. "If you can't contribute anything better than that, go away." In childhood she had always been the leader, Rachel the rebel. Now she could see from Liz's face that she wanted to agree with her, show solidarity, but somehow could not.

"Look . . ." Liz sounded both placatory and desperate. "We could go on and on about how awful it is – it is awful – but the question is, what are we going to do about it?"

"And is it up to us to do anything?" They were all looking at her and Rachel tried desperately to explain her words. "It's not that I don't care. It's hateful and I can see what it's doing to Mum, no matter how she covers up. But it's up to her, surely. It's her life . . . her marriage."

"That's true," Liz said, but she sounded doubtful.

"It'll probably blow over," Rachel urged. "If we all rally round, let them sort it out, it'll pass. He isn't seeing the woman again, Mum said that last night."

"It'll blow over. Of course it will." Vanessa's voice was heavy with sarcasm. "Until next time . . . and we know there'll be a next time because we know Daddy. Except that next time he'll be – what? – give it eighteen months . . . He'll be sixty-six and Mum will be sixty-two. Sixty-two! For God's sake, should a woman of sixty-two have to go through an indignity like that? If she doesn't leave him now she'll have to leave him eventually, you know that, and the longer she waits the older she'll be."

"Where would she go?" Liz was plucking at the flowered bedspread.

"*She* shouldn't go anywhere." This time Vanessa and Rachel spoke in unison. It was left to Vanessa to finish the statement. "It's not up to her. She's not the perpetrator in this. She's the victim. I'm not saying that they should break up but if they do I'm crystal clear about who should have to leave. The one who caused the trouble in the first place."

"Well, I think we should wait." Rachel felt that everything was moving too fast. Time to call a halt. "If it's all over . . ."

"Oh, Rachel." Vanessa shook a weary head. "There's *so* much you don't know. Of course it's not over. These things are never over. Their effects do lasting damage. And if you think he isn't still seeing the woman, where was he yesterday? Where has he gone now? Grow up, Rachel."

Rachel and Liz left Vanessa without making a decision

and went to their room. "It's ghastly, isn't it?" Liz said, when they were safe inside it. "And it brings back bad memories for me of Steve, the bastard."

"It's bad luck," Rachel sympathised. "But you mustn't let it spoil things for you. This should be the happiest time of your life. You are happy, aren't you?"

"Very." Liz's face softened at the thought of her future. "I just have the feeling that this time I'm going to be all right. What about you?"

Rachel felt an impulse to confide, which had to be fought against. Things were complicated enough without adding something that wasn't necessary. Leigh was a workaholic but they would work it out.

She gave her reassurances and went downstairs, hoping to find one of the phone extensions deserted. She wound up in the morning room, doors closed behind her, and dialled the Global TV number. "Newsroom please," she said, when she got through. It was eleven fifteen. He'd have settled at his desk by now and sorted the day ahead. The ring ceased. "Leigh Barnes, please." There was a pause and then his voice.

"Barnes." He sounded flat, almost bored.

"Leigh?" she said. "It's me."

"Hello." Just the one word and then an interrogatory pause.

"I'm not interrupting you, am I?" Already she was regretting the call. Why hadn't she waited until tonight?

"No . . . Well, actually I'm up to my neck in shit. Clive's gone down with some bug or another so I'm doing his interview tonight."

"Who is it?"

"William Hague. Welsh Office. Not exactly class one but better than nothing. So I've Welsh affairs to mug up. Was there anything important?"

"No . . . nothing special."

"Everything OK?" Already she could feel him cutting off from her.

"Yes, fine. Everyone sends love." Couldn't tell him about Dad, not now.

"Good. Me too to them. Well, if that's all . . ."

"I love you."

"Me too. Take care." The click at the other end came before she had taken the receiver from her ear and she felt tears sting her eyes. Which was silly, really, when she knew that he was so engrossed in work and had just had an extra interview dumped on him.

She and Liz went for a walk before lunch, the family Labrador, Sally, padding in front of them. They breasted the rise behind the house and saw the county of North Yorkshire spread out before them.

"Nice," Liz said. "It always gets me when I see a scene like this. England! Why do people go abroad?"

"Because they don't want to freeze to death?" Rachel suggested drily.

"Nonsense. You're getting soft, living down south. This is good bracing Yorkshire air."

Around them the sky was blue, flecked here and there with white clouds, which moved swiftly eastwards. The fields were a patchwork of brown and green and gold, bounded by hedges of darker green, speckled here and there with sheep. "Not so many cows now," Liz said sadly. "Poor beasts. Wiped out because we got scared."

Ahead of them a man had emerged from a thicket, closely followed by a black and white dog. "It's Tom Lattemore," Liz said. "Is it? Yes, it is. You remember Tom?"

"Of course I do," Rachel said drily. "I didn't have so many boyfriends that I could forget one." She and Tom had been close for two years, in the fifth and sixth forms. And then he had gone off to medical school, and a year after she had left for art college and somehow what had been between them had dwindled.

"He's in practice here now," Liz said. "Everybody likes him."

"He always said he'd come home eventually. What happened to Emma?"

"His sister? She's in America now. Married a boffin. Tom's still free, if you're interested."

"Wash your mouth out, I'm spoken for. And lower your voice, he'll hear you."

"Morning." Tom was bending to attach a lead to his dog's collar and Rachel took hold of the Labrador as Liz greeted him.

"Tom? How are you? Still playing rugby? You remember Rachel?"

He looked at Rachel. "I do." He held out a hand and clasped hers. "You're cold," he said, as he let it go. "And, yes, I'm still playing rugby." But as he answered Liz his eyes were on Rachel.

Rachel was struggling to hold back Sally, who was

keen to make friends with the Collie and it was a relief when Liz took control of the situation.

"Give me the dog," she said. Rachel surrendered gratefully and smiled at Tom.

"You're based in London, aren't you?" he said. "And in TV. I've heard the local gossip but it's always vague. Apparently one of you is getting married?"

"Yes, I'm in TV, and it's Liz who's getting married. How's Emma?"

"She's well. Had a baby last month. In Ohio. I've just been over to stand godfather. That's why I'm not at the surgery today. My freedom lasts till Sunday. Incidentally, how's your brother-in-law, Trevor? We were tennis partners at one time."

"He's coming for the wedding. Vanessa's already here, Trevor and the kids arrive tomorrow. You must come over while he's around. Saturday night, after the wedding. It's open house in the evening."

"I couldn't intrude . . ."

"You wouldn't be." Rachel was turning away as she spoke. "It's not formal, just anyone who's stayed on after the reception. Do come. It'll be good for Trevor to have someone to talk to and we can catch up on one another's news — I'll tell him to expect you."

"He's still keen," Liz said, as they climbed a stile to take the footpath.

"Don't be silly. He was just making conversation."

"OK. Don't listen. But I know what I saw. Still, if you and Leigh really are an item don't let me encourage you to stray. There's enough of that going on in the family already."

Rachel was keen to avoid discussion of both elements in this conversation. "I expect it'll settle down. And yes, I've got Leigh."

Ahead of them the field was newly ploughed and neat as corrugated iron. If only life could be like that. She appeared to have quelled her sister's fears, at least for the moment, but in her heart of hearts she knew that the chance of things settling down in the near future was decidedly remote.

There was an uneasy truce as they helped to prepare dinner. All afternoon they had stayed apart, meeting only briefly for a cup of tea round the kitchen table. Now, as the women moved back and forth in the blue and white kitchen the atmosphere grew tense, especially when their father came in to uncork the wine.

"A nice Graves, I think. I brought it up from the cellar as soon as I knew it was halibut. And I've a rather nice Sauterne to go with dessert."

"Excuse me." Vanessa was clutching a chopping board, waiting to get access to the bench where her father was operating. He moved and she clashed down the wooden board, but as she turned she found her way still blocked by his figure. "For God's sake, Dad—"

"Vanessa!" Her mother had appeared in the kitchen doorway, her face pale except for two bright spots of colour, one in either cheek.

"I'm sorry, Mother. I've tried, I've really tried, but it's becoming a farce. All of us pretending, moving around, making conversation, all the time knowing exactly what's going on. It stinks, Mother. It really stinks!"

"Calm down, Van." But it was too late for Liz's words to have any effect. Vanessa had turned on her father now, tears streaming unchecked down her cheeks, her fists balled and raised in front of her.

"How can you? How can you be such a pig? How can you do this to our mother, who's worth fifty of you? How could you, *could you, could you*—"

"Hush." Rachel put her arms around her sister and tried to draw her away. It was the wrong thing to do. Vanessa twisted away from her to confront her father once more. "Didn't you do enough damage the first time? Wasn't that enough? Haven't we all paid, all these years?"

"Vanessa!" This time her mother's voice cut like a whip and Vanessa's head slumped on her chest.

"I'll go." Her father was putting down the still corked wine. "She's right. We can't just pretend nothing has happened. I'm sorry, Dodie."

"Hush, Philip. No, perhaps you'd better all go for the moment. Liz, take Vanessa upstairs. I'll put dinner back an hour. Perhaps if we all calm down we can have a civilised meal. Run along, Rachel, off you go. I want my kitchen to myself."

Rachel took refuge in the morning room, leaving the light switch alone, feeling her way towards the luminous patch of the window, lifting the telephone receiver even as she lowered herself into a chair. But the telephone in the London flat remained unanswered.

It was seven fifteen and she had hoped he would have come home for a shower before his broadcast. She dialled the number of the TV company but when she reached the newsroom it was already too late. "He's gone down to the studio, I'm afraid. You won't get him now until after the programme."

They ate in semi-silence, speaking only of the excellence of the food, the way dietary habits had changed in the last few years, the prospect of a change of government. Liz mentioned their encounter with Tom and her mother seemed pleased that they had invited him to the evening reception.

"He was always fond of you, Rachel. And they say he's a wonderful doctor." At nine thirty Rachel excused herself and went to switch on the TV in the drawing room.

Leigh was there, on the screen, immaculate in pink shirt and maroon tie under a grey suit. "It will be hard for the Conservative Party to retain a presence in Wales, Mr Hague. How does that reflect on your tenure as minister?"

The Welsh Secretary's face was creased with earnestness, making him look more than ever like a new baby. But there was a quiet authority there and Leigh was not having things all his own way. She switched off the set when the interview was over and returned to the dining room. They would be having drinks in the green room now. No point in ringing yet.

Her mother and father were nowhere to be seen, her sisters were still slumped morosely around the table.

"Not every marriage is perfect," Liz said, obviously countering a previous argument. "But you see it through, you don't just run away. I stuck it out with Steve until there was no point!"

"Precisely!" Vanessa's tone was triumphant. "Isn't that what Mother's done all these years? Stuck it out? And there's no longer any point for *her* to stay!"

"It's not up to us to say that," Rachel countered.

"Fine words." Vanessa's words were spat from between narrowed lips. "What you mean is that Mum should stay because it's better for you. You're not married, you like the idea of home still being here. Better for you. Better for Dad. Not better for her. She's going to get into his bed tonight, lie beside him – for all I know they still have sex – and you want her to do this knowing he's been with . . . he's sleeping with . . . another woman?"

"I don't want her to 'do' anything," Rachel said desperately. "I'm not even sure she should stay. If she wants to go . . . I just don't want you to push her. Any-way . . ." Her words tailed off as she caught sight of Liz's face, eyes already brimming with tears. "I think we're all forgetting that tomorrow is the eve of Liz's wedding day. Which ought to be a happy day for her. I suggest we stop bickering, stop hounding Dad and get on with what we came here for, to celebrate something. On Sunday, when it's all over, we can talk about it, if everyone still wants to, that is."

"I won't be here." Liz was blowing her nose and folding her handkerchief back into a square. "But for what it's worth I think Dad should move out for a while. He can have my flat in Harrogate. There's still eight weeks on the lease and I won't be using it. If they have some space, perhaps they can work things out."

7

Fenton Marske, Friday, 4 April 1997

Daylight was filtering through the curtains when Rachel woke, but the still hush of the household told her it was early. She turned on her side to look at her travelling clock. Five fifteen. She was about to roll back into sleep when a wave of nausea overtook her and then a sudden brackish rush into her mouth. She lay back on her pillows, praying for it to end, feeling only pity for herself. What had she eaten last night? Was anyone else ill?

She closed her eyes and had almost given way to tears when she heard the noise, the unmistakable noise of the front door closing and then the sound of a car starting up. Someone had left the house, was even now negotiating the drive, turning out into the road, making an escape.

A few feet away, in the other bed, Liz was slumbering like an exhausted warrior. Who had gone out? No one was due at work today and none of her Mum's charitable efforts required a dawn start. Her speculation was ended by another wave of nausea.

She lay still for a moment and then she flung back the covers and got out of bed. A bath would help, as it always did. She shut herself in the bathroom and relaxed into foam-filled water.

There was the smell of coffee as she descended the stairs and then, as she drew nearer, the hum of the radio. "Mum?" Her mother was sitting at the kitchen table, a mug held in her clasped hands. She wore a blue candlewick dressing-gown and her auburn hair, flecked now with grey, was tucked behind her ears.

"What are you doing up, darling? There's coffee on the stove."

"Thanks." Rachel poured a cup and added milk from the pan on the Aga. "Who was that I heard driving away?"

"It was your father. He's gone to an hotel until the wedding. Oh, you needn't gasp. He hasn't gone for good. But I won't have him stay here to be hounded in his own home. I won't have it, Rachel. Whatever he's done or not done is between your father and me. We talked and decided it was easier for him to go. He'll be here for the wedding and come back for good when the house is quiet again."

"Oh, Mum." Rachel sat down at the table, uncertain of what to say.

"It's all right." Her mother was suddenly determinedly cheerful. "We're not going to spoil Liz's day. Tomorrow will go off well, Dad will be here for the high-jinks and then everything will be back to normal."

"How do you know he's gone to an hotel?" It was out before Rachel could stop it.

"Because he told me." Her mother's face and voice were both earnest. "Because I trust him. He's never lied to me, Rachel. I've always known when . . . well, when things weren't right. And I've always known it would pass." She was smiling but it only served to make her look more weary, more vulnerable. "Oh, I know Vanessa would say, 'until the next time,' but, don't you see? these aren't real affairs he has. They're just little attempts at being a rogue, a roué. It's his way of saying he's free. That he could go if he wanted to go. I understand that."

"But he humiliates you." Alone here, in the blue and white kitchen, it was suddenly all right to be honest, and desperately important that they should be.

"A little . . . but there's a price for everything in life, darling." Her mother reached out and clasped Rachel's hand. "What I get from your father, what I've always got from him, has been worth whatever pain there's been. Besides," she let go of Rachel's hand and patted her arm, "he gave me you. And the others . . . but you were the baby."

"Aren't you ever angry with him? I ask because I don't know how I would cope if Leigh was unfaithful to me."

Her mother considered for a moment, her eyes steady, only the mug, turning round and round in her hand betraying agitation. "Perhaps I was a little angry the first time. Hurt, certainly, and incredulous. How could he do this to me? The children. You weren't born then but Van was and Liz was on the way. But then I looked at my options. You must always do that in life, set out your alternatives. I could stand on my pride and lose him – lose not only a husband but a father for my children – or I could set about mending things. You know which I chose."

"But what about the next time, and the times after? What about now? He's never going to change, is he? How can you bear it?"

Her mother put up a hand to push back the hair that was falling on to her forehead. "God only knows, darling, if I'm truthful. I just – I just get on with it, with things, then it's over and he's mine again. It's amazing how much easier life is if you live a day at a time."

"Well . . ." Rachel said doubtfully, and sipped her coffee. The sick feeling had gone now but she felt deflated. This was supposed to be a happy home-coming and it was all going away.

"Cheer up," her mother said. Her eyes were moist but twinkling nevertheless. "It'll be all right, you'll see. We'll have a lovely wedding and things will settle down. Dad loves us – loves us all. Never forget that."

They hugged then and separated, one to turn to the sink, the other to mount the stairs to her bedroom, wondering when her world would cease to rock upon its foundations.

How do I feel, she wondered, lying on her bed, glad that for a while at least Liz was asleep. I have to face the fact that my father is a shit, to my mother at least, and yet I still love him. She turned on her face then, burying it in the crook of her arm, trying to work out why you could forgive things in those you loved that would seem unforgivable in anyone else. If she was honest with herself, she was critical of her mother's attitude. She had spent a lifetime pandering to a man's ego. Or had she? Was it simply that she had decided, quite ruthlessly, what she wanted out of life and gone for it? And, if her mother had been weak, was she any better? What would she do in a similar situation?

It was a sober enough thought to bring her to her feet. What she needed was some fresh air.

The sun was shining but she wrapped up warmly. She intended to find a spot out of the wind where she could sit and think positive thoughts. What better than to take inspiration from the unfolding spring around her.

She settled in the lea of a big elm tree at a place where four fields met. Against her back the bark seemed almost cork-like. The sun was strong enough to warm her cheeks and fingers and there was only the sound of wind riffling through spring grass and occasional agitated chatter from birds to disturb her. But she did not draw from the life around her. Instead she thought of the Tuileries gardens, the budding iris against a faint suggestion of water. Paris had been brief but wonderful. She luxuriated in memory, her mind returning only now and then to the turmoil she had left behind at home and her own dilemma.

She felt the dog before she saw it, its breath hot on her cheek, its tongue reaching out to caress. "Budge!" She looked up to see Tom Lattemore frantically trying to seize his dog's collar as it ploughed through the gloves she had placed on the ground at her feet.

"It's all right, I like dogs — don't I, old fellow?" The

dog's muzzle was grey, its eyes almost rheumy. She fondled him while Tom stood watching.

"Do you mind?" He was indicating the bank beside her and she shook her head.

"Not at all. The grass is quite dry." His legs in their golden corduroy cladding were long and ended in sensible boots. "You've obviously been walking."

"I do it when I can. I'm a one-man practice so chances are limited. I've got a locum at the moment, a friend from med school who's off to South Africa soon, so I'm a little intoxicated with freedom. Back to the grind on Monday. What about you?"

"I've just finished a series. I'm on leave till my next assignment. I went off to Paris last weekend and I'm here for a few days."

"Paris! Very swish."

"No . . . I was there . . ." Something made her choose her words carefully. "I was there with a friend, just for forty-eight hours. Do you know Paris well?"

"No. I've been, of course, but it was strictly the Sacre Coeur and the Moulin Rouge and back on the plane. In my student days. I seem to remember it through an alcoholic haze."

They laughed then and talked of student days until it was time to rise, brushing grass from their clothes. "I'll see you on Saturday night," he said, when they parted. "If you're sure it's OK."

"I'm very sure." As she made her way home, Rachel reflected on how pleasant the meeting had been. He had put her at ease, no easy thing at the moment, and somehow the years had slipped away. She decided it was his bedside manner and would have made a joke of it to her mother and sisters, if it had not been for the fact that when she re-entered the house they were embroiled in a family row.

Liz was seated at the kitchen table, her fists clenched in front of her, a look of desperation on her face. The contest was between Vanessa and her mother.

"If that's how you feel, my dear, then perhaps you should go.' Her mother's face was calm but her voice trembled.

Vanessa was far from calm. Her voice, when she spoke, trembled on the verge of hysteria. "I can't believe you're saying that to me. I'm your daughter!"

"And your father is my husband. I think that's something you forget sometimes."

"Forget! There's precious chance of forgetting! Things keep reminding us."

A look almost of terror crossed her mother's face then, and Rachel rushed to intervene. "I thought we'd agreed to put all this behind us. Why are we spoiling things for Liz?"

"Exactly!" her mother said.

Vanessa turned to Rachel, her eyes starting out of her head. "That's right. Sweep it under the carpet. Say it's in the past. Why should he get away with it? That's what I'm asking. Why do men like him always get away with it?" She was weeping but no one went to comfort her. At last she raised her head to fire a parting shot. "You say leave it alone. It's over. How can you say it's over, any of it, when we've been living with the consequences for twenty-eight years?"

At that moment there was a muffled, "Hello," from outside, and then Hugh was stooping through the doorway. "Any room for a bridegroom?"

"Darling!" Liz was pushing back her chair to rush into his arms, and Vanessa fished for a handkerchief to blow her nose. But the tears continued to flow and, with a gasp of frustration, she hurried from the kitchen. Rachel would have followed her but her mother's hand was on her arm, almost vice-like. "Leave her alone," she said. "She's better on her own for a while."

Rachel bade Hugh welcome, then excused herself. Not to follow Vanessa. Her mother's eye was on her making that impossible. Instead she went to the morning room and dialled Leigh's office. To her relief he was there and free to speak.

"Hello, darling. How are you?"

"Did you see the interview last night?"

"Yes, it was marvellous. Well done."

"I thought you might have rung to tell me what you thought of it."

"I'm afraid I couldn't. Things are a bit difficult here."

She had expected him to pick up on that, make solicitous inquiries, but he was still obsessed with his job and the limited chances he was being given to do it.

"Have you missed me?" she asked, fearful that the phone-call would end without endearments of any sort.

"You know I have." It was not reassurance, it was a reproof. "Why do you ask questions like that? What am I supposed to say? 'No, I never noticed you'd gone. Was I alone in bed last night? Did I miss a screw?' For God's sake, Rachel."

Her eyes were brimming over now. "I'm sorry. I just wanted you to say you'd missed me."

"Of course I've missed you." His voice was gentler. "Would I live with you if I wasn't going to miss you? Don't be a goose. But I've got to work, darling. Just as you've got your responsibilities — family, and your own work. Have you rung in yet?"

"No. I'll do it next week. Tell me how things are going, then."

They parted amicably enough but she had a strong feeling that he was glad to be rid of her, not because he didn't care for her but because, just now, he cared more for his work. As she mounted the stairs to her room she remembered a poem she had read at school by Shelley or Yeats; something like . . .

The heart of man is capable of
Forty different kinds of love.
And the heart of woman is just an ocean
Of jealous, immoderate damp devotion.

By the time she came downstairs glorious smells were emanating from the kitchen and her mother was bustling between sink and stove. "Lay the table, dear. Trevor and the children have arrived so we'll be eight. They're upstairs now, settling in."

Rachel made rapid calculations. "So Daddy isn't

coming?" Again she wished she had bitten back the words but her mother's response was unruffled.

"No, darling. Not tonight. He'll be here in the morning in plenty of time. Now, what did I do with that strainer?"

Rachel had found the missing implement and was about to leave for the dining room when her mother spoke again. "Don't take too much notice of what Vanessa says, darling. Not at the moment. She's rather overwrought. I hope things are all right with Trevor. Perhaps we'll be able to talk before she goes off on Monday."

Rachel half turned, amazed at her words. There was only one thing wrong with Vanessa, fury at her father's behaviour. Why could Mummy not see that?

"What do you mean, don't pay attention?"

"Well." Her mother was intent on straining broccoli. "Nothing especially. Just . . . well, some of the things she says as though they were fact. Well, they're just . . . well, silly."

Inside Rachel's head something registered. There was meaning in those words. But what? What had Vanessa said that was not to be believed? Was Daddy innocent after all, the whole thing a horrible mistake? They both knew it was not. She might have stayed and questioned her mother but at that moment Liz appeared.

"Are we eating tonight or not? The table's not set in the dining room and I'm famished. I hope you've made Yorkshire puddings, Ma. We haven't had them for ages."

_____ 8

Fenton Marske, Saturday, 5 April 1997

Rachel awoke once more to overpowering nausea, a
sensation of sickness that caused her to cover her mouth,
sure that the urge to vomit would shortly overcome her.
She had been all right last night, the sickness of the
morning forgotten. Now she was sick again, exactly like
yesterday. She lay still, trying to control it. Perhaps it was
just imagination. But the sensation was all too real . . . and
there was something else, something she had noticed
yesterday but pushed aside. She put up a hand and
pressed her breast. It felt tense, although there was no
pain. I am pregnant, she thought and felt her senses reel
until her ears sang. Why had they never talked through
the possibility of its happening? After all, it was the
constant danger of love-making. What had Princess Anne
called it? "The occupational hazard of being a wife."
They had felt so safe, so clever, so totally in command of
their lives, that was why they had not considered risk.

Now she was brought face to face with it and it was awesome. Except that it couldn't be true. The pill was 98 per cent safe, if taken properly, and she had always been punctilious.

I'm not ready to have a baby, she thought. And neither is Leigh. Not now, when he's at a career crossroads. Not now, when her own family life was in crisis. Not now, when she had suddenly begun to doubt that relationships could endure. Still, she couldn't be pregnant. It was an impossibility! She pressed her breast again but this time it felt OK.

She was lying still, trying to make sense of it all, when her mother entered the bedroom. "You're awake, darling," she whispered. "Good. Let Liz sleep on if you can. It's just that we'll have to stagger the bathrooms if we all want a bath — and we must keep Liz and Hugh apart. That's vital. Trevor will see to Hugh if you look after Liz — check on the landing and that sort of thing. I don't expect she'll want to come down, and I've told Trevor to get Hugh dressed and down as soon as possible. He's in the bathroom now. You can use mine — I should go in now if I were you, before Vanessa and her tribe grab it."

"Are you all right, Mum?" Rachel couldn't resist the question. No one could be as all right as her mother looked, not in the circumstances.

"I'm fine, darling. Or I will be when I see everything under way. There's coffee and eggs in the kitchen when you get down."

So that's how it was going to be, Rachel thought. Vanessa had got it right after all. There was to be a papering over the cracks, a refusal to admit that the fox had got into the hen-house. My mother is amazing, she acknowledged, but her emotion was not entirely admiration.

"OK," she said. "I'll have a quick bath and be down directly."

She set her alarm-clock on the side of the bath. She could wallow for ten minutes, no more. As steam filled the bathroom and misted the tiles she let her nightdress fall to the floor and dipped a tentative toe into the water. It was then that she caught sight of herself in the mirror. There was something different about her body, though at first she couldn't decide what it was. She turned this way and that before realising what had changed. It was her breasts, not fuller but somehow riper, darker around the nipples. She stared again, sure it must be imagination, but no, she did look different. She was pregnant and already her body was adjusting to its altered state. She lay in the scented water, telling herself to be calm. This could be handled. There were options.

Chill words like termination and adoption flitted through her mind, except that neither of these dread alternatives would be necessary. This baby, if indeed it was a baby, might not be an expected one but that did not mean it would be unwanted. After all, it was the product of love.

By the time she rose from the bath to dry herself on one of her mother's thick, velvety towels she had come to terms with it. There was never a perfect time to have a baby, not in the average life. This would be as good a time as any.

Before she slipped into her robe she stood erect for a moment, one hand on her belly. It was there, no bigger than a grain of sand and already sending shockwaves throughout her system. Throughout her life! When she left the bathroom she was smiling.

In the bedroom Liz was sitting up in bed, a breakfast tray in front of her. "I'll never get through all this!" There were eggs and bacon, a rack of toast, preserves and butter, even a tulip in a vase.

"You can't disappoint Mum. She's building you up for the ordeal."

"You'll have to help me, then." Together they picked at scrambled eggs and crispy bacon, soft-centred toast that crunched deliciously when liberally spread with marmalade, and drank hot English breakfast tea.

"This is like old times," Rachel said. "Remember supper trays?" They had been treats after exams or other hard days, times when they were cosseted and treated with care. "Mum was an angel, wasn't she?"

"No wonder Van's taken this badly." Liz's face was mournful. "Mum doesn't deserve it. But what can we do?"

"I suppose Van thinks Mum's to blame a bit — always forgiving him, I mean. I know about that teacher and the girl at the stables but there must have been others."

Suddenly Liz's eyes dropped. She wiped her mouth with an index finger and gave a rueful smile.

"I suppose so. Still, no point in going over it now. I expect it'll sort itself out. I only hope Van doesn't launch forth at the reception — not in front of Hugh's family."

"She won't." Guiltily Rachel remembered that she had been given charge of the bride's welfare. Mustn't get into discussions that might upset her. "Now, is there anything I can get you? Shall I water the pot? No? Right, then, I'll move this tray and you can have your bath. But not until I've spied out the landing."

"I'm going to be happy," Liz said suddenly. "This time I know it. Steve didn't have it in him to be faithful. Hugh is different."

Rachel was inspecting the landing. "Right, coast clear, in you go. And don't come out till I come for you. You can take as long as you like – well, half an hour at least. The hairdresser's booked for eleven so there's bags of time."

When Liz was safely ensconced Rachel carried the breakfast tray downstairs. Her mother was at the sink, the draining-board piled with rinsed cups and saucers and plates. "Let me help," Rachel said, and then, emotional, "Oh, Mum, we do love you, you know."

They stood facing one another, each knowing that what was being offered was sympathy as well as affection.

"I know," her mother said at last. "I do know. Now, there's a tea-towel on the radiator. Let's get this lot out of the way before the caterers arrive."

Around them the house throbbed with life, doors opening and closing, laughter and the sound of children. This is what a family is, Rachel thought. Life going on all around you.

Perhaps she would have three children like her mother but, if not, one would do. "I'm having a baby," she said, but only in her head. Leigh must be the first to know. After that she would share it with everyone.

Chores accomplished, she went upstairs to shepherd the bride back to her room. "Should I put on my dress before the hairdresser comes?" Liz asked anxiously. "I don't want to get anything smudged."

"I'd stay in your undies until she's done your makeup. Then the dress, then your hair." The dress hung in front of the wardrobe mirror, a column of warm colour. On the dressing-table the hat looked ready for lift-off, a confection of tulle and ribbon and silken flowers.

"I'm cold," Liz said, clutching her bare arms. "I expect it's nerves, which is silly, really. It's not as though I'm a virgin bride."

"This is the most important day of your life." Rachel was draping her dressing-gown round her sister's shoulders. "I'd be worried if you weren't nervous."

"I suppose he is still here?" Liz was only half joking.

"The last time I saw him Trevor had him in an arm-lock," Rachel said reassuringly. "The family won't let him get away." She crossed to the window, ostensibly to watch out for the hairdresser, in reality to hide her eyes from her sister's searching gaze, for suddenly and sharply she had realised that she might never stand at an altar or before a registrar. In all the time they had been together Leigh had not once mentioned marriage. He had talked of the future, of children, even, but never as part of a legal bond.

It was a relief when the hairdresser arrived to set out her tools in her mother's bedroom. Rachel scooped up everything Liz needed and conveyed her across the landing before going back to her own, now empty, room.

She had bought a pearl-grey suit for the occasion, to be worn with a violet shirt. When she had done her makeup and hair and clipped in huge pearl earrings she looked at herself in the mirror. Would they know her secret? Her eyes seemed huge and dark, her face thinner. The effects of pregnancy, or illusion? She was still regarding her reflection when her mother appeared, dressed in her own cream suit, a smear of lipstick her only makeup, her hat not yet in place.

"Come here and sit down," Rachel said firmly. "You've been so busy looking after everyone else you've forgotten you're the mother of the bride." As she made up her mother's face, conscious all the time of her victim's desire to escape and get back to her duties, Rachel pondered the state of motherhood. It made you forget that you were a woman – or, rather, a woman of vanity and frivolity and selfish desire. It made you, instead, a carer, a guardian, someone who would always put another first. Had her mother stayed because she wanted to keep a husband or a father for her children?

"There now," she said at last, the question unanswered. "That's better. You look lovely." It was the truth. The tired eyes were transformed with shadow and mascara, the good skin enhanced with foundation and blusher.

"Thank you, darling," her mother said. "I can face the world now. You've done wonders." She left the room, but a minute later she was back. "Coast's clear, groom's gone.

You can bring down the victim any time you like."

There was little left to do for Liz. The apricot dress was in place, hair and makeup immaculate. Only the hat to lift and settle on the piled-up curls. They stood together, looking in the mirror. We are not alike, Rachel thought. She had always been the odd one out in the family but today the difference was pronounced. Liz's warm beauty was in sharp contrast to Rachel's own pallor and it was easy to see who was the bride, for Liz's face wore an almost exultant expression. "Happy?" Rachel asked, and was rewarded with an emphatic nod.

They went out on to the landing then, the hairdresser hovering behind. "Have I got everything?" Liz said anxiously.

"Yes. You don't need anything. Your flowers are downstairs. I've got makeup and pins and a handkerchief in case you cry. Let's get a move on."

They were on the stairhead now and Rachel felt her throat convulse. How much longer could home go on? They were all drawing away from it, one by one. Perhaps Mum and Dad would separate and there would be two houses to visit. Two small houses, probably, with no opportunity for them all to get together.

Suddenly she heard a swift intake of breath and saw that Liz's face had tensed. She followed the direction of her sister's gaze and saw her father, immaculate in dark grey suit and regimental tie, waiting at the foot of the stairs.

Both women halted. They had known he would be there eventually but his sudden appearance, almost barring their way, was an embarrassment. Rachel was desperately seeking a remark, anything to defuse the situation, when her father acted. "Darling, you look wonderful." He was mounting the stairs two at a time, holding out both hands to his daughter, and then they were all being swept along in the wake of his charm. But for Rachel there was a tinge of resentment. He *was* charming but he knew it, he used it. He manipulates everyone, she thought. Especially Mummy.

It was not a pleasant thought but there was no time to explore it. Everyone else was assembled in the hall. Cars were waiting to whisk them away and then they were entering the Civic Centre and a hush fell upon them.

The service was short and fairly unemotional until, towards the end, the registrar recited a poem taken, he said, from a Native American wedding ceremony.

Now each of you will be warmth to each other,
Now there is no more loneliness,
Now you are two persons but there is only one life
   before you,
Go now and enter into the days of your life together,
And may your life be long and happy upon the earth.

Rachel glanced carefully at her family. Her mother's face was alight, her father's full of pride. Only Vanessa stared straight ahead and Trevor's hand on her arm looked more like a vice than a caress. What was going on? Beside her parents her niece and nephew gazed intently at the ceremony, eyes wide. They were thirteen and eleven. Old enough to sense grown-up tensions.

When the ceremony was over they all flooded out of the chamber. "It was lovely, wasn't it?" Liz said, as they came face to face. And then she was being whisked into the waiting car and they were off to the reception at Greystones, a country-house hotel where carpets were sumptuous and flower arrangements of orange-grove proportions.

The resentment Rachel had felt on the landing resurfaced when it was time for the speeches. She dared not look to where Vanessa was sitting, fearing what she would see in her sister's eyes as her father rose to his feet to speak of "my family" and "my beautiful daughters".

But it was the way he paid tribute to "my darling wife" that turned resentment into a kind of fury. She tried to tell herself that he was simply doing his best for Liz, but the look on his face was one of complete satisfaction with his life and his lot. Could anyone be that good an actor? Or was he simply a selfish shit? It was a relief to Rachel when at last it was over and they could go home.

"Thank God," Vanessa said, as they shared the back seat of Trevor's Mercedes. "How I kept control through that I'll never know."

"Hush, dear." There was a warning in her husband's voice, a consciousness of the two children in the car.

"I'm tired of hush!" It was said with a venom that surprised even Rachel.

"That may be but this is not the time or the place." He was angry now, and Rachel was uncomfortably aware that she was witnessing more than anger over her father's behaviour. This was something unpleasant between husband and wife. Her heart sank at the thought of more discord.

"Cheer up," she whispered, and patted her sister's beringed hand.

Vanessa sighed. "I wish I could." Her voice was low but Rachel could see that the children were straining to hear every word. "I've lived with this for too long, and now . . ." She raised her voice. "I hope everyone — everyone — realises I won't live with it again!"

"What?" The question escaped Rachel's lips before she knew she had formed it. "What have you lived with?"

"Things," Vanessa said enigmatically. "Things that should never have been . . . never kept secret anyway. It's so unfair." She spoke even lower. "I won't have any more of it. I hope everyone realises that."

What *is* going on? Rachel thought, for there was no doubt that Vanessa's remarks were directed at her husband.

They were all at the house now, spilling out on to the drive, scurrying in before the evening guests arrived. The carpet had been lifted in the drawing room and when Rachel peeped in she saw that the band engaged for the evening were already setting up their music stands.

"Have you heard?" Trevor had come up behind her, eyes wide. "There's been a bomb scare at Aintree. One of the guests heard it on his car radio. The National's been called off."

"The Grand National?" It was a stupid question. What other National was there?

"They're going to terrorise us from now to the election," Trevor said gloomily. "You mark my words!"

Rachel looked into her brother-in-law's face. Was he having an affair, as Vanessa's behaviour in the car had suggested? He didn't look like an adulterer but, then, what *did* adulterers look like? "I do hope not," she said. "Life's difficult enough without the IRA."

To her relief the morning room was empty. Soon people would spill into every area of the house. If she was to ring Leigh she should do it now.

To her relief she got through straight away and she could tell from the sound of his voice that he was in a rare good humour. Now she could tell him, share her secret, tell everyone.

"Darling . . ." She was about to launch into her tale when she heard what he was saying. Someone – someone prestigious – had been in a car crash. "He can't be back for weeks, no way, they've asked me to stand by. That means I'm lined up to replace him. I'll get it all, interviews, details . . . Oh, God, I'm so – so . . ."

She wanted to say, "I need you, Leigh, I'm having your baby," but somehow her news seemed insignificant now, an irrelevance. "That's marvellous. Well, you know what I mean." Mustn't make waves, must understand. Every article she had ever read on relationships had stressed the need to give equal importance to your partner's feelings. "But what about me?" she wanted to say, and couldn't. But neither could she help feeling an irritation that was almost anger.

"How did it go?" He had remembered at last that this

was a special day.

"Fine . . . wonderful. We're back home now, getting ready for the party. I wish you were here."

"Me too. Still, have a good time."

When Rachel put down the phone she felt wretched. She ought to be pleased for him, so why did she feel like crying?

She huddled in an oversized armchair and tried to pull herself together. Nothing had changed. If anything, things had improved. The better Leigh's career prospects, the more likely he was to welcome the baby.

"It's OK," she told herself, trying to switch her thoughts to the evening ahead. This was Liz's day, after all. But even as she thought of Liz she realised that this was no ordinary wedding. It had been overlaid with mystery, resentment, animosity.

What had Van meant in the car? Had her words about things kept secret for too long applied to her father or to Trevor? That first night, at dinner, she had said about twenty-eight years. That would be 1969. The year I was born, Rachel thought. And yet there had been an animosity in Vanessa's voice that had been directed at someone and it could only have been Trevor.

She fished for her hanky and blew her nose. Time to get on, think of someone else. Where was Mum? But tears threatened to overcome her again and however much she dabbed at her eyes they could not be stemmed. Was she being wet or was this what pregnancy did to you? If so, she didn't like it.

Terror took over then. The house was filling with

guests. They would find her here, eyes like puddings — everyone would stare! Her worst fears were realised when the door was pushed slowly ajar and a figure appeared.

"Hello." It was Tom Lattemore. He was dressed in a dark suit and a well-cut shirt. "I'm sorry." He had seen her face and was starting to back out but then he changed his mind and entered the room, closing the door behind him. "Is something wrong?"

"No," Rachel said. Then, knowing her answer had been ridiculous, "I'm just, it's just . . ." She meant to say, "Weddings. You know what I mean," but the words wouldn't come. Instead she just shook her head from side to side in dumb misery.

"Here," he said, holding out a folded handkerchief. "Wipe your eyes. I'm going to go and get us both a drink. There seems to be lashings of it out there."

He brought pale sherry in schooners and settled himself opposite her. "Better?" he said, when she had sipped.

"Yes. Thank you."

"Anything you want to share?"

"Now you're treating me like a patient," she said, but she smiled. It was the smile that undid her. It triggered off sobs that rocked her chest and caused her to splutter like a child.

To her relief he didn't move. Just went on sipping his sherry and waiting for her to regain control. At last he spoke. "I think you'd better tell me what's wrong. There's obviously something and I just might be able to help.

We're old friends, remember. Let me help!"

"You can't. No one can — and it's not just one thing, it's everything."

"Well, you've got to start somewhere," he said equably. "What's the first problem?"

"I'm pregnant," she said, at first cursing her runaway tongue and then discovering what a relief it was to tell someone. "Well, I think I am."

"That's not the end of the world," he said. "Do you want the baby?" But before she could answer the door was flung open and she saw her mother and Trevor framed in the opening.

"So this is where you are," her mother said, looking quizzically from one to another.

Useless to dab her eyes or wipe her running nose. It was plain to see that she had been weeping. Rachel was searching for something — anything — to say when Tom stepped in.

"Blame it on the wedding, Mrs Trewhitt. Apparently it was a marvellous ceremony, really moving, and your daughter is overcome with the euphoria of it all. I've been consoling her with your excellent fino."

"How kind." Whether or not her mother believed him, she appeared to accept what he said. "Run upstairs now, dear, and powder your nose. We're going to get the speechy bit over first and then we can all relax."

As Rachel passed Tom on her way to the door he smiled reassurance and mouthed, "Later." The next moment he was engaging her mother in conversation and Rachel escaped.

9

Fenton Marske, Sunday, 6 April 1997

Rachel was awakened by bells summoning people to church. It was Sunday, but downstairs the debris of yesterday's wedding party was awaiting attention. Rachel groaned and turned on her face, slipping her hands under the pillow, trying to block out the day.

Last night had been an ordeal. It had been a brilliant party for guests, but for family, those who knew of or were part of the underlying tensions, it had been a struggle to keep smiling. Rachel had watched her nephew and niece, had seen that even their young faces were strained behind the amiable party expressions.

Only her mother seemed truly at ease, the perfect hostess, the doting mother. Above all, the contented wife, her arm linked through her husband's whenever they stood together. "How does she do it?" Vanessa had asked, in a bitter aside, and Rachel had not had an answer.

Now, for her mother's sake, she dragged herself from

bed, giving thanks that there was no sign of sickness, and located jeans and a T-shirt, ready for the fray. At least, she reflected as she sluiced face and hands in the bathroom, family crises took your mind off your own troubles. Was she pregnant? This morning it seemed doubtful, and she couldn't decide whether that was a relief or a disappointment. But when she stripped off her nightdress she could still see the changes in her body.

She found her mother already up, hands in a sink full of suds and wine-glasses. "I'll leave them to drain. Let's clear the dining room," she said, as she dried her hands. "I want us to have a nice lunch before Vanessa leaves."

The idea of a "nice lunch" with brooding tension as the main course was far from appealing. Rachel was longing to ask if her father had stayed the night and, if not, where he had slept. Instead, on an impulse, she asked, "Is something the matter with Van? Other than being upset with Daddy, I mean."

"Why do you ask?" Her mother was scooping up mats and tablecloths and avoided meeting her eye.

"She seems so . . . well, jumpy. And in the car yesterday she and Trevor seemed to be having a spat."

"I should leave well alone, Rachel." Her mother faced her now, arms full of damask, brow furrowed. "It's never wise to interfere."

Rachel felt herself bridle at the rebuke in her mother's tone. "I don't want to interfere. I'm just worried about Van – about you."

"I'm sorry, darling." Her mother had put aside the cloths and moved to embrace her. "I'm sorry, forgive me, I know you care. It's just that things between Vanessa and Trevor are so difficult at the moment. I'm terrified that anything might tip her over the edge."

"Over the edge? Do you mean she might have a breakdown?"

"No." Her mother was shaking her head emphatically. "No, nothing like that. But I don't want her to leave him – well, not precipitately."

"Is there someone else? Has he been unfaithful?"

Her mother was turning away again, gathering up the soiled tablecloths. "No one serious. A silly little nonsense. Best forgotten. In fact, it's probably all in Vanessa's imagination. Trevor says it is, and I think she should believe him."

So that was why Vanessa was so bitter against her father. It gave her the chance to criticise the crime of adultery! "How do you know it's nonsense?" Rachel was amazed at how disapproving her voice was but she carried on. "Perhaps it's serious. Perhaps she should leave him."

They faced one another, the daughter critical, the mother defiant, both knowing it was not really Vanessa they were discussing. The impasse was dissolved by the ringing of the telephone. "It's for you," her mother said, holding out the receiver.

Rachel felt her heart leap and then thud uncomfortably. It could only be Leigh. No one else would track her down here. But when she took the handset it was not Leigh's voice she heard. "Hello," she said, hearing Tom Lattemore at the other end. "Did you get home safely?" She sounded as disappointed as she felt and could only hope it didn't communicate itself to the listener at the other end.

"Yes. Nothing like a brisk walk to sober you up. Are you OK?" There was genuine concern in his voice and she warmed to it, but her mother's presence in the background was disconcerting. What if Tom mentioned what she had told him last night? How could she answer without giving the game away to her mother?

At that moment she understood the depth of her own indecision. Yesterday she had been almost happy about her pregnancy, longing to tell Leigh and then the world. What had changed her? As she asked the question she answered it. The phone call to Leigh had changed things. There had been no room in their conversation for the momentous news, just as there would be no room in their lives for a baby.

She was roused from her musing by Tom's voice at the other end. "Hello? Are you there? Or has my suggestion driven you screaming from the phone?"

"I'm sorry. I just — what were you saying?"

"I was suggesting dinner tonight. If you'd like it, that is. We could talk." He was being nonchalant but she knew what he meant. She was about to make an excuse when she thought of the alternative. If she stayed at home it would either be a meal with her father and mother or alone with her mother with her father's absence looming over everything. If it was the former her father would be cocky as ever, dominating the table and arousing resentment within her. If the latter, what could they talk about that wasn't dangerous?

"I think that might be nice. I'll just check." She turned to her mother. "Tom's asked me to have dinner with him. Do you need me here?"

Her mother's look of relief was fleeting but unmistakable. "Of course not. That's a lovely idea. You used to be so close."

They arranged a time for him to pick her up and then she got on with clearing the party debris. Her mother went off to the kitchen to prepare lunch and Rachel tweaked chairs into place, took the leaf from the dining-table and found an unstained cloth. She was still longing to check on her father's whereabouts but it would probably be unwise. According to her mother, he was at an hotel but that was hard to believe. Her father liked attention. Sitting alone in a hotel room, however plush, was not his style.

When Vanessa and her family surfaced, Rachel went upstairs to have her bath. When she had turned on the taps and tipped in oil she went back on to the landing and stood at the head of the stairs listening to the murmur of conversation from below. As soon as she identified her mother's voice she went straight to her mother's bedroom and pushed open the door. To her relief the bed hadn't yet been made and she could see clearly that only one side of it had been slept in. So Daddy had not stayed the night and left at dawn, before Vanessa got on the warpath! Where the hell had he slept?

In the bath she indulged in a fantasy of seeking him out in his love-nest, presumably Esme Parkin's rambling mansion if it was true that her husband had walked out. "How dare you seduce my father?" she would say, and lead him, contrite, home. Except that the seduction had probably been the other way round.

That led to an uncomfortable line of thought. Everyone talked about genes nowadays. They were responsible for everything, if you believed the experts. What if she had inherited an adulterous gene? At the moment every bone in her body ached to be faithful. She regarded her stomach, submerged beneath the bathwater. Once you had a child everything changed, so even if she had been inclined to stray she would have reformed. Except that she might not have this child. Might not be allowed to have it . . . might have to choose.

She escaped from the hell of indecision by finishing her bath in record time and then sprinting through dressing to hurry down to the kitchen to help with lunch. When thoughts were unbearable, work was the only escape.

Lunch was a strained affair, conversation about everything and anything innocuous.

"These courgettes are scrumptious."

"I've always liked courgettes."

"Yes, they're a much undervalued vegetable."

It seemed that courgettes could be an everlasting topic passed from hand to hand or mouth to mouth for ever. The very best thing about courgettes was that they were about as far removed from fathers as was possible.

From time to time she regarded her niece and nephew. Evan was the elder and, at thirteen, there was a faint down on his upper lip, while the bony wrists that protruded from his cuffs were more those of a man than a child. He looked pretty miserable, but most teenagers looked miserable so that was not a reliable pointer to the state of her sister's marriage.

Joanne was eating steadily, almost greedily, as if food was all-important. Normal eleven-year old greed, or the sign of emotional deprivation? You could drive yourself mad trying to analyse your family.

"How did your series end?" her mother asked, when coffee had been served. It was obviously an attempt to continue innocuous conversation and Rachel tried to respond.

"Quite well, I think. Viewing figures were high so we're all in good favour."

"Will you go back?" Trevor was pitching in now, trying to help. "It starts up again in the autumn, doesn't it?"

"October. I'll probably do a drama in the meantime. It depends what I'm offered."

Vanessa was holding her cup to her lips with both hands, but her eyes stared fixedly ahead as though to show contempt for such a transparent attempt at diversion.

"What does a floor manager do? I've never been sure."

"That depends on the production. And the director. Some directors are happy for you to do the lot, decide the order of shots, co-ordinate effects and stunts, others like to do the whole thing themselves."

"It sounds complicated." This was her mother, who was looking fairly desperate now.

"Well," Trevor said, coming to the rescue, "I hate to

break up the party so soon after a great meal but we really ought to be on our way."

They assembled on the step to leave or wave goodbye. "I'm sorry, Mum," Vanessa said at last. "But you know why . . ." She turned to Rachel, eyes filled with tears, then back to her mother. "Oh, Mummy, Mummy . . ." She was a child again, needing her mother's arms. "How did you bear it?" She was looking into her mother's face now, wanting answers. But there was an impatient toot from the car where Trevor and the children were already installed and her mother put her gently away.

"Off you go, darling. Don't worry. Ring me tonight." There was much waving and shrill calls of love and goodbye. Rachel had to hold back Sally the labrador, who wanted to go for a ride. It was a relief when at last the car disappeared and she and her mother could go back into the house.

Rachel was in the morning room when Leigh rang. He was still euphoric. "I did Hewitt last night. Which Hewitt? Patricia, of course. One of Blair's gurus. You know, Aussie do-gooder. She has that same look of professional tolerance that Virginia Bottomley had. As if she's saying 'Poor little pygmy, how can you be so wrong?'"

Rachel tried to be interested, even glad for him, but it was difficult. There was a forthcoming election out there yet it seemed remote from the reality that was her life now, here. The call came to an end without her saying anything of note. "I'll try and ring you tonight," he said. And then, as an afterthought, "Love you."

She took the dog for a walk, hoping there was no possibility of running into Tom, glad that she need speak to no one for an hour or so. She tried to make order of her jumbled thoughts. It seemed unfair that Dad should get away with it all, slip back into the comfort of married life, perhaps even keep his "bit on the side". But if that was what her mother wanted, who had the right to gainsay her?

As for Trevor and Vanessa, she had never really cared for Trevor but life with the Drama Queen would not be altogether easy. "Never one to make a molehill out of a mountain," Liz had said once, and it was true. Had Trevor had it off with the au pair or merely glanced at a fellow party guest? With Vanessa you could never be sure. It was only when Rachel remembered her niece and nephew's strained little faces that she grasped that whatever was happening in her sister's life it was more than a pinprick.

She walked on, enjoying Sally's obvious pleasure at every scent and sound, every nook and cranny in the hedgerows. Above, the sky was an even blue flecked with white cloud, nimbus or cumulus, she never could remember. She paused, watching each puff of white drift lazily eastward. The dog had wriggled under a gate and she climbed over to join her.

It was then that she saw the flowers, tiny blue star-shaped flowers, nestling close to the ground, half hidden in the rough grass. How wonderful nature was that such a fragile thing could flourish. She felt tears prick her eyes. Hormones. It must be hormones. She was not naturally so emotional. She whistled up the dog then and turned for home, wondering why she was suddenly such a wimp. Because everything was different and she was no longer sure what was going on. That was why.

She wore a grey wool dress for dinner with Tom. She found it in the back of the wardrobe and, to her delight, it still fitted. "That's nice, dear," her mother said, when she came downstairs. She had added a red suede belt and red earrings, and they seemed to give the dress a new lease of life.

"Forgive my asking," her mother said, "but is this simply a meal with a nice man?"

Half of Rachel's head thought the question perfectly understandable. She had lived with Leigh for four years, it was natural for her mother to wonder why she should want to dine alone with another man. A man, moreover, for whom she had once cared. But the other, perverse half was angered. Her mother was quick enough to demand privacy for her own affairs. "Leave it, let it go," was her mantra. Why didn't she apply that to her daughter's business? Rachel managed to make a noncommittal reply and then they made small-talk until Tom's knock came at the door. But she couldn't resist a parting shot, "Will Dad be home tonight?"

The moment the words had left her lips she regretted them, but it was too late. She saw her mother's teeth catch her bottom lip and then her face came up and she met her daughter's eye. "I don't know," she said. "We'll have to wait and see."

Rachel turned and moved back to embrace her. "I won't be late," she said. "We'll talk, if you want to."

"Off you go." Her mother's habitual smile of reassurance had returned. "Have a good time."

There was a pleasant smell in Tom's car, a subtle fragrance that caused her to wrinkle her nose in appreciation. "Oh, Lord," he said. "It's not that strong, is it? I used some stuff Emma gave me for Christmas. Is it dreadful?"

"It's rather nice. What's it called?"

"I don't remember. Initials, I think."

"CK?"

"Could be, anyway . . ." When she looked sideways she could see that he was grimacing with embarrassment.

"It's lovely," she said, relaxing into her seat. "Stop worrying."

"I thought we'd try the Falstone." He seemed anxious to change the subject.

Rachel had not felt hungry for days but it would be nice to sit somewhere without waiting for a row to erupt. "Good," she said. "They say the food is marvellous." They were silent then until they reached their destination.

"Look," Tom said, as they turned into the pub car-park. "I suggested this because I thought you might want a chance to talk about your pregnancy."

She was glad that he said it straightforwardly. No euphemisms, no beating about the bush. "Thank you," she said. He was helping her out of the car now and she felt the warmth of his hand. "I can't talk to Mum at the moment and there's no one else. But, please, I don't want to fill your last evening off with yet another problem. I can sort it out."

"I don't doubt it, but let's sit down and have a drink and then we'll talk as much — or as little — as you'd like. I promise you I won't be bored. I haven't been a GP long enough to grow tired of the human race — not yet, anyway."

They were given a table in a dimly lit corner, the waitress obviously under the impression that they were lovers. Rachel looked up and saw that Tom had reached the same conclusion. He grinned. "Remind me to hold your hand between courses. We mustn't disappoint her."

But between courses they talked. About the election, about his job and hers, about the wedding and their respective families. She would have liked to be honest about the family crisis but it wasn't her secret to impart.

"It's funny," she said, as they ate pudding, "we haven't seen one another for eight or nine years and yet . . ."

"We've picked up where we left off? I feel that too. But an awful lot's happened in between — to both of us." He was reflective now, almost sad, and she might have probed if he had not forestalled her.

"Now," he said, leaning back in his seat, "what about you?"

"I think I'm pregnant. No, I know I am."

"You know? Have you had a test?"

"No, but my period is late, my breasts look different and I feel pregnant. I'm on the pill but I still feel sure." He was holding her eye and it was easy to be frank.

"Well, you should have a test. The pill doesn't normally let you down. I can arrange that for you. Do you want a baby just now?"

"I don't know. I have a partner. We've been together for four years and children were pencilled in. We discussed them occasionally, but only in the distant future. He's in television. His name is Leigh Barnes and he does *Agenda*. Reporting, mostly, but he's presenting it at the moment."

"I know him, I think. Tall, dark hair. Uses his hands a lot?"

"Yes. He's under a lot of pressure right now."

"So are you," he said gently.

"I know, but it's different."

"It's not."

The waitress was wafting by. "Everything OK?" she said.

"Fine, thank you." He turned back to Rachel. "There's no greater pressure than feeling your body changing. That's why it's so important that you have support. I can't tell you what you should do, but I can set out the options. Do you want me to do that?"

"Please. I think I know what they are but it'd be a help to have them listed."

He leaned back and smiled reassuringly. "You can take the pregnancy to full term and bring up the baby. Would he support you?"

"I suppose so."

"That means you're not sure"

"No, I am sure. We love each other . . . It's just . . ."

"You feel he'd rather not take on parenthood yet?" She nodded. "OK. I can understand that. We all have times like that." He was not being judgemental and for that she was grateful.

"I know he'd never ask me to have an . . ." She was about to say "abortion" but couldn't bring herself to use the word. Instead she said "Termination. If I did it, it would be my choice."

Now he was nodding and pouring more coffee from the cafetière. "Termination is a possibility. Technically you should have physical or psychological reasons but you'd find someone to do it."

"And if I did?"

"How would you feel? That depends. If you'd thought it through and it was what you *really* wanted you'd probably be all right. If it wasn't a voluntary decision you'd be in trouble."

"And in the future? Other children?"

"Done properly, no complications. No effect on future pregnancies. There's a third option."

"Adoption?" She had known he would raise this. "I don't think I could. If I had the baby I'd have to keep it."

"I know. It's just that I find it ironic that a patient can come into my surgery and say, 'I'm pregnant – I can't bear it,' and the next patient has come for the result of her fertility test. I say, 'No chance,' and she says, 'I can't bear it.' In the early days I had this compulsion to round up the unwanted babies and give them to those empty arms. Is that crazy?"

"Idealistic. You said 'unwanted'. It isn't that I don't want this baby . . ." Her voice died away and he leaned forward.

"You feel Leigh doesn't?"

"He doesn't know. I haven't told him so how can I tell?"

"For God's sake, why not?" He had thrown himself back in his seat and was looking at her with amazement.

"There hasn't been an opportunity." It was a lame excuse and they both knew it. After a while he leaned forward again and put a hand on hers.

"Tell him right away, Rachel. You can't begin even to think about this, much less make decisions, until you do. He was part of the beginning, he has a right to a say in the conclusion."

How could she tell him she had shirked telling Leigh, was afraid of his reaction? That would show him what a wimp she was, totally unable to do what must be done, utterly incapable of being a mother. Instead she said, "How do you feel about termination? Ethically, I mean."

He frowned a little at her question before he answered. "I'm not sure I have an ethical view. Each case is different and needs a different solution.

"You don't see it as a sin?"

"Not unless it is done for utterly selfish reasons . . . or used as a form of contraception by people too lazy to get it right in the beginning."

"I thought the pill was infallible," she said guiltily.

"It is, if you take it properly. You haven't had antibiotics lately, have you? Or a bout of gastritis? Sometimes if you vomit . . ." He grimaced as he saw her look of horror.

"I had food poisoning last month. Shellfish. I was very sick."

"That's it, then. You throw up the pill and forget to replace it. It happens quite often.

"I should've thought about it," she said.

"You're doctor should have warned you," he said firmly. "Don't blame yourself." He drank from his cup, then pushed it away. "Sometimes the decision to terminate can be the right answer, the only answer. Not only for the mother but for the baby. There are worse fates than not being born. It's the motive for a termination that matters. Some women do it for love of the child or, rather, for fear of its future. That's a world away from doing it because its birth would be an inconvenience."

"And worse fates than dying?"

"Yes," he said. "That too. Now, for the last few minutes, let's talk about something less serious. We can return to the hard facts of life at a later date. Let's get the test done, then take your time over your decision and don't regret it." They talked of films then, and music and sport, and found that their tastes were remarkably similar.

At last they came out under a starlit sky and walked over crunching gravel towards the car. "Call in at the surgery tomorrow," he said, as he folded her into the passenger seat of his Audi. "Bring a specimen and we'll arrange that test. I'll tell the receptionist to show you straight in, no need to give explanations." He smiled. "And don't look so tragic. In my experience these things always work out better than we fear."

_____ *10*

Fenton Marske, Monday, 7 April 1997

Amazingly, Rachel slept well and woke feeling refreshed. She had not arrived at any answers, but Tom's calm exposition of the facts had helped her to see things more clearly. If she kept calm — and, above all, if she brought Leigh into the decision-making — they could sort it out.

She went downstairs after her bath, expecting to find her mother in her usual place, the kitchen. But there was no sign of her, although the table was laid for breakfast and the kettle steamed on the Aga.

Rachel was about to go in search of her when she heard a car draw up outside and then crisp footsteps on gravel. "Hello." Her mother was smiling as she entered the kitchen, so all was well.

"Where've you been?" It was only eight o'clock, no shops were open. It seemed a fair question, but Rachel half expected an evasive answer.

To her surprise her mother answered easily. "To see

Daddy. He's been staying in Bardsage. I want him to come home." She had shrugged off her coat and was warming the tea-pot, lifting the kettle, scalding tea. They moved into chairs either side of the kitchen table, the tea-pot between them, and Rachel sensed that her mother was ready to talk.

"Are you sure, Mum? That you want Daddy back, I mean. I know you love him — I love him too. But I love you, and I don't like to think of you being unhappy."

"Darling . . ." Her mother was clutching together the edges of her blue cardigan. Above it her face was creased with the effort to explain. "I wish I could make you see. If Daddy comes back — and as far as I'm concerned he never left, it was his decision to go to save unpleasantness for Liz — there may be times when, well, when I'll be hurt again. But if he goes, if we separate, there's no doubt that I'll be unhappy *all* the time. The choice is between the possibility of pain and the certainty of it. Can you see that?"

"Yes." Rachel said it grudgingly but she couldn't avoid agreeing. "Yes, I see. And I know it's your choice and your choice alone. It's just . . ." She took a deep breath and plunged. "It's not one crazy slip with Daddy, is it? I knew about some things but, talking to the others this weekend, I can see that there's more than even I know——"

"What do you mean?" Her mother's question cut through her words. "What have they said?"

"Well, nothing definite. Vanessa said something the other day about twenty-eight years ago. I didn't understand that because it obviously happened before I was born or round about then."

"Rachel," her mother was rising to her feet and moving to the bench where the toaster stood, "I must have some toast. Shall I make you some? There was an affair all those years ago. I was pregnant, things often go wrong then, it was nothing. Now, marmalade or honey?"

The conversation was definitely over, Rachel thought, as she began to leaf through the papers she had collected from the lobby. Any intention of taking her mother into her confidence about her pregnancy had gone too, at least for the moment, and it was probably just as well as she had yet to have a proper test. This morning, in the calm light of day, it was impossible to believe she was pregnant. Why make unnecessary waves?

She made small-talk with her mother throughout breakfast and then, on the pretext of shopping, she borrowed her mother's car and set off for Tom's surgery, a tiny bottle of early-morning urine safe in her handbag.

The receptionist had evidently been warned of her visit. As soon as Rachel gave her name the woman's face was wreathed in smiles. "Doctor's expecting you. If you just take a seat till he's finished with his patient . . ."

A few moments later Rachel was in Tom's consulting room. He took the specimen from her and began to fill in a card. "It won't take long. I've marked it urgent. Try not to think about it too much in the meantime. I know it's not easy but you won't make anything better by worrying – or hurrying things up. Get out and get some fresh air. I only wish I could come with you."

He walked with her to the door of the surgery, lifting

his face to the sun when they were outside. "God, I'd really like to be free today. Having time off doesn't build you up, it thoroughly discontents you. Still . . ." He put a hand on her arm. "You get yourself home. I'll ring as soon as I get the result. And don't worry. If anyone else answers I'll flannel it and you can ring me later."

"I'm really grateful, Tom. I know I should've seen my own GP but that means——"

"Hush. It's done. Anyway, you're here on holiday so I'm entitled to treat you. And I'll look forward to seeing you next time you come home. One way or another, this will be solved and you'll be happy. I'll look forward to meeting Leigh, too." And then he bent and kissed her cheek.

He stood waving as she reversed and headed out of the car-park. He's a nice man, she thought, and he was a good friend she intended to keep. As she drove back towards the house she ran through her girlfriends, thinking of possible matches. Except that matchmaking never worked. Everyone knew that.

Once she had banished wedding bells from her mind, old doubts resurfaced. Even if the problem of pregnancy vanished overnight with a negative test, the problem of her parents remained. Vanessa would not let up and, if the ominous signs were anything to go by, her sister would probably be back home before long, children, worldly goods and all. And if Mum and Dad patched things up, as they probably would, how could any of them behave towards her father as though they were unaware of his . . . she sought for a word and came up with "peccadilloes".

She was uncomfortably aware that she had always

loved her mother best. She loved her father, too, had admired him in many ways, the handsome figure in uniform, a commander of men, but it had been her mother who held the family together, was always there, put everyone and anyone first. If it came to a crunch Rachel knew where her loyalties would lie.

But before she made a firm decision there must be honesty. Her mother had shied away from something this morning. "And I have to know what," Rachel said aloud. Outside the car the countryside was green with spring, hedgerows bursting into leaf, everything pregnant with summer growth. It was a good time for the uncovering of secrets.

Her mother was alone when she got back to the house. "Only you and I for lunch, darling. Will salad do?"

Rachel seized the opportunity. "Good. I'm going to see if I can catch Leigh, and then I want to talk, Mum. I can't go away with so many questions unanswered. I have to find out from you . . . or else I'll have to ask Van. She'll tell me." Her conscience pricked at the sight of her mother's griefstricken face but her resolve did not weaken. "I'll make my call and be back in a tick."

She reached Leigh without much difficulty but his greeting was abstracted, as though his mind was elsewhere.

"I'm coming home tomorrow, darling." She had expected at least a muted enthusiasm but it was not forthcoming.

"Oh, well, if you're sure . . . I mean, I'm OK. I can manage. To tell you the truth, I've barely touched the flat except to get a shirt. So if you want to stay . . ."

"No." The resolve she had formed earlier was still in evidence. "I'll be home tomorrow, tea-time at the latest. I'll make dinner, something that'll keep so don't worry. I know you're under pressure. It's been hectic while I've been here so I could do with some time to myself."

"Well, as long as you know I won't be at home much. You can't imagine how crazy it is here. Word is that Major's gone up to Aintree for the race — you knew the re-run was today — so we've had to cover it. And the place is heaving about Martin—"

"Martin?" He obviously expected her to know who he was talking about but she knew at least four Martins.

"Martin Bell. You know, the war correspondent. He's standing against Hamilton in Tatton. Came forward yesterday. They want me to go up there for his press conference tomorrow. Rumour has it Hamilton's wife might turn up."

"I see." She had a dim recollection of Neil Hamilton's candidacy being threatened because of his purportedly unethical dealings with Mohamed Al-Fayed and someone suggesting Labour and the Lib-Dems might unite to get rid of him by tactical voting, which seemed an attractive idea until you really thought about it and realised it was undemocratic.

She could tell that he thought it would be better if she stayed in Yorkshire. In some other man she might have expected another woman but this was Leigh, whose only thought was work.

"When will you be back from Tatton?"

"I can't tell – we're in a state of flux here, because of Baz being *hors de combat* and the election and the Irish thing. But they'll have it all battened down by the weekend. They'll have to. Then we'll have proper hours again – well, almost – and I'll make it up to you, promise."

But until then you'd like me to dematerialise, Rachel said, but only in her head. Aloud she said, "OK. I suppose it makes sense to stay on for a while and Mum could do with a bit of TLC. I'll ring you tonight."

"Good girl." He was relieved: she could hear it in his voice. "I'm missing you like crazy but I've got to give this one hundred and ten per cent. You do see that, don't you? If I can come good now, when they're up to their necks in shit, it won't be forgotten. I've seen it happen to others. 'You can always depend on so-and-so.' You know the thing. So it's for us, really. So you can stop working those little fingers to the bone and just look after me."

"I like my work," she protested.

"Only joking – don't go PC on me. You know how much I value your career. But I'd like you to be free to work when you want to – and only on stuff you enjoy."

Should she tell him now? Had he made an opening? "Well, speaking of giving up work . . ." she could say. "How would you feel about me being a full-time wife and mother?" Except that she was terrified of letting the genie out of the bottle. Once out, you could never get it back in.

Outside, the garden was a riot of yellow, forsythia, daffodils, tulips. The colour of spring. If she was pregnant her baby would be born at Christmas. A picture of holly and poinsettia was replaced by the thought that before the forsythia had faded the baby might be no more. They would have to make a decision. She said goodbye, put down the phone and went back to the kitchen. One thing at a time.

She had wanted to tell her mother about her extended stay but she had gone. Because I said I wanted answers, Rachel thought, and grimaced at the idea that her mother wanted to avoid her. She decided to go for a walk but when she whistled there was no sound of eager paws and when she looked she saw that the lead was missing from its hook behind the door. Had her mother fled with the dog or was Daddy back?

Upstairs she decided to go through her wardrobe. The grey dress had been an unexpected find. There might be other things there she could take back to London and use. If not, she would throw them out. If the situation between her parents worsened, the house might have to go. Mummy would never throw Daddy out but what if he opted out, chose the younger woman and set up home with her? Mum would have to let go then.

The thought of her parents being locked in a divorce settlement was unbearable. She had friends whose parents had divorced and they had survived. So would she if she had to — except that she had always been family-oriented. She had had friends at school, at college, had friends in London now, women and one or two men, whose company she valued and enjoyed. But it had always been the family she had thought of first, wanted to confide in, needed to depend on. Until now.

Now she was nursing the biggest secret of her life and

she couldn't tell them. Couldn't tell anyone except, perhaps, Jago, who was lovable but only a neighbour, after all. And Tom Lattemore, who was virtually a stranger after so many years apart. And yet he didn't feel like a stranger. She found she was grinning almost fondly at the thought of him and shook her head at her own foolishness.

She sat down on the window-seat, looking out at the spring landscape. Somewhere out there, in the newly green meadows and hawthorn-edged pathways, a mother was hiding from a daughter, a father was living with strangers and fifty miles away a sister was probably weeping into one of the immaculate lawn hankies that were Vanessa's trademark.

What a mess, Rachel thought. What a bloody mess. Because she was no better off than the rest of them. She had been careful about contraception but not careful enough. If she got out of this, if it was only a scare or if she had to choose termination, she would make sure she was never in this situation again, unless it was planned.

The ambivalence of her thinking about the possibility of a pregnancy amazed her. One minute she was almost exulting at the idea, the next deploring it. One minute planning abortion, the next designing a layette. Only when she was discussing it with Tom did she feel calm.

She could see him tonight . . . except that it wasn't fair to foist herself on him night after night. He had a life of his own, after all. That first day, after they had met him in the field, Liz had said he was very attractive to women. "Emma says they hurl themselves at him. But there was a love affair when he was at med school, some girl who died of an aneurysm. Quite tragic. Emma says he's never got over it." He had not mentioned it when they talked, which probably meant it was still painful.

Poor Tom. Poor Mum. Poor Rachel, come to that. At least she could leave her mother in peace today. When Dad comes back, when it's all settled, I'll ask her then, Rachel vowed, and went back to sorting out her wardrobe.

11

Rachel kept her vow to give her mother space. They ate alone at the dining table, chatted about work and the joys and woes of country living, drank a bottle of her father's excellent claret. Neither of them referred to the upheavals of the last few days until they carried their coffee into the living room and settled either side of the fire.

"I miss Daddy," her mother said, reflectively, stirring her cup clockwise and then anti-clockwise, although the sweetener she had put in it must long since have dissolved.

Rachel did not answer directly. Instead she said, "I envy you."

"Me?" Her mother's face creased with merriment. "I can't imagine why."

"Because you're serene. Because you know what you want. Because you're never afraid." But now her mother's face was crumpling, ageing before her very eyes.

"Oh, I'm afraid, Rachel. Frequently. And I don't think

I'm serene. But I am determined. I've always known what I wanted. A home and a family. I've done whatever I needed to do to preserve that. If that makes me ruthless, I suppose I am. I would call it loving, being in love. Putting that above everything. Is that what you feel for Leigh?"

"I don't know. I love him, I know that. But I'm not sure if . . ." She hesitated, trying to find words that would not offend.

Her mother smiled. "You're not sure you could accept, as I do? Perhaps you couldn't. But it's children who make the difference. Wait until you have children, then you'll understand."

This was it, the moment to confide. Rachel felt relief flood over her but before she could assemble the words to describe her state of perhaps-pregnancy, the telephone rang.

"See who that is, darling. It's probably for you. Leigh usually rings in the evening, doesn't he."

But it was not Leigh. It was a woman, sobbing uncontrollably. "Rachel? I want Mummy. Where's Mummy?" And then, before Rachel could reply, "He's admitted it, Rachel. It's gone on for weeks. He says it never meant anything but that was always Daddy's excuse, wasn't it? Well, I won't let Trevor get away with it like Mummy did. I won't live with the scar for thirty years. Not me."

"What is it? Is it Vanessa?" Her mother was at her side, eyes anxious, almost elbowing Rachel aside in her eagerness to take over the phone. She listened to her daughter's outpourings and put a hand over the mouthpiece. "Go to bed, Rachel. Leave everything. We'll see to it in the morning. I'll deal with this."

It was not a suggestion, it was an order, and Rachel obeyed. But she spent a restless night replaying Vanessa's almost incoherent statement over and over again. "I won't live with the scar for thirty years." Thirty? It had been twenty-eight. Did that mean there had been something else, or had it been a slip of the tongue? Vanessa had never been a model of exactitude.

Light was beginning to filter in through the curtains when she wondered if Tom would ring today with the result of her test. Why hadn't she simply driven into Harrogate and bought a home pregnancy test? Still, it was done now. She told herself she would hear today as she drifted off.

Her sleep was troubled and brief. As soon as she woke, she showered and dressed and went downstairs. Her mother was there in the kitchen, standing with her back to the Aga.

"Please sit down." She saw her mother flinch at the tone of her voice but unless she was brusque, cruel, even, it would be the same old weave and dodge. "I have to know everything, Mum. Even the things that happened before I was born. I was already suspicious and last night clinched things. I'm tired of hints. If you won't tell me I'll ask Dad, I'll ask Van, I'll ring Aunt Sue in Alberta, if I have to. Someone must know, someone will tell me."

"Don't do this, Rachel. Leave well alone." Her mother's hands were twisting around a mug, right and left, left and right, and it was a shock to notice how loose and wrinkled the skin on the back of her hands had become. She's getting old, Rachel thought. She's getting old and I never noticed.

"I have to, Mummy. Not just for my sake, for yours too. For everyone's . . . including Daddy's. He can't be happy about the way things are. But before this family can heal, before we can be together again as a family, we have to be honest with one another."

All of a sudden she was seized with a sense of her own hypocrisy. She was urging truth on her mother while withholding truth herself. Except that she might have been truthful, might have sought solace in her mother's arms if it hadn't been for the business of Esme Parkin and, after that, last night's phone call. It isn't fair, Rachel thought, and folded her arms in front of her. "I'm waiting." It was her turn to come first and all she wanted was a little truth. That wasn't much to ask.

"Don't say I didn't warn you." Her mother's voice had dropped to little more than a whisper. "I suppose I might as well tell you. If I don't, Vanessa will. She sees it as a weapon with which she can punish your father — and me."

"What is it?" Inside Rachel a knot of fear was forming, a feeling that she had prised up the lid of Pandora's box and might be sorry she had done so.

"Before I tell you," her mother began, "I want you to know how much I love you. You do know that, don't you?"

"Yes," Rachel said, trying not to sound impatient. "I know how much you love me — and I love you. That's why I can't stand this mystery, Mum. It's coming between us."

"Nothing could come between us. Nothing."

"I know," Rachel said. "But please, Mummy, just tell me. It can't be half as bad as my imaginings."

"Your father was stationed near Hamburg. We went there in 'sixty-seven. You were born in 'sixty-nine," her mother said, her voice calm now, almost flat. "In the August of 'sixty-eight a girl came to me. She was a corporal, assigned to the adjutant's office." Her fingers were writhing now and Rachel put out a hand to still them.

"She told me she was carrying your father's child. I laughed. Impossible, I said. I laughed when I told your father . . . and then I saw his face. I had two children – if there was a scandal, a whiff of his misbehaving with a lower rank, we would have lost everything. I arranged – I bribed the girl to leave the service on the grounds of pregnancy, father unknown. It happened quite often so no one was curious."

She paused and was looking down at her nails, examining them as though for flaws. The kitchen stayed silent except for the ticking of the wall clock with its pattern of leaves and flowers. So that was it, Rachel thought. A half-sister or -brother somewhere. Well, worse things had happened.

"What then? Were you pregnant too?"

Her mother smiled, almost pityingly, but she took up her story where she had left off. "I arranged for her to be boarded in a small hotel in Kensington. I visited her every week. I can't say I came to like her but I knew she had probably been more sinned against than sinned herself.

And there was no possibility of her looking after the child. Not as I would have liked, anyway. She was young. Twenty. She felt she hadn't lived." There was a faraway look in her eyes now, the pain of remembering.

"I asked what she intended to do. Give up the child for adoption, she said. This was your father's child, remember. Besides, as weeks went by I felt a bond with it, poor little thing. Conceived in folly, about to be cast out, God knew where. I realised then what I had to do. I told your father. I laid down my terms. Either he acquiesced or I left him. He didn't argue. I think he was probably relieved."

"What did you do?" Rachel asked, eager now to know the outcome.

"When the baby was almost due we travelled to Britain, Freda and I. That was her name, Freda. She checked into a hospital but she gave my name, my details. I was ten years older but no one queried anything. I had a thousand pounds, a legacy from my grandmother. When she came out of hospital with the baby I gave her one thousand pounds. She gave me the baby."

"What did you do with it?" Rachel was agog now. Somewhere there was a child, a half-sister or brother. "And why did she pretend to be you?"

"I needed a certificate, a legal right to the baby. What did I do with it? I kept it, Rachel darling. I kept it and I came to love it as though it was my own."

Only the ticking of the clock. Only the slow and terrible stirring of an idea. "You don't mean . . . was it a boy or a girl?"

"It was a girl." Again the clock, but louder now.

Unbearably loud.

"It wasn't me? I don't believe it was me."

"It was you, Rachel. And what I said about loving you is true. You know that. You are so dear to me I sometimes fear I love you more than the others."

There was silence for a long, long time and then she heard her own voice as though far-off. "What did you say to people? To the others?" Her ears were ringing but she tried to grasp at facts.

"Liz simply accepted that I had had a baby. Vanessa was twelve. Pointless to lie to her. I told her it was our secret. Your father had arranged a transfer. When I came back to Germany it was to a new location. I said I'd had a baby recently. It was accepted. Even now I don't know how we got away with it but we did."

"What happened to her?" Rachel couldn't bring herself to say "my mother". She had no mother. Not now. She didn't wait for an answer. "I can't believe this." She was rising from the table but her legs were threatening to betray her. "It means I'm not one of the family. Liz and Vanessa are not my sisters. How could you lie to me all these years?"

"I did it for the best . . . and of course they're your sisters. Your father is their father. You have his genes, just as they do."

"I don't want them! How can you expect me to bear this?"

Her mother's eyes had strayed to the door. It was opening and a figure was framed there.

"I've left the car out, Dodo. I need to get my bags. Any

chance of a cup of tea?" He noticed the faces then, the tension around the table.

"How dare you come back? How dare you?" Rachel would have attacked him with her fists, but what good would it have done?

"She knows, Philip." Her mother had got up. "I had to tell her. If I hadn't Vanessa would . . ."

For once her father looked uncertain. "Rachel, oh, darling, I am sorry you had to find out like this. Let me explain . . ."

He was moving forward, leaving the door open. Rachel had only one overpowering desire: to run from this place and never see any of them ever again.

"Wait." He was reaching out and she struck at his hand as she passed him. And then she was running across the gravel, over the lawn, dropping down the ha-ha behind the house, not knowing or caring where she was going as long as it was away from here. She didn't stop until she had climbed the field to the copse and could look back and see that there was no one in pursuit. She lay down then, on the soft pine needles, smelling leaf mould and soil, crying until her eyes hurt and her chest ached with sobbing. I want to die, she thought, and knew that even that was beyond her control.

She stayed in the wood for hours, sometimes sleeping, sometimes weeping. She stayed until the light began to fade. She couldn't go back home but where else was there? She had no money, no handbag. Her shoes were flimsy and she was already so cold that she wondered if she was still able to move.

It was the cold that brought her at last to her feet. In the dusk the colours of the countryside had merged and there was no sign of life. No smoking chimneys, no lighted windows, only the lights of the main road far over to the left.

For a while she thought about finding a phone-box and summoning Leigh. Perhaps she could thumb a lift back to London. She even contemplated feigning amnesia and being admitted to hospital, to lie tranquilly between crisp white sheets and refuse to answer questions.

In the end she turned towards the village. Tom's house lay in that direction. Three miles away. Perhaps four. She started to walk, slowly at first then quickening her pace until at last she was moving into the dark porch and raising a hand to the knocker.

12

It was strange to wake up in a bedroom she had seen only dimly by lamplight. In daylight she could see that it was a delightful place, full of furniture that glowed with the patina of years and stood out against the pale walls and flower-sprigged curtains.

There were odd, and probably valuable, pieces of china here and there, a nodding mandarin in white porcelain, a pink lustre jug and, on the walnut dressing-table, a bisque cherub. So he likes to collect, Rachel thought, and then cringed as the horror and embarrassment of the night before flooded back to confront her.

She had arrived on his doorstep, teeth chattering, not caring about anything but getting away from home and what had come to light there. He had drawn her over his step and piloted her to a chair by the fire. A real fire, if she remembered correctly, spluttering and crackling as wood flared and sparks flew up the vast chimney.

"Have you taken anything? Booze, pills, any kind of drug?" His voice was kind but brisk. When she shook her head he moved away, then returned with a glass of water.

She sipped gratefully and then, aware that there must be some explanation, began to stammer out a story. "I had a shock. At home. I had to get away."

"I don't want to pry but – well, is there anyone else to worry about?" She laughed then, a high-pitched, hysterical laugh. There were plenty of people to worry about, but who were they? Mothers who were not mothers, sisters who were only half of what they had been before.

"No," she said at last. "Not in the way you mean. I found something out, about myself. It shook me."

He relaxed into his chair. "That happens to all of us at one time or another."

"It wasn't like that. It was a – I found out that I was adopted." No need to tell him everything.

He pursed his lips. "That's tough. You should have been told long ago. From the beginning." He looked down at his glass. "Look, it's probably a good idea if everyone cools off. Do your parents know you came here?"

"No. I just ran out."

"Then I'm going to ring them and tell them you're OK and you're staying the night. Tomorrow it will all be easier to deal with. OK?"

She hesitated but there seemed no alternative. "If you're sure I won't be a nuisance?"

"Not at all. Let's get that sorted, then. Finish your

water and then we'll think about food. I'm no cordon bleu but I'm not bad."

It was a relief when he came back and nodded that all was well. She had pictured her mother insisting on coming over, taking her home . . . And it was a blessed relief that someone else was handling things.

"You didn't tell me you left home hours ago. They were pretty distraught."

"But they haven't called the police?" Her voice was bitter. Of course they wouldn't have called the police. Mustn't make waves.

"They were about to do just that. I caught them in time, fortunately." He smiled then. "There's no need to look so woebegone. You look like a defiant little street-urchin and you've grass in your hair. Let's get you cleaned up and then we'll eat."

She washed face and hands in the cloakroom leading off the hall and tried to brush down her clothes as best she could. Her hands and feet were burning now as blood returned to them and her eyes seemed like embers in a too-white face. But when she emerged the smell of food was in the air and the fire had been banked up. She let out her breath in a long sigh and then looked around the room.

There were sporting trophies on a sideboard and team photos on the walls. That was when she noticed the picture of the girl in an off-the-shoulder dress, pearls at her throat and ears and a smile upon her lips. That must be the girl who died, Rachel thought, and was sad for him.

She managed to eat a forkful or two of the excellent stir-fry Tom produced, and sipped gratefully at coffee and

Benedictine. Then, to her amazement, she felt her eyelids droop. For one crazy moment she wondered if he had given her something in the coffee but it was only the exhaustion of too much emotion.

"Come on," he said, pushing back his chair. "You need sleep." He half led, half carried her up to the spare room, then disappeared to return with a towel and a pair of silk pyjamas. "Emma's," he said. "I don't have other lady guests. Well, not usually."

"I'm sorry," she said apologetically, but he simply turned back the duvet.

"Don't be. It's rather nice, I find. Now, bathroom's across the landing, spare toothbrush in the drawer. I won't disturb you again." She sluiced face and hands at the wash-basin in the corner and tumbled into bed. Sleep came as her head touched a pillow scented with herbs.

Now she lay in a room lit by sunlight filtering through the curtains and wondered how on earth she was going to face the embarrassment of the day.

"You have to go home," he said, as they sat at the breakfast table. "Practically, because you need your clothes and possessions. More importantly, because the longer you wait, the harder it will be."

"I know." It would have been a great relief to tell him the truth, that hers had been no ordinary adoption. But the story was not hers alone. "I don't owe them anything," said a voice in her head. "Why should I keep their secret?" In the end, the pull of remembered hugs and love and sympathy was too strong. She kept her counsel, and discussed the pros and cons of adoption with him as though hers had been a classic case.

"There's something else," he said at last. "The result of your test. It's positive."

"Oh!"

It was a small explosion of breath rather than a reply, and he looked at her quizzically. "Well? Good news or bad?"

"Good," she said slowly. "Good – or, at least, it will be when it's sorted out, when I've told Leigh."

"I'm glad." He took a step forward and put his arms around her. "For old times' sake," he said. "You look like you need a hug right now." She nodded but she did not speak. She simply stood there, enjoying being held.

"I have to go," he said at last, glancing at his watch. "Surgery awaits. Stay as long as you like, unless you'd like me to drop you off now?"

If she stayed a while she might stay for ever. "Perhaps I'd better have a lift," she said. They exchanged phone numbers before they drove off.

"Try to keep calm," he said, as he opened the door of the car in the driveway of her home. "It's tough on you, bearing in mind your pregnancy. In the meantime, chill."

She stood waving until his Audi disappeared, then lifted her chin and went into the house.

Her mother was coming down the stairs, her arms full of bedding to be washed. "I'm glad you're back," she said, as though nothing had happened.

They followed one another into the kitchen, each knowing that something must be said and reluctant to be the one to begin.

"Can we talk?" her mother asked, when she had brewed tea and they were seated at the kitchen table.

"We have to," Rachel said, and was surprised at her own weary tone.

"Do you doubt that I love you?"

She had not expected that to be her mother's first question and it threw her. The sun blazed through the window, haloing her mother's head but throwing her face into shadow. "No," Rachel said at last. "No. I know you love me . . . but I also know now that you lied to me. My whole life has been a lie. Nothing is what I thought it was."

"Your father is still your father."

Rachel contented herself with a look of contempt and waited for her mother to continue. "You know who your father is, your sisters are still joined to you by blood, and they love you."

"Does Liz know?"

"Yes." A faint flush mottled her mother's cheek. "Yes. Something Vanessa said set her thinking. When she was about twelve she asked me outright. I had to tell her the truth — not about Dad. I simply said I wanted another baby and you were there and I loved you. She accepted that."

"So she doesn't know I'm her half-sister?" Suddenly she was swept with anger. "Is she another of Dad's by-blows? Is Van yours or has he collected a family of bastards?" She saw her mother's tears but she couldn't stop — until she remembered that she was flaying the wrong person and that this person had already been punished too much. "I'm sorry," she said, and rose from the table.

She had almost finished packing when she heard her father's tread on the landing.

"You've upset Mummy," he said, without anger.

"I know." He was stooping through the doorway and she had to repel him. "That was wrong of me because it's not her fault, is it? We know whose fault it is. Yours. You are the selfish, arrogant . . ." She sought a bad enough word but there was not a word base enough to describe him. ". . . prick," she said at last. "You are the shit who caused all this so can you get out of my room? Oh, it's your house so it isn't my room. But get the hell out of it just the same because I can't bear to be within four walls with you."

He turned and left then, pausing only to throw the keys of the Rover on to her bed. "You'll need transport," he said. "I'll pick up the car from the station later. Lock the keys inside. I have a spare set."

She kissed her mother's cheek as she left. "I'm sorry," she said. "I shouldn't take it out on you. I just can't understand why you didn't tell me sooner. We'll talk about it later. When things have settled down." She would have gone then but her mother restrained her.

"Whatever happens, Rachel, whatever you decide, never doubt that I have loved you from the first moment I held you in my arms."

At times Rachel could scarcely see the road through her tears. Only one thing consoled her. This baby, hers and Leigh's, would know its origin from the onset. "No lies," she promised it, touching her still-flat belly with one hand, holding the wheel with the other. Anything was better than being lied to. Even termination.

She thought about the future all through the train journey. At York she tried to telephone Leigh but he was unavailable. "I think he's gone home," said the voice at the other end, filling Rachel with dreams of an evening together, a listening ear, the comfort of loving arms around her. She would tell him then and see his face light up at the prospect of a child, a son. She had a feeling that the child she was carrying was a boy.

Strange that what she had so feared at first had become so desirable.

She had hoped to find Leigh at home when she arrived, the flat warm and noisy with the radios and television he liked to have burbling permanently in every room. She even sniffed for the aroma of coffee or one of his exotic concoctions spluttering in the wok. But the flat was silent, the rooms chill. If he had been at home while she was away, his visits had been fleeting.

For a moment she wondered if there *had* been someone else, some other woman who had taken him into her home and her arms. Was every man like Daddy? Vanessa had believed it of Trevor and it had been true. Was Leigh different? A wry smile came to her lips. Other women were not her rivals, not where Leigh was concerned.

13

They made love in the early-morning light. Hungrily, because they had been separated but without the usual laughter and lazy pleasure that accompanied sex between them. Last night Leigh had arrived home at two a.m. and tumbled into bed with little more than a muttered "Welcome home." He had claimed to be overcome with fatigue but his breath had smelt of whisky and there had been the odour of tobacco about his clothes. If he had been working he had been relaxing too.

During her long wait Rachel had rehearsed and rerehearsed her announcement but when he stood before her there seemed no point. Not even the news of imminent birth could animate those lacklustre eyes. Leigh had made for the bedroom, apologising as his eyes closed. Then, in the dark, he put out a hand to pat her rump. "Good to have you back . . . in the morning . . . masses to tell . . ."

She lay in the darkness listening to his breathing as it

evened and deepened and told herself that the secret was worth keeping. Perhaps she would tell him tomorrow. Perhaps she would save it until they had their first meal together without the need to eat up and go.

Now they lay in bed, tired but sated. "How was the wedding?" he asked, although they had already discussed it on the phone. She trembled on the verge of telling all but something held her back. He had been working hard, they were just reunited. Why submerge him at once into a family crisis?

"It was fine. Liz looked wonderful, Hugh was beaming, we all cried."

"It sounds a happy occasion." His voice was mocking as it always was when they discussed anything in the least sentimental.

"The party in the evening was good."

"Same people?"

"Some . . . Some who couldn't be accommodated during the day. Not family, neighbours mostly, and one or two of the people we knew at school."

"Ah!" He was teasing her now. "Old schoolfriends. Female?"

"Mostly. One or two men."

He growled and raised himself to hover above her. "So, you didn't spend all your time wishing I was there?"

Under her hand his shoulder was smooth and firm. "Oh, yes, I did," she said.

"Good!" He lay back on his pillow. "Who were these men, then, the ones you didn't fall for?"

"Philip Gedge was there. We shared a pony once. And

Tom Lattemore. He's the local doctor, and he and I were an item once. But it was his sister who was the most ravishing thing you've ever seen, who had all the boys drooling."

"With you around? I can hardly believe that."

"It's true. And you couldn't even hate her for it because she was so nice. So is Tom."

"Tom!" He had roused himself on an elbow again and was leaning to tease her. "Tom! I'm not sure I like the way you said that."

She felt a delicious pleasure at even this mock-jealousy. She mattered to him. "He's an old friend. That's all." She was turning into him now, twining her legs around his, seeking his mouth. In the early days they had made love twice, thrice . . . even more.

But he was gently disentangling himself. "Sorry, darling, the spirit is willing but the flesh, as you'll have noticed, is weak." He was swinging from the bed, stretching, rubbing his face, scratching idly at belly and sides. "I hope to God a shower perks me up. We've a planning meeting this morning. God's coming. Baz will apparently be out for at least six weeks. It's a pity for him but from my point of view it's manna."

While he showered she cooked breakfast for him, half of her fretting at the lack of opportunity to talk, half relieved that she could escape it. How would she begin? "I'm pregnant—oh, and by the way you know my mother? She's not." If she spoke about it she would cry, and she knew how he would react to tears at this juncture, when his body was with her but his mind was already at work.

They listened to the radio as he ate. "My God," Leigh said with relish. "The Tories are in the shit, good and proper. Listen to Humphries making rings round them — it's like shooting rats in a barrel." He was equally scathing about Labour. "Anything and everything, as long as it gets votes. Wait till they have to keep their promises. That's when the brown stuff will hit the fan." The Liberals he dismissed as "chancers". "As for Paddy Pants-Down, a hanger-on if ever I saw one." And all Rachel could think of was how little the disintegration of the Tory Party mattered alongside the disintegration of her own family. "Cheer up," he said at last. "A few more days, three weeks, and then, unless you've been reassigned, we'll take off somewhere special."

When he had gone, on a welter of goodbyes and promises, Rachel sat contemplating his half-cleared plate. It was eight twenty and the day yawned in front of her like a chasm. Eventually she poured herself a drink, gin and tonic, ice and lemon, but it tasted foul in her morning mouth and she poured the remains of it into the sink. She watched the ice, collected in the plug-hole, melting as it was dripped upon from the hot tap. She felt mesmerised by the spectacle. How long would it last? Would it melt entirely or would slivers remain to fall through the grating and float, still frozen, in the sewers? Why had she poured gin at this hour? She didn't even like it much, it was just that she needed something! She stayed watching long after the last fragment had melted into nothingness and it was a relief when she heard Jago's impatient rattle at the door.

"It's not sugar this time or milk. It's gossip. Hot off the press!"

The hot gossip concerned the mysterious Italian lady who occupied the upstairs flat opposite and entertained sinister men in dark glasses who arrived in chauffeured cars. This time she had flown off to God knows where with an enigmatic look in her eye, or so Jago's sources were saying.

He was stretched on the velvet sofa now, head propped on a sweatshirted arm, spiky hair framing his freckled face. Leigh thought him an amusing inconsequence, Rachel knew, but she was fond of Jago. He was gentle and remarkably perceptive at times.

"Why are you so interested in her comings and goings?"

"Well," Jago waved an elegant hand, "she's beautiful. She dresses divinely. But don't let the eye-liner and the stilettos fool you. If it came to the push, she'd turn her hand to anything. I want to see her happy. If that lot she hangs out with will ever let her be happy."

"What would make her happy, then?"

"A man who puts her first, a Porsche, world peace and a tab at Versace. It's not a lot." He swung his legs to the floor and straightened up. "I thought you said there was coffee?"

"Coming up." She had forgotten it in her need to talk.

"Anyway," he followed her to the percolator, "what is 'happy'? I mean, who has ever succeeded in defining happiness? For you it's Leigh and a house with a garden. For me it's a guy with good pecs in an Armani jacket.

Horses for courses."

"Drink this." She held out his cup. "It's too early in the morning to philosophise." But as she dressed for a shopping expedition she pondered what Jago had said. Who had defined happiness? Who could? And even when you thought you had it, didn't it slip through your fingers like melting snow?

By eleven thirty she had bought the few small articles and some items of food she needed. She ought to go home and do some work, but if she did she would simply mope around. She was moving idly from counter to counter in D. H. Evans when nausea overcame her. In the cloakroom, mercifully empty, she leaned her face against the mirror and tried to retch. If she held on it would pass. She vomited a little, only waterbrash that burned her throat and tongue, but the nausea continued.

She had sluiced her face with water and reapplied lipstick when she realised she had not eaten apart from half a slice of toast at breakfast. No wonder her stomach was in revolt. Normally she would have snatched a sandwich in Lewis's or Debenham's but today she wanted peace and quiet, a place where she could restore her mind as well as her soul.

She walked out into Oxford Street and made for Portland Place. A few months ago Leigh had taken her to the Heights, a quiet spacious restaurant on the fifteenth floor of the St George Hotel in Langham Place. She had scarcely looked out over the rooftops of London so animated had been their conversation but, if her memory served her, there had been a wonderful feeling of tranquillity up there, looking down on the dome of All Souls, seeing the Langham Hilton across the way, Broadcasting House bustling with activity on the right.

When she was safely ensconced at a table by the window, she knew she had made the right choice. Nearby tables held sharp-suited men, huddling over their meal to exchange business confidences. No one was taking any notice of her. She ordered eggs Florentine and halibut, and sipped an excellent dry white wine.

As she ate she felt better. The last few days had been unbelievably traumatic. Uncertainty about her own state, anxiety about her parents' marriage and then the bombshell. No wonder she felt disoriented. But the reality was that she had her own life now. Whatever her parents did, she could neither influence nor change it. And the anger she had felt at her mother's — impossible to call her anything else — deception was evaporating as she began to comprehend the gesture she had made in taking another woman's child as her own.

I was the living proof of her husband's infidelity and she never let it affect the way she treated me, Rachel thought. She sipped her wine and contemplated the depth of that self-sacrifice. Could I love like that? she wondered. Even my own baby?

As she pondered she saw a plane in the sky above, making its way to Heathrow. Mesmerised, she followed it across one vast plate-glass window, losing it behind the frame, watching for its reappearance. That was the way to escape, take to the skies. As soon as everything was settled, before her pregnancy was too advanced, once the election was over, she and Leigh must get away, have a few magical days somewhere where no phones rang and no one pricked the bubble of your security with news that all was not what it seemed.

When she left the restaurant she made her way into All Souls and sat in its cool depths to pray for calm. Amazingly it came. She sat on for a while, letting peace flow over her, and then she emerged into the bustle of the London streets.

She took a cab back to the flat, feeling at last a sense of purpose. She had bought salmon steaks and asparagus in Selfridges. Now she set about making an elaborate meal, preparing everything with Delia Smith-like efficiency and, when it was done, wallowing in a scented bath. She kept an ear alert for the phone to ring but there had been no call by the time she was dressed and made-up.

She put the salmon ready to poach and prepared the vegetables, one eye on the clock. If Leigh came in in time she would tell him about the pregnancy. She might even tell him about *her* birth.

She met him in the hall, a glass of Chablis in one hand, his slippers in the other. "How's that for devotion?"

He kissed her forehead and moved past her into the living room, flung himself into his chair and reached for the remote control. She wanted to way "Don't, not now. Let's have one night without it," but she knew his compulsive need for news. He was flicking through Teletext, clicking his tongue, groaning, although he would have had details of the latest developments before he left his office.

"How was your day?" he asked, without taking his eyes off the screen.

Her positive mood was still upon her. "Good — I shopped, ate, relaxed. Are you bathing or eating first?"

"Bath," he said, draining his glass in one swallow. "It's been a hell of a day but interesting. The Tory EMU policy is a shambles. Heseltine at odds with Major over the free vote, according to the scuttlebutt. And that's only half of it. Give us a kiss and then let me get out of these clothes. I'll tell you everything over supper."

As he vanished into the bathroom she hoped she would be able to reciprocate, tell him everything and get it off her chest. But with revelation, as with sex and everything else, the important thing was not to do it quickly but to do it well.

14

"Go on, then." They had settled in the living room of Jago's flat, Rachel with feet tucked up on the sofa, Jago sprawled sideways across an armchair. Around them the walls were studded with photographs, posters, theatrical memorabilia, and mementoes of his travels. This flat was his base but he was an itinerant musician, and a clever one at that. At first Rachel had wondered how he could keep clean in such clutter. Now she just accepted that he did.

"Go on," he said again. "I know you're sitting on something. I knew it yesterday. Might as well lay it, ducks. You'll feel much better if you do."

What would his reaction be if she said she could lay two eggs if she chose? She settled for one at a time. "You know I went home for the wedding?"

He nodded. "Family gatherings! Recipe for disaster. What happened?"

If she waffled he would say, "Get to the meat, Rach,"

or "Get to the nitty-gritty."

"I'm adopted," she said baldly. "Well, it's not even that simple. I'm not my mother's child but I am my father's."

"You mean you *are* your mother's but you're *not* your father's?"

"No. I mean what I say. My father made someone pregnant. My mother – Dodo, who isn't my mother although I thought she was – took me in as her own."

"She adores you!" For once Jago had been taken by surprise, his habitual worldly wise expression replaced by one of astonishment.

"Yes. She's been the most wonderful mother—"

"So who told you? I mean, is it true?"

"It's true. It was Mother – I can't call her anything else—"

"Nor should you," he interrupted. "Sod the labour pains, I say. It's the one who tops and tails you who's your real mother."

"Precisely. Anyway, she told me but only because Vanessa kept hinting. There was seven kinds of hell going on over my father. He's had an affair – another – and this time I think Van had just had enough. Also, well, her own marriage isn't a hundred per cent at the moment."

"Hmmm. She quite likes stirring, that sister of yours. Still, I suppose it had to come out some time. What does Leigh say?"

"I haven't told him!" She had expected scorn, even anger but his silence was even more hurtful. "There hasn't been time," she said at last.

"Balls. It took two seconds to tell me. You live with the

man, Rach. Don't kid me — and, above all, don't kid yourself. If you can't turn to Leigh when something like this crops up, you have to ask yourself if this relationship is going anywhere."

"I *can* turn to him." She was seized with the need to defend her lover. "It's just that he's so stressed now. I was going to tell him last night but I could see he just wanted to relax."

"Oh dear!" Jago said. "Stressed! Poor thing. It must be stressful getting all that money for talking to the good and the great three times a week."

"It's not like that, Jago, and you know it. Just because he appears on screen for five minutes that doesn't mean that's all the job entails. He works all the hours God sends. You know that."

"I know what time he gets home. The two are not necessarily the same thing. Half these BBC types spend the day propping up the bar in TV Centre."

"He's not BBC," Rachel said.

"You're nit-picking now because you know I'm right. If miners and trawlermen top the hard-work scale, TV journalists are a poor hundred and thirty-third. And you're far too easily impressed by his aura. I've watched you, hovering round, pandering to his whims. You're making a rod for your own back, Rachel. You won't listen to me now but you should. Assert yourself!"

And then, in one of the mood changes that made him such fun to be with, he leaped from his chair. "Enough of the Anna Raeburns! I've got a nice drop of vodka in the kitchen. I know it's too early but sod the rules."

"There's something else," Rachel said.

He turned instantly. "Well, spit it out."

"I think I'm pregnant. No, I know I am."

"Oh, God." Jago was silent and then he grinned. "What a turn-up! Still, it'll keep us all young. I've wanted to go to EuroDisney for ages. Now I've got an excuse."

By the time Rachel was back in her own flat, good humour was restored. She was glancing out at the weather, wondering whether or not to go out, when the phone rang.

"Rachel?" It was her mother – Dodo – Mother – liar! The names chased through her head.

"Yes. It's me."

"Are you all right?"

She wanted to say, "No, I'm bloody well not all right, thanks to you," but it came out differently.

"Yes. I'm fine. I'm sorry if I was – well, over the top yesterday."

"It's all right." As ever, her mother was rushing to reassure. "I understand. And I'm glad it's out at last. I should've told you before. At first I didn't want to confuse you. And then, suddenly, you were grown-up and I was afraid to tell you."

"In case I blew my top," Rachel said ruefully. There was a beep-beep in her ear, the signal that another caller was trying to get through. It might be Leigh. "Mum, that's another call. I think it's someone about work – I was expecting them to ring. Would you mind?"

"No, of course not. I just wanted to make sure you were all right."

"I'm coming home soon, very soon. We'll talk then. I love you, Mum." And then she was depressing the receiver stand and the other caller was through. She had hoped for Leigh. What she got was a penitent Vanessa.

"I'm so sorry, Rachel. I could cut my tongue out. When Mum rang this morning and told me she'd had to tell you I howled. Please, please don't let it make a difference. You're my sister, Liz's too. You know that."

"Of course." She tried to reassure her sister and keep any note of resentment out of her voice. In the end, Vanessa had done her a favour. It was better to know the truth. "Are you all right?" At the other end of the line there was an audible sniff.

"I'm bearing up. I've pulled myself together since yesterday. Things aren't good here . . . It'll be a relief to talk to someone. So I'm coming up tomorrow. We'll talk and talk and get it all sorted out." Rachel woke up to the fact that Vanessa had just made a lunch-date with her and they were meeting at King's Cross at twelve thirty tomorrow.

"See you, then," she said, and put down the phone.

She was pulling on walking shoes when it rang again.

"It's me, darling. Leigh. I've been thinking, we haven't had a moment together since you got back. I can see some free time coming up around one thirty. Could you come over here and we'll grab a pub lunch?"

"Oh, yes. That would be lovely." Euphoria carried her through to the bedroom to rifle her wardrobe for something sensational. Meals out were usually at her instigation so this was a treat. "He does care," she told herself triumphantly, and then was brought up against the unpleasant certainty that until now she had half feared he didn't.

They ate in a pub around the corner from the studio. "The scampi's usually edible. Don't have the chilli. It's vile." It was a second-grade pub with a smoky atmosphere, but they were opposite one another in a glass-walled booth and the food was like manna because they were together.

"I've got something to tell you," she said at last, forking the remaining scampi around her plate.

"That sounds ominous." His smile suddenly faded. "You're not pregnant, are you?"

Her tongue felt huge in her mouth and her ears rang with anxiety. Why had he said that? "It's not that." Even to herself she sounded as though she was lying. She had avoided the truth and it troubled her, but Leigh's face had cleared and he was looking at her expectantly.

"There were some rows at home over the weekend," she continued. "I told you that, didn't I? Vanessa was furious with Dad because he's been having an affair with a woman from the village."

Leigh threw back his head and feigned horror. "Randy old sod. How old is he?"

"Sixty-four. Anyway, that's not it. Vanessa got mad and kept making veiled allusions to something in the past, round about the time I was born."

"Go on." She had his attention now. Around them, the hum of conversation had receded. They were alone in their own world. "She kept saying things about twenty-eight years ago—"

"Don't say your mum had a bit of tit-for-tat and you were the result?"

"Not exactly." It was hard to find the right words, at least not as quickly as he liked.

"What do you mean, not exactly?"

"It was the other way round." He looked uncomprehending and she continued, "He had the affair and I was the result."

She watched him closely as enlightenment dawned, only to be replaced with disbelief.

"So how did you get to be one of the family?"

"She took me in. The girl — my birth mother — was a servicewoman my father got pregnant. She gave me up and my mother, Dodo, that is, took me in. She felt I should be part of the family so she took me in. Adopted me. Not legally. Not as far as I know. Her name was put on my birth certificate—"

"How?" The journalist in him was interested now.

"The girl gave my mother's details when she went into hospital. My mother was ten years older but no one queried it. I was registered as Dodo's child and my father as the father. The girl went off somewhere and my mother went back to Germany." She would have to stop calling her birth mother "the girl". It somehow seemed wrong but she could summon up no sense of the woman as her mother.

"You mean they simply fixed the whole thing?" He whistled softly. "It's a hell of a story!"

"You mustn't tell anyone."

"Don't panic. I'm not likely to, am I? It's hardly front-page stuff. Still, I didn't know they had it in them." He contemplated the ceiling. "Where does this leave you legally? Do the others know?"

"Yes. Van always knew, Liz found out later."

He was pushing aside his plate and wiping his lips. "Good God, it beats Catherine Cookson. Your mother . . . God, this has to be a first." He wrinkled his brow. "What about the other one?"

"I don't know," Rachel said aloud, suddenly wondering why she had never asked about the woman who had given her life. At least, she had asked but not waited for an answer.

"Probably best to let sleeping dogs lie." He was looking at his watch. "I've got to fly now but I'm glad we did this. It's a facer, but she is fond of you. Dodo I mean. That much is evident."

"I know." She wanted him to put his arms around her, there in the centre of the pub. Hug the breath out of her, promise to let nothing at all harm her. Above all, she wanted him to say he wouldn't mind if she was pregnant. But he was already planting a swift kiss in the direction of her cheek. "Got to dash. God, I've heard some stories — we'll talk tonight. Take care." And he was gone.

The fact that she had lied about the pregnancy was still scary. Why hadn't she told him the truth? Because I'm scared of his disapproval, she thought. That's why. As she travelled home by tube, she tried to tell herself that Leigh had been as supportive as time allowed but in her heart she knew he hadn't and it hurt.

When she got home she changed into jeans and got down to work. If she was spending time with Vanessa tomorrow she must get something done now. She worked well, spurred on by relief that at last one of her secrets was out. Leigh knew and Jago knew. She could talk to them whenever she wished now. And there was no point in becoming obsessive about her parentage. She could change nothing and if her mother . . . again she hesitated but then ploughed on . . . if her mother and Van were to be believed, their attitude to her had not changed. They would all go on as well — or as badly — as they ever had.

As for Daddy, she had meant the insults she had hurled at him yesterday, but what was the point? He was what he had always been, an amoral, conscienceless charmer. I don't even like him, she thought, and was amazed at the revelation. So much for ties of blood. And yet . . . She put a hand to her belly. This baby was flesh of his flesh.

She was struck by a thought. Some woman, faceless as yet, had once laid a hand on her belly, just like this. And I was the life within.

She went through to the kitchen and made coffee in a mug. What had she been like, the woman? Impossible to think of her as Mother. She had been young, twenty years old, a servicewoman, lower ranks. She could have had an abortion, Rachel thought. But she chose to keep me.

She carried the coffee to the window and stood looking out over the rooftops. Where was she now, the girl in khaki, lisle stockings and a peaked cap? She would be forty-eight. Still young. Married, probably, with children. She could be dead. That was a possibility. I have to find her, Rachel thought suddenly. I have to see her face.

15

London, Saturday, 12 April 1997

The sun was shining as Rachel travelled to King's Cross. The pavements were filled with people uncertain whether to dress for winter or spring, and Rachel had deliberated before putting on a lightweight suit. Better to be chilly than overheated, especially when her heart was already beating a rapid tattoo.

They had arranged to meet at the arrivals board in King's Cross. Rachel checked Vanessa's train as soon as she entered the great echoing concourse and saw that it would be on time. It would come into platform three but she decided to stick to the appointed meeting-place. If there was a rush to disembark they could easily miss one another and then their meeting would start in a flap. Not a good idea in view of the way she felt already.

"It can't be any worse. You already know that. She'll only fill in details," Jago had said, comfortingly, as she left. But how could she be sure he was right? How could she be sure of anything now? She stood, watching the computerised arrivals board clatter with each change, Vanessa's train coming nearer and nearer to first place with every shift and rumble.

She made a conscious effort to put her imagination on the back burner and thought about practicalities. Vanessa had agreed they should lunch at the Heights. If they took a cab they'd be there in ten minutes. Afterwards, if there was time, Vanessa wanted to go into Oxford Street.

The board clicked again. Another arrival, and then Vanessa was coming towards her, looking harassed and contrite and almost middle-aged, arousing compassion in Rachel.

"Van, good to see you." They embraced, not caring about the people scurrying past them, aware only that they belonged. Whatever the revelations of the past few days, they still belonged.

"I'm sorry, Rachel. I am a bitch to let it come out like that. And I can't say it slipped out. I knew what I was doing, edging nearer and nearer the brink. I just wanted to hurt him, wipe the smile off his face."

Whose face? Rachel thought. Trevor's or Daddy's. Aloud she said, "Let's get a cab. We can talk when we get to the restaurant." They held hands in the taxi, aware of the driver beyond the open partition, but no confidences were exchanged until they were in the lift, whooshing up to the fifteenth floor. "I'm so sorry, Rachel. I can't forgive myself for upsetting you. I can only plead that I was upset myself but that was no excuse for involving you."

"I'm glad you did," Rachel said, as the lift doors

opened. "I wasn't at first. Now I think it was for the best."

They chatted then until they were settled at a table, looking over the London skyline, their starters before them. "Now," Rachel said, "tell me what you remember. I need to know, Van. I really need to know. Afterwards, we'll talk about you and Trevor. If you want to, that is."

"Well," Vanessa said slowly. She put a forkful of food into her mouth and chewed. "I was twelve, wasn't I? I remember we were all out in the garden. The house near Hamburg. The gardens there were beautiful but, of course, you were never there. This woman turned up suddenly."

"What was she like?" Rachel couldn't contain her curiosity.

"Quite ordinary. I only saw her once but I knew something was terribly wrong so I do remember her. She was average height, quite a pretty face and nice hair. Wavy and falling down over one eye. She kept pushing it back, I remember that. She asked for Mummy and I went out to the garden to get her. We were always told to invite people in so I'd settled her in the drawing room. Very polite and grown-up I was then. Mummy went into the room. She didn't close the door and I heard the woman say something but I couldn't hear what, and then Mum said something, and as the woman was replying Mum came back and closed the door. I knew then that something was wrong. I don't know why but I did."

"What happened next?" A waitress appeared and topped up their glasses from the wine in the bucket.

"Thank you," Rachel said, and looked expectantly at her sister.

"They were in there for ages. I tried to hear what they were saying but I couldn't, although sometimes their voices were quite loud. I kept expecting Mum to come out and make tea because she always did for visitors. And then I heard Liz crying in the garden and I went to see to her. She was my pet, you see, a baby coming along when I was a toddler. She'd fallen from the swing and hurt her knee. When I'd sorted her out I came back. The door to the drawing room was open and Mum was just sitting there. The woman had gone and Mum was just sitting and looking into space. I asked her if she was all right and she started to cry."

"What did she say?" Rachel asked.

"She said not to take any notice, she was just being silly — you know Mum, never wanting to upset anyone. She must've rung Dad because he came home unexpectedly — not at his usual time — and shooed me out to join the others. We had a maid called Heini and she was in the garden with Liz so I went out to them."

"What happened when you came back?"

"Mum was making tea, Dad was smiling and helping her but I knew something was wrong — the way kids just *know*. My two know things aren't right at home. Still, mustn't lose the thread. Nothing happened then, not for weeks, but I still knew something was wrong. Liz did, too, although we didn't talk about it much. I think we were scared of comparing notes and finding something awful. That's all that matters when you're a kid, keeping the status quo. If I didn't know that, I'd've walked out on Trevor a week ago."

"Did you see the woman again?" Somehow, without knowing it, Rachel had drained her glass. Now she refilled it. Vanessa's was untouched.

"No. A long while after, Mum went away. She said she was going to Gran's and couldn't take us because it was term-time. We moved to Sennelager then, with Dad and when Mum came back she had a baby — you. She took Liz and me into her bedroom and showed you to us and then she sent Liz out on some pretext and she put her arm around me and hugged me. She said it wasn't her baby but she loved it and was keeping it. I supposed she told me because I knew about the birds and the bees and wouldn't have accepted some tale about finding you in a box on the step."

"How could she know you wouldn't tell?"

"She told me it was very important that we told everyone this was our baby. I agreed. I was keen on the idea. The baby — you were lovely. I was very anxious to demonstrate ownership. We used to push you round in your pram, Liz and I, proud as peacocks."

"So you thought it was just a straightforward adoption?" Rachel asked.

"Yes . . . at first. But something had changed between Mum and Dad. Not on the surface but underneath. He was anxious. It was the first time I'd ever really seen him play up to Mum. He was penitent, I suppose — and grateful. She could have ruined him, instead she was making everything smooth-going, the way she always has." She put out a hand to Rachel. "And he wanted you. Don't ever doubt that. Mummy brought you into the family but he wanted it too."

"So when did you realise—" Rachel was seeking for words when Vanessa forestalled her.

"I knew there was something else. And I'd never forgotten the woman's visit because it was so odd. I puzzled over it for a while and then I tackled Mum. I asked her if the baby belonged to the woman who came to the house that day. I could see her struggling, wondering whether to admit it or not. In the end she did."

"What made you link the two things – the woman and the baby?"

"They were both so – so full of significance. When I worked out that nine months had elapsed I knew they had to be connected. And then, of course, I started to wonder about the father. Why did Mum take the baby? Why did Daddy let her? And by then there'd been another of his dalliances. It wasn't hard to work out."

"Did you tell her you knew?"

"Not at first. Not until I was, oh, fifteen or sixteen. I'd been away at school, I came back rebellious, we had a row – over nothing but you know adolescents – and I threw it in her face. I'll never forget her expression. Of course, I'd've given anything to take it back but it was too late." She grinned ruefully. "I did it again last weekend, didn't I? I haven't grown up much with the years."

"It was an awful secret for a teenager to keep," Rachel said. "You couldn't be blamed."

She waited until they were through dessert before she

asked about Trevor. "Do you want to talk? I don't want to pry."

"It's a familiar story. She was coming to my house, butter wouldn't melt in her mouth, 'We're such chums, you and I, Vanessa,' and all the time, behind my back . . ."

"Who is she?"

"The membership secretary at the golf club. 'I need to speak to Trevor about subs,' that was her mantra." Vanessa's eyes closed in misery. "Rachel, what did I do to deserve this?"

"Does he want to leave?"

"He says not. It's Dad all over — 'There's only you, Vanessa. Never again, Vanessa.' But all the time I keep seeing poor old Mum down the years, over and over again."

Rachel did what she could to console until it was time to make for the shops. "Don't do anything in haste," she said finally. "It's up to you to decide, but take your time. You know we'll all be there for you."

"This is an amazing place," Vanessa said, as she insisted on paying the bill. "I never knew it was here, tucked away behind All Souls."

"I'm glad you came," Rachel said, as the lift descended. "We'll do it again soon."

The sun was shining as they walked to John Lewis. "I want some apricot silk chiffon," Vanessa said, as they turned into Oxford Street, and Rachel was amazed to think she could think of dressmaking at such a time. But it was a comfort to finger the fine fabrics, see the great falls of satin and chiffon and summer cottons in all the colours of the rainbow.

"Are you all right?" Vanessa asked anxiously, as Rachel saw her on to the train. "We've talked a lot about me but you're the one who's had the shock."

"I'm fine. It takes coming to terms with but I'm almost there." It wasn't true, but Vanessa needed reassurance.

"You won't try to find her, will you?" Neither of them needed to say who they were talking about.

"I don't suppose so," Rachel said, and then stood back as the train doors shut. But as she prepared the evening meal she thought again of the woman who had appeared on the doorstep of the Army quarters in Germany twenty-eight years ago. Where was she now? There were mechanisms for finding birth parents. She had heard a television agony aunt talking about them once, urging caution but saying it could be done. Last night she had been sure she wanted to search. But now . . . Best to let sleeping dogs lie, probably.

She made a tomato and mozzarella starter and opened a bottle of red wine, leaving it to breathe in the warm room. It was six thirty. With luck Leigh would be home soon.

She showered, then checked the chicken roasting in the oven before she dressed. She was leafing through a magazine and wondering whether or not to start the vegetables when the phone rang – probably Leigh to say he couldn't make dinner. But it wasn't. It was Tom.

"I thought I'd ring, just to ask how you were."

"I'm fine, but it's nice to hear from you."

"Have you told Leigh yet?" She had known that question was coming but still she squirmed.

"Not yet. I know it sounds crazy but there hasn't been a chance . . . not a real chance. I don't want to do it unless we have time to discuss it."

"I think you need to talk to someone," Tom said. "I don't want to intrude but I can't help feeling you're not sure about your attitude to this . . . and talking does help. Are you sure you're not shirking telling Leigh?"

Rachel felt a flush of embarrassment. He must think hers a peculiar partnership, close enough to conceive but not to confide. "I wanted to be sure. Now that I am it's just a question of finding the right moment."

"Of course. Well, I'm here if it helps. Or there are organisations, help-lines — you don't even need to give your name."

"I'm coming home," she said suddenly, unaware until she spoke that that was her intention. "Perhaps we could talk then. I'd be grateful — if it's not an imposition?"

"Not at all. I'll look forward to it. And if you can't make it to Yorkshire I could come south. I do sometimes."

She was hovering over the chicken again when the phone rang once more. "Sorry, darling. Something's come up. Apparently Labour are using a bulldog in their next broadcast. The Tories are livid. Serves them right for using that bloody chicken to chase Blair. Anyway, they want me to track down Mandelson, if I can."

She carried the wine down to Jago and was heartily relieved to find him in. If he had been out to whom would she have turned?

"Leigh's been held up. If you're sure I'm not keeping you . . ."

He shook his head and took the bottle from her. "You look peaky. Pregnancy does that."

"Yes, Dr Kildare."

"Ooh, you're showing your age now, darling. Chamberlain's out. Clooney's in. Or that divine doctor in *Dangerfield*. Very cruel mouth. I'm glued. Anyway, never mind telly, are you allowed to drink?"

She hadn't given a thought to that and a chasm opened before her. If she went ahead with this pregnancy, everything would be changed. For ever! Her mother was still a mother twenty-eight years on. Both her mothers!

"What are you thinking now?" Jago asked, kindly. "You look stricken."

"I was thinking about my mother. My birth mother. This is her grandchild. It's strange, but you never think about your antecedents, well, not seriously, but something like this makes you conscious of them."

"Chain syndrome." Jago had poured the wine and now took up his favourite position on the sofa. "I've seen it before. Had it myself when I realised what I was. That there'd be no children. You suddenly discover you're a link. Not a self-contained entity but a link in a chain. One behind you, one in front of you. Well, at least you've got the opportunity."

"So could you. Gays do father children."

"Some do. Not me. I've made my choices. Now it's your turn." There was silence and then he continued, "I wouldn't blame you, you know, if you decided on a termination. I'd back you up."

"You're a darling," Rachel said, suddenly tearful. "I

158

want this baby, I really do. It's just that we weren't intending it, not yet."

"Come here." He was sitting upright now, arms outspread. She went to him, and they sat, wrapped in one another's arms. "There, there," he said. "There, there. It'll all come out in the wash. It may run a bit at the edges but it always comes right in the end."

She was in bed when Leigh returned, lights turned out because her eyes were sore with crying.

"Are you awake?" Through her closed lids she could sense his dark shape in the lighted doorway. If she spoke he would come to her, take her in his arms, comfort her. She could tell him then.

"Are you awake?" It came again, but she neither spoke nor moved until she heard him tiptoe away from the door and it was safe to turn her face into the pillow.

16

London, Sunday, 13 April 1997

They slept late, waking to grey skies. "What shall we do today?" Leigh asked, switching on the radio and turning towards her. She felt his hand on her breast, her belly, her thighs.

"I've something to tell you," she said, and felt him tense. She had an uncomfortable feeling that he was afraid she was going to say she was pregnant. Any thought of telling him about the baby left her then and she scrabbled desperately for something to fill the gap.

"I've missed you," she said, and turned towards him, seeking his lips, pressing her body against his, anything to avoid the truth, aware all the time that it was a truth that eventually would out.

"Me too," he said, sliding his arm under her head, drawing her towards him, placing his mouth on hers so that there was no more need for words. "Yes," he said, when the kiss ended. "Oh, yes," and then he was touching her and feeling her body respond until he could enter her easily.

He's all I want, she thought, as the climax came. This is what she knew, Dodo, my mother, that having your lover is all that matters. She went on thinking that as they lay in warm, odorous, post-coital contentment. It was only when at last she left the tumbled bed that she wondered.

Towelling her body after her shower she thought about the future, gazing at a sombre reflection in the steamy mirror. Today she must tell Leigh the truth, then she could feel at ease again.

"Now," she said, when she returned to the bedroom, "tell me what you'd like to do. I'm easy, as long as we're together."

"Well . . ." His brow furrowed. "I could do with catching up on a few things — but what the hell? There's the Argentine grand prix on the box, not to mention the golf and . . ." He was glancing at the weather outside, blue skies with only a hint of the earlier cloud. ". . . it's the Marathon today. I'd quite like to see them pass."

They stood at Tower Bridge to watch the runners go by, some of them dragging legs already weary, others steely-eyed, determined to finish. "God," Leigh said. "I'd never have the guts to do that. I'd like to think I would but . . ."

"You would if you wanted it enough," Rachel said. "They just have different goals. We can all be single-minded if we want something."

He was taking her hand, drawing it through his arm, making her feel special as only he could. "Come on, then," he said. "We've had our exercise for the day. What next?"

They decided on a trip out to Windsor. "We'll have a pub lunch and read all the papers," he said, seizing her in a bear hug. "And then we'll go walking and I'll hold your hand and tell you I love you. I'll even get down on one knee. Seriously, though, I don't do that often enough. Especially at the moment. Things will be different as soon as this lot's over."

As the car sped towards Windsor Rachel made her plans. She wouldn't say anything before lunch. But afterwards, when they were mellow with food and wine, she would tell him. She rehearsed it carefully. "How would you feel about a baby?" she would say. She pictured his face, surprised at first, then incredulous, then suffused with delight as the truth hit home.

They found a pub with a garden. "Is it warm enough to sit out?" Leigh asked, and she nodded. Better here, away from the hubbub of a Sunday hostelry. He came back with wine and began to riffle through the pile of papers they had brought with them. He whistled at the front page of one of the broadsheets. "God, the Tories have a death-wish. They're at it again, sniping at one another. Gunning for Clarke and he's their biggest, if not their only, asset."

"I thought John Major was their biggest asset?"

Leigh shook his head. "Everyone likes him. Almost everyone trusts him. Hardly anyone thinks he has a political future. Too much compromise. He's fallen over himself to keep everyone on side when that was a plain impossibility. You can't keep an aggressive Eurosceptic like Redwood on the same team as a pro-European like Clarke. Major has tied himself in knots trying to achieve unity and it hasn't worked. No taste for the knife, that's Major's trouble."

He read on while Rachel studied the menu, a choice of roast meats with vegetables. At last he folded the final paper and pushed them aside. "Let's order," he said, "and then we can talk."

Rachel felt her heart leap. Here it was, the moment to share her secret. He went into the bar to place their order, and then he returned to his seat. "This is nice," he said, reaching for her hand. "I'm glad we did this today because I need to talk to you."

Fleetingly she wondered if he had guessed, if he was about to tell her he knew and was pleased, but as he began to speak she knew that he had not. "We've been happy together, haven't we?" he said.

She felt her heart begin to thud uncomfortably. What was coming next?

He didn't wait for an answer. "I've never lived with anyone before, not for any length of time. I wondered if it would work, if there was anyone who could put up with my lifestyle. And if I could make someone else happy. Well, it has worked. Triumphantly, as far as I'm concerned. What about you?"

Rachel felt relief flood over her. She licked her lips as a preliminary to speaking but Leigh had not finished. "The way things are going I think there's going to be something for me soon . . . a foreign posting, a big one. Washington, probably, or the UN. If that happens I'll be back just as often as I can."

"I could come with you." The words left her lips of

their own accord, and she regretted them as soon as they were gone.

"You could, but I doubt you'd get a work permit. What would you do alone all day in a foreign city? You think the hours are bad here. There, with time difference, it's crazy. They'd expect interviews at their time, whatever the cost to me. This is when I have to make my mark, Rachel. Once I've done that it'll be different. I'll be back here, behind a desk probably. I quite fancy management — eventually. We'll talk about things then, the future, kids, a house, the works."

A waitress was advancing on them with steaming plates but Rachel felt bile sour in her throat. He didn't want her — let alone a baby. She felt anger burning in her chest, her throat. But she mustn't lash out now. This was too important to blow. She picked up her fork and tried to eat.

"Come on," Leigh said, after a while. "Eat up. It may never happen. If it does I'll come to you. You'll come to me. It's just now that I need to be focused. You do understand, don't you?"

The beef was ashes in her mouth and she chewed it for a moment before she replied, "Yes," she said. "I understand."

"Tell him now," said the voice in her head, as they drove home. "Tell him now, make him see, make him face up to his responsibilities." But it had been her responsibility to see to contraception, he had made that clear from the start — or, rather, it had been the unspoken acceptance from the start. It wasn't fair to blame him. She had said that she was on the pill and would remain on it.

"You're very quiet," he said, as they neared the flat.

"Just tired," she said. "I think I'll have an early night."
If she could get to her bed, burrow beneath the duvet and
shut out the world, perhaps she could think it all through.
Perhaps, if she was lucky, she would fall asleep and wake
to find it was all a dream.

It was six o'clock when they entered the flat, too early
to escape yet. "I think I'll have a bath," she said. "Do you
want supper?"

He was in a magnanimous mood tonight. "Only you,"
he said. He reached for her face, sliding his hands either
side until they cupped her ears and her face was held
between them. "I'll make supper," he said. "You have
your bath and I'll conjure up some ambrosia. As for
dessert . . ." He kissed her mouth. "I just might have you."

She tried to smile but tears were not far away. He was
on a high, exultant about work and therefore about life.
She could wipe the smile from his face in a second if she
told him about the baby but she was afraid to tell him.

In the warm, scented water she tried to work out why.
Because he might flinch at the news. Because that joyful
expression he wore might be replaced by one of
displeasure and she couldn't bear that. I am afraid of
rejection, she thought. And yet she had lived without him
before so she could do so again. She had friends, good
friends. She had a career of her own, for God's sake,
which rarely seemed to enter the calculations. But even as
she thought defiance, fear fell upon her like a cold finger,
a fear that was unbearable. She rose from the water, put a

towelling robe over her still-wet body and went through to the kitchen.

"I've something to tell you," she said, from the doorway. "I'm pregnant. I know we didn't intend it but it's happened. I'm glad now that I'm over the shock. I hope you will be too." But his expression was not of joy or even acceptance. It was at first an expression of horror, and then of distaste.

17

Daylight was entering the bedroom when Leigh's arm crept around her. "I'm sorry, darling. I was a pig yesterday. You took me by surprise and . . . I didn't think."

She had cried in the night until her eye-sockets felt on fire. She turned now and put her face into his shoulder, sliding her right hand up and over his chest, feeling the hair curl beneath her fingers, the rib-cage solid and smooth. "And?" she said.

"What do you mean — and?"

"You've had time to think now. So what *do* you think?"

His body tensed beneath her fingers. "I think we need to talk," he said cautiously.

She felt bile rise in her throat, but whether it was nausea or revulsion she could not be sure. "Talk, then," she said.

"What do you want to do?" It was a reasonable enough question, but somehow she knew that for Leigh there would be only one acceptable answer.

"I don't know." She tried to be as dispassionate as she could. If they talked they would arrive at a proper answer. "Sometimes I think one thing, sometimes another. I could see it would be difficult—"

"There's no room here — and if you had a child to care for, how would you work? We'd need two salaries to afford something better, unless we moved out — into the suburbs."

It was said dolefully, as though he was contemplating a move to Outer Mongolia.

"Other people manage."

"Oh, yes." He sat up in bed now, punching a pillow behind his head, crossing his arms on his chest. "I've seen them manage. His suits smell of sick, she whinges at being cooped up all day with no one to talk to, he stays at work because there's nothing to go home for — I've seen people cope!"

"It doesn't have to be like that." But even as she spoke she knew it was futile. "I'm not getting up," she said. "I feel sick. You'll have to get your own breakfast."

He looked in to say goodbye before he left. "I'm off." His voice softened. "We'll talk tonight. Stay in bed if it helps. I'll tell Jago on my way down. He'll look in on you. I'll leave the door on the latch."

The phone rang almost as soon as he closed the door. "Darling?"

"Hello, Mum," she said, and shuffled up on her pillows. "I was hoping you'd ring."

Rachel ignored the implied reproach. "I was going to

later. Anyway, how are things? Are you OK?"

"I'm fine!" Her mother's voice was bright and upbeat.

She's amazing, Rachel thought. If I didn't know better, I'd think her life was perfect.

She listened as her mother enthused about the weather, the time of year, the state of the garden and last night's TV. And then it came, the reason for the phone-call.

"I've been worried about you, darling. I feel so guilty — I should have told you sooner, years ago."

"I'm fine," Rachel said firmly. Outside, the sun was shining. It ought to be a good day. She was young and alive . . . and pregnant. "I'm sorry, Mum," she said at last, "but I really have to go now. Work calls. I'll tell you more when I see you."

She had just come out of the shower when she heard Jago's distinctive tap at the door. "Well?" he asked, putting both arms out to the door-jamb. "Have you or haven't you?"

"Come in," she said. "I've got coffee on." When they were seated, she said, "I told him last night."

"And? God, it's like drawing teeth."

"He doesn't want it," she said flatly. "It's the wrong time work-wise and in every other way."

"So he wants you to get rid? Selfish sod! You do what you want to do, petal. I'll stand by you. God knows, that's not much but it's there for you."

She went to him then, loving the comfort of a pair of arms, a wholehearted hug. "It's not as easy as that, though, Jago. In fairness to Leigh—"

"Oh, sod fairness! That's your trouble, Rach. Too much seeing the other feller's point of view. There are times when tunnel vision comes in handy, that's what I say." Above the open neck of his buttoned T-shirt his rueful face looked as though it belonged to a child.

"Come on," he said, seizing her round the waist. "The sun is shining, the birds are singing, I'm sick as a parrot of sharps and quavers. Let's go out!"

She couldn't be bothered to argue, knowing full well that Jago would not take no for an answer. Fifteen minutes later they were in a cab and on their way to the South Bank, where Jago had work to deliver to LWT.

They ate lunch in the open air at a bistro in Gabriel's Wharf. "That's better," Jago said, as she relaxed and sipped white wine. "Now, feeling better?"

"Yes," she said. "It's done me good to get out."

"What are you going to do, then? Made any decisions?"

Rachel shrugged. "I don't know. I'm just marking time, waiting for things to happen, work out so that I don't have to *do* anything."

"That's no good, ducks. There's a train thundering down on you, got to get your act together." He sipped his drink. "There are agencies, you know. Help-lines."

"If I decide to terminate it'll be easy enough to fix things. It's the decision that's the hardest part, not finding a clinic."

"I don't mean clinics. I mean people who help you make up your mind. They don't urge you one way or another, they just let you talk." His face had wrinkled up in earnestness and, in spite of herself, Rachel smiled. "Oh, yes," he said, "you can smile. Seriously, Rach, what I mean is that you already have the solution. You just haven't worked it out. These people let you bash your ideas off them until you see the way out you want."

The trouble was that she couldn't believe there was a way out. If she kept this baby she would probably lose Leigh. She would certainly strain their relationship to breaking point. If she had a termination she might find she had ended her one and only pregnancy. If she lost Leigh, she would be absolutely alone.

"Penny for them." Jago had risen to his feet and was holding out a hand. "Come on, Dolly Daydreams. We're going on the river."

They caught the pleasure boat at Westminster Bridge and sat side by side, watching the murky waters of the Thames roll by. "Mucky old river," Jago said, but Rachel was drinking in history as it unrolled. The Palace of Westminster, Traitor's Gate, the mass of Canary Wharf, new but still splendid, eventually the beauty of Greenwich as they approached it.

She was silent on the homeward journey. "Thank you, Jago," she said, as they disembarked. "It's heaven to get away like this. I don't know what I'd do without you."

"Get out of it, soft girl," he said, but she could see he was touched. "Keep your pecker up," was his parting shot when they separated on the landing, and she smiled and nodded. But once she was inside the flat with the door shut her smile faded. In an hour, maybe less, she and Leigh would be either side of the table. They would have to talk then, whether or not they liked it.

She was stirring the contents of the wok when he came home. She did not turn as he came up behind her, put his arms around her, nestled his cheek against her hair. She felt first a wave of relief and then joy. It was going to be all right!

"I'm sorry, darling. It's damned bad luck. Still, they say it's quite simple — and afterwards we'll really talk about a baby. God knows, I don't understand the little blighters but I'm not against them.

She pulled free of him and turned to face him. "What do you mean, Leigh?"

"We'll talk," he said. "About the future." But he was avoiding her eye.

Behind her she could hear the wok spitting but it seemed not to matter. "What about now, Leigh? I'm pregnant now."

"We can't keep it," he said. "You can see that. In this flat? Now? With both of us working flat out? Be reasonable."

She was still not sure how she felt about the child she was carrying, but of one thing she was certain. It merited discussion.

"This is a baby, Leigh. It's not a culinary failure, something to be tipped in the bin without a moment's consideration."

"Oh, God," he said. "I'm sorry. I'm an insensitive pig and I'm sorry. But you do see, don't you?"

"I see," she said. "Only too clearly I see." She turned to the cooker and began to serve up the dinner. They ate — or rather pretended to eat — in silence until the stir-fry was cleared away.

"I think you're being a little unfair," he said. "You took me by surprise. You've had time to adjust. I'm still shell-shocked."

His attempt to get sympathy annoyed her. "Go and sort out the election, Leigh. Leave me to sort out the rest."

He shook his head then, as though in amazement at the unreasonableness of her behaviour. But this time she was not prepared to feel in the wrong. She began to clear the table as he wiped his lips on his napkin and drowned his words with the swish of water into the washing-up bowl.

18

London, Tuesday, 15 April 1997

She was retching in the bathroom when Leigh's knock came at the door. "Are you OK?" He sounded penitent and anxious, and she wanted to comfort him.

"I'm fine. I'll be with you in a moment."

He turned from the cooker as she entered the kitchen. In the background John Humphries was haranguing some hapless politician, but this time she had Leigh's undivided attention. "Were you being sick?"

"A bit."

He came to her then and took her in his arms, rocking her to and fro. "I'm sorry."

"It's not your fault. Anyway, it's nothing." She felt a sudden uplift at the thought that he cared, that he had changed his mind. Her euphoria was short-lived.

"The sooner it's over the better, darling. I know it's tough. We'll be more careful in future. Let me know exactly when and I'll make sure I'm here to take care of you."

She sat down at the kitchen table. "You're taking it for granted that I'm going to have a termination, aren't you?"

He moved to sit opposite her. "It's the best way, Rachel. You must see that. How *could* we have a baby here? You've said it yourself — we live out of suitcases there's so little room. Later on, when we've got a better place — and we'll start looking as soon as I get the election over — it'll be different then. I *want* kids."

"But not this one?"

His voice sharpened. "That isn't fair. It isn't a baby yet. It's a — a cell. You can't even be sure you're pregnant, that's how early it is. Be fair."

She got to her feet, feeling heavy and weary. "I'm trying to be fair, Leigh. And I am pregnant. I've had a test. Now, if you don't mind, I'm going to get myself a cup of tea."

"I've made coffee."

But her stomach lurched at the thought of coffee. Even the smell made her feel ill. She scalded a tea-bag in a cup and carried it, milkless, to her room.

When Leigh had left for work she got up and dressed. An idea was already forming in her mind. She had far from resolved the situation of her own birth. She had the bare outline now but that was all. What had gone through her mother's mind when her conception was discovered? What had gone through either mother's mind, come to that, so that they had embarked on what was really a crazy plan? The fact that they had got away with it for so long was a miracle. What motivated them? Rachel wondered. What made one bear me and give me up? What made the other accept me? If she uncovered their reasoning, perhaps she could find some of her own.

She left a note for Leigh and another for Jago, who couldn't be roused. An hour later she had fuelled the Citroën and was weaving her way out of London.

Leigh had come home with her only three times in four years, so what was different about today? Rachel asked herself as she headed north alone. Besides, at the moment his presence would have been more an encumbrance than a support. She had rung Tom and asked if they could talk over the options he had mentioned. She had listed them for herself, abortion, adoption or acceptance, with or without Leigh, but somehow it would help to talk them over again with someone knowledgeable and far enough removed to be dispassionate. And she wanted to know more about the circumstances of her birth. Her parents owed her that much at least, to tell her all they could.

It was a relief when she was out on the AI, the route she preferred. Norman's Cross, Doncaster, and then she was navigating the by-roads that led first to Tom's house then to her home. She called from a phone-box, half expecting him to be out, even half hoping he would be, but he answered on the fourth ring. "I was expecting you," he said. "The kettle's already on the boil."

They carried a tray of tea into his garden and settled at a table in the lea of an old stone wall. "This is lovely," she said, and meant it. Ahead of her the garden stretched away as far as the eye could see, ending in a wooded copse. On the right, it was terraced and planted with heathers and alpine plants. On the left, water trickled from somewhere out of sight into a small pool where lily-pads floated, glossy and unreal like something in a fairy-tale. "I must draw those," she said, and smiled as he nodded assent.

"Have you reached any conclusions?" he asked at last.

"No. But I've told Leigh." The other secret must be kept. "He wants me to have an abortion. I can't decide."

"It won't go away, Rachel. That's the one thing of which you can be certain. You are pregnant. You must do something, even if it's arranging ante-natal care. I've already set out the options. Keeping the pregnancy, having a termination or giving the baby up for adoption. That's seldom done nowadays. Nevertheless it's worth considering. You've had a good life as an adoptee, haven't you?" His voice was even and unemotional.

She managed a rueful grin. "I keep hoping for a fourth option – closing my eyes until it all goes away."

"Not on, I'm afraid. But let's take number one first. It divides into two. You and your partner bringing up the child, or you bringing it up alone."

He was speaking gently but she felt as though he had struck her. "You mean Leigh might walk out on me?"

He didn't rush to deny it, as she had hoped. Instead he said, "Something like this brings you up short. You look at your relationship, look at it hard, sometimes for the first time. And when you do that you sometimes find it wasn't what you thought it was, what you wanted. I don't only mean Leigh. Be honest, aren't you thinking furiously at the moment, wondering, conjecturing?"

It was true, and she nodded dumbly as he continued. "If you go ahead you'll cope. You're well placed to cope and you will — but only if it's what you want to do. Nothing can be worse for a baby than sensing it wasn't wanted. I know you would never be unkind, never say a wrong word, but children sense things. So don't assume that if you go ahead you'll automatically love the baby. That only happens in fairy stories. If you choose the second option you'll have to go through a procedure. I can help you with that. If you go privately it will be quicker and less complicated, but there will be questions. No need to go into that until you decide it's a possibility. And thirdly you can give up the baby for adoption. It's a noble thing to do, it will bring endless joy to a couple somewhere, but only certain women can do it. And increasingly there's research to show that adoptees need to seek out their origins. Could you cope with that twenty years on?"

"I don't know," Rachel said. "Probably not."

"Well," he stood up and moved to free a shoot that was entangled in a wooden trellis, "it's early days. You have time to think, time to talk to Leigh. It's his baby too, remember. He's sure to have views."

She kissed his cheek as she left. "Thank you," she said. "You've been a great help."

But the calm that her spell in the garden had brought about vanished as she drove the mile and a half to her parents' home. She was warmly welcomed, the table was set for three and her father was ready with a brimming glass but the eyes that met hers were wary. She felt her heart thud in her chest and knew that the sooner it was over the better. "Will lunch keep? We need to talk."

"Look . . ." Her father was the first to speak, but she knew that if she let him he would steer things his way and she couldn't afford that.

"I've made up my mind," she interrupted. "I want to find my birth mother. I need to find her because I need to see for myself. There are reasons, I can't explain them now, why I need to know who and what I came from. Can you understand that?"

Her mother's eyes were wide with fear. It couldn't be shock for she must have known this day would come. "It's no disrespect to you, Mummy. I always thought you were wonderful. Now I know how wonderful. And I understand — at least, I think I do — why you kept it from me. But I know now and I have to do something about it."

"This is crazy." Her father was standing, one elbow on the mantel, a well-shod foot on the brass fender. "We're not going to see you off on a wild-goose chase. It's thirty years, for God's sake. Thirty years. For all we know she's emigrated — dead, even."

He was refusing to name the woman. "She": that was all he could say and it infuriated Rachel. "I don't need your help. There are organisations. I'll employ a detective . . ."

But her mother was rising from her chair and crossing to the bureau. She turned back and handed Rachel an envelope. "There," she said. "That's where she was the last time I heard of her. It's a long time ago but at least it's a start."

The envelope was addressed to her mother in a round, almost childish hand. Rachel lifted the flap and took out the single sheet of paper it contained. It was a letter to her mother, beginning "Dear Dorothy". It was signed "Yours sincerely, Freda".

Rachel lifted her head and looked at her mother. "Freda who?" she asked.

"Fielding. Her name was Fielding." As she spoke Rachel's mother's eyes flicked towards her husband. His brows were down, his eyes fixed on the letter in his daughter's hand. Suddenly he made an involuntary move, as though he would snatch it up, and instinctively Rachel clutched it to her chest.

"How long have you kept that?" he said, with a disapproving cluck.

He turned to Rachel then. "I'm sorry, darling." His hands came up in a gesture of appeal. "I was wrong — very wrong — to Mummy, to you . . . but it was a long time ago."

"What about her?" Rachel struggled with the name. "Freda. What about Freda? Did you wrong her — or was she of little consequence?"

She had shaken him. She saw it in his face, in a tensing of his fingers. But, as always, he bounced back. "I don't want to speak badly of anyone, Rachel. But there are lots of things — so many things — that you don't know."

His hair was silver at the temples now, his skin the golden bronze it had always almost magically been. And although there were crows' feet around his eyes they seemed only to augment the blue of his irises. He wore a brown leather jerkin over a blue sweater with a Paisley cravat at his neck. It looked casual but it made a perfect combination.

"You know your trouble, Dad," she said. "You're just too damned handsome for your own good."

19

Rachel slept fitfully, waking with a start only to drift into nightmarish sleep. "Freda." She searched for the faceless figure in her dreams but, lying awake in the early morning, she had no illusions about the woman who was Freda. She had no desire to find and embrace her, to install her as some warm mother figure, still less grandmother to a baby who might or might not be. If a mother figure existed it was Dodo. "I just need to know," she told herself. The figure in her mind was a girl of twenty in a service uniform. Whatever the reality turned out to be, if indeed it could be located, it would not be that.

She switched on the bedside radio: Will Self had lost his job on the *Observer* after he had been accused of taking heroin on John Major's plane, and the EU rift in the Conservative Party was widening. Nothing new about that.

As she munched dutifully on cereal and toast at a tense breakfast table, she planned her escape. "I need to leave before lunch," she said. The address on the letter had been Middlesbrough, sixty or seventy miles north in Cleveland. "I'll take Sally for a walk first and then I want to get straight off."

"While you're out I'll look up a hotel someone recommended," her mother said. "It's just outside Middlesbrough and apparently it's wonderful."

"Look!" Her father's knife clattered to his plate. "Be reasonable, Rachel. Where's the sense in going off at half-cock to chase up some address she probably left years ago?"

"She." He still wouldn't give the woman a name and Rachel had to drop her hands to her lap and knot them to contain her fury.

"I'm sorry, Dad. I know it must be upsetting for you, and especially for Mummy, but it's something I have to do. Like it or not, I now have a mother — a blood relative — I have never met. Or am not aware of meeting. I don't expect there'll be much rapport between us . . . What do they call it? Bonding? But I have to see for myself."

When she left the house Rachel headed for the fields, but once out of sight she scrambled down the bank to the main road and made for the phone-box next to the pub. "Tom . . . no, I'm OK but, well, if you're free . . . if I'm not being a nuisance . . ."

They arranged to meet in the car-park of a pub as soon as he finished his surgery. "We can have lunch," he said. "I was thinking of going out. I don't feel like cooking and

I didn't have time for breakfast but eating out alone is a pain so you've saved me from a lonely meal hidden behind *The Times*."

As she walked the dog Rachel wrestled with her conscience. Was she latching on to Tom because she was scared of turning to the man who should support her? If she was honest, she had always been a little afraid of Leigh or, perhaps, afraid of losing him. Suddenly the extent to which she had pussy-footed through their relationship struck her. They had never had a row, not a real one that would have tested their relationship, because she had always kept the peace. And now she was carrying his child and that meant they were tied together for life. Even apart there would be a bond between them. The enormity of what was happening was terrifying. She whistled up Sally and made for home.

Knowing that she would soon escape and be with Tom made things easier when she got back. She was able to embrace her mother, say a civil goodbye to her father, then she was in the car, the safe armour of its bodywork around her, and all she needed to do was wave.

Tom was waiting outside the pub, the sunlight glinting on his red hair. They settled in a corner. "Let's order," he said, "and then we can talk. I can see you're bursting to tell me something." They settled for a traditional roast and vegetables and a half-bottle of red wine. "Try this one. It's Romanian. I spotted it on their list a while ago and I like it, but only one glass, I'm afraid." It was rich and fruity, almost fortified, and she smiled appreciation. "Right," he said. "Fire away."

"I told you I was adopted, that it came as a shock?" He nodded. "Well," she continued, "I've decided to find my mother — to try to find her, that is."

He whistled softly, then pursed his lips. "You've thought it through? It doesn't always work out happily."

"I know. I'm not looking for some rosy dream. I have curiosity rather than longing."

"How will you begin?"

She told him about the letter. "I'm going there now. It was dated nineteen ninety. Mum sent her a picture when I graduated."

"Seven years?" he asked, pursing his lips. "How often does the average person move?"

"About every seven years," Rachel said. "With my luck I'll arrive to find she left yesterday, destination unknown."

"And you might arrive to find her there, ready and waiting. Ideally I'd like you to wait a little while, have some counselling, sort out what you really want, but I can see that I could more easily hold back the North Sea."

"I know you're right. If I had time I would wait, but time is running out."

There was silence and then he leaned forward, putting his hands together under his chin. "Let me get this straight. Has this need for haste something to do with the fact that you're pregnant?"

"Yes. Call me crazy, but I want to see where I came from, who I came from. Then I can make decisions."

"And you may opt for a termination?"

"Yes," she said. "There are other factors and I need to

talk to Leigh, but I feel I've got to get this out of the way first."

"Is it possible you're simply running away from the real decision, whether or not to have this baby?"

"I don't know. I don't think so. I know I have to decide soon. How long have I got?"

"In practice, although it is possible to get an abortion on the NHS after twelve weeks, it's very difficult and it's rare for a doctor to perform an abortion if the pregnancy is twenty-two weeks or more, counting from the first day of the woman's last period. They use an ultrasound scan so that the doctor can find out the exact age of the foetus."

"What will happen? I know vaguely but I'm not really sure."

"If an abortion is carried out in the first nine weeks of pregnancy, counting from the first day of the last period, a woman can be given an abortion pill, mifepristone, and a drug called prostaglandin. This is called a medical abortion because it doesn't involve surgery. After taking the mifepristone she'd have to return to the clinic thirty-six to forty-eight hours later to have a tablet of prostaglandin placed in her vagina. These two drugs will end most early pregnancies within the following four hours. It feels like having a heavy and rather painful period." He paused, then continued. "Most abortions before thirteen weeks of pregnancy are by vacuum aspiration, the suction method. For this method the woman has either a general or a local anaesthetic. The abortion is performed through the vagina, and there's no wound and no stitches. It takes only a minute to remove the pregnancy by suction. Healthy women take only an hour or so to recover and most go home the same day."

He had spoken in a formal voice and she knew that was to make it easier for her.

"Thank you," she said. "So how far on this pregnancy is is crucial?"

"Yes. We guess you're five or six weeks but we need to be sure. You should see a doctor as soon as you get back to London. Do you get on with your GP?"

"I've hardly ever seen her, but yes, I could talk to her."

"Good. Now, I think this is our lunch. I think we'll have water. I have to drive and you shouldn't drink too much at the moment."

They were careful to talk about anything and everything except emotional trauma in the hour that followed. To her amazement Rachel found herself laughing uproariously at some of his tales but suddenly she sobered. "It's odd, isn't it? The way you can still laugh and enjoy life when you have, well, other things on your mind."

"It's called sanity," Tom said wryly. "Or it's what saves your sanity. When I was a houseman we used to clown about all the time off duty. It was a reaction to what we were seeing on the wards every day. Now, if I have a grim surgery I come home and enjoy a good malt whisky. God knows what proportion of GPs have an alcohol problem." But his eyes were clear and bright, his skin with its faint dusting of freckles had few lines. He didn't look like a man with an alcohol problem.

"I can't tell you how grateful I am," Rachel said, as

they emerged into the sunshine. "You wouldn't let me pay so there has to be a next time. I'll come back and we'll have a bonanza, nothing spared."

"I'll look forward to it. But get things sorted out first."

"I will, I promise." This time he kissed her cheek and she kissed him back. He was waving as she left the car-park and turned towards the AI, marvelling that she could have come so close to Tom so quickly after such a lapse of time.

She left the AI at Dishforth and turned on to the AI9. It was raining now, and ahead of her lay the Cleveland Hills, dark against the horizon. What would she discover once she got beyond them? In spite of herself she felt a shiver of apprehension but there was no going back. Not now.

Her mother had told her of a white horse etched into the hillside. "Look to your left as you leave the AI and drive towards the hills," she had said, and there it was, clear against the dark grey-green of the hillside. "They struggle up there to restore it year after year," her mother had said, almost in awe. But how simple restoring a white horse seemed, compared with opening what might turn out to be a can of worms. At times she had been tempted to tell Tom the whole truth, but in the end it had been simpler to let him think that hers had been an ordinary straightforward adoption.

At Thirsk the road swung north. The hills were on her right now, separated from her by fields studded with sheep. The rain had ceased but clouds scurried along and a kestrel hung in the air like one last black, brooding raindrop. Middlesbrough was no more than twenty miles. Soon the hotel should be in sight.

At last it was there, a grey stone house with myriad windows, another stone building beyond. A sign swung on a wrought-iron frame: The Cleveland Tontine Inn. Its walls were ivy-clad in parts, flowers bloomed in the garden, and she drove in through a courtyard, past an arch that should have had ostlers plying for trade. She parked in another yard, flanked on two sides by grey stone, on the third by a long greenhouse that must have been there almost as long as the grey stone walls.

"One bedroom left," the receptionist told her. "You're lucky." Rachel looked around her. It was a house of arches leading from one room to another. There were green plants everywhere, and big, sloppy chairs and sofas rioting with cushions. Nothing matched but everything blended.

It's a warren, Rachel thought. She could hear voices but glimpse no one, only the suggestion of figures flitting beyond an arch somewhere out of sight. Better than a warren, it was a womb, a sanctuary, a place in which she could hide.

She sat in one of the arched rooms to drink tea from a fragile china cup. "It's chilly after the rain." The woman who had been at Reception had appeared with matches. Sparks flew in the great chimney as logs crackled and took fire.

This is heaven. She snuggled into cushions of velvet, damask and chintz, a wonderful hotch-potch of colour and comfort. There was wood panelling half-way up the walls and a curious air of timelessness about the place.

"Eighteen-o-four," the receptionist said, when Rachel enquired. "It was built as a coaching inn and then the Stockton–Darlington railway was built in eighteen twelve and coaches were no more. It's had a chequered career since then, but we love it."

Afterwards, alone by the fire, Rachel closed her eyes and thought of what lay ahead. It was nearly six o'clock. Too late to go looking for a stranger in a strange town.

Tomorrow she would set out on her quest and then, please God, be free to go back to London and get on with the rest of her life. She would have to make a decision then, but finding her mother would make it easier.

Except that, once found, a birth mother might not go away. What if she was a harpy, a leech, someone who would cling? Worse still, she might be ill, failing, in need of care. In spite of herself Rachel chuckled at the mental picture of herself pushing a forty-eight-year-old woman in a wheelchair for the next thirty years. "Wait and see," she told herself as she drifted into sleep.

20

Cleveland, Thursday, 17 April 1997

Rachel awoke to find it was eight forty. She had slept for nearly ten hours, unheard-of, especially lately. She had slept for an hour in the lobby but as soon as she had eaten dinner she had been ready for bed. She climbed from the bed and padded to her bathroom. It had a black and white tiled floor and a cute black cat for a light pull. Before dinner last night she had lain in the white bath for an hour, soaking in deep-green pine-scented water that seemed to take all the tension from her limbs. Now she looked at her face in the mirror. Already she seemed less tense.

Before she climbed back into bed she pulled back the rose-patterned curtains and looked out. Green fields, with drifts of white sheep, the brooding hills and roads going nowhere and everywhere. It was having a curious effect upon her, this Tontine, making her feel of this world and yet out of it.

195

Her newspaper was beside her plate when she went down to breakfast. She ordered fresh fruit and orange juice, toast and tea, and skimmed through the headlines. William Hague, the Welsh Secretary, was three to one favourite to win the leadership contest when Major went but the *Independent* thought it unlikely. And yet Leigh had enjoyed interviewing him. Rachel put aside the paper as a plate was laid before her containing two kinds of melon, fresh pineapple, mango, prunes and kiwi fruit. She had not felt hungry before but her mouth watered at the sight.

As she ate she looked out at the hills. Here they were tree-covered but on the top of one she could see a cluster of scanners and satellites. And the kestrel was still there, cruel against the blue sky. Rachel looked away quickly lest she see his sudden drop.

She ate two pieces of toast, drank her tea and then went upstairs to fetch her bag. It was ten o'clock. Time to begin her quest. The receptionist lent her a map and waved away an offer to pay. "I'll have it back when you've done with it."

The hills were quite close on her right-hand side as she started off. Signposts flashed by – East Harlsey, Ingleby Arncliffe, Ingleby Cross – musical names, but everywhere Triffid-like pylons were on the march and gradually the hills were lost to view. Yarm appeared on the signposts – almost there. The hills reappeared and then the town, Middlesbrough, cooling towers and chimneys touched with a sunlight that turned them into enchanted castles – until you saw the smoke and realised that this was a town where everything was subjected to the needs of industry.

The map showed Keeler Street leading off from Newton Street, and she found Newton Street behind the railway station in an area that was obviously being redeveloped. Here and there a solitary building stood like a single tooth in an otherwise empty gum. On one the roof had gone, leaving the rafters skeleton-like against the sky. But someone had made an effort to improve things, planting shrubs along a fence, laurel, cotoneaster, wild rose and lime.

Newton Street was grim and desolate, a corner shop at one end with half its windows shuttered, some houses with boarded windows, looking for all the world like blind men. Her heart sank then, as she realised the unlikelihood of her mother still being here after seven years. She nosed the car round the corner, into what should have been Keeler Street, to find only a wasteland covered in weeds. She parked the car and got out.

There had been houses there, and recently, for there were still isolated bits of rubble here and there. She could see where the front steps had been. If she counted she could find the eleventh doorway – except from which end of the one-time street should she count, and what would be the point?

She turned and surveyed the area. In the distance she could see building work in progress. One day this would be a new estate or a business park. Perhaps there would be factories but, whatever took its place, every trace of Keeler Street would be obliterated. She got back into the car and turned on the engine but she did not engage the gears. Instead she tried to analyse her feelings.

She was disappointed. It would have been satisfying to find a door to knock at, a face to identify. But she also felt relief. I'm not sure I want this confrontation, she thought. But I can't avoid it. Not now that I know a huge piece of the jigsaw puzzle of my life is missing.

It was a pity that this secret of her birth had come to light now. She ought to be concentrating on her pregnancy and whether or not it should continue. If it did not, their lives would go on as they had before. And one day, when he felt more secure, they would commit to one another and children would follow.

We are already committed, she reminded herself. Or, at least, I am.

She let out the clutch then and drove away from what remained of Keeler Street. The only thing she could do was write a letter to Freda Fielding and address it to her at Keeler Street. The Royal Mail might have a forwarding address. They always tried to deliver letters, she knew that. But she also knew that the odds were high that the letter would come back marked "Not at this address". If she had any sense she would pack her bags and go straight back to London.

But for reasons she could not explain, even to herself, she parked the car in an hotel car-park and went walk-about. She passed houses where prams stood outside, one with a mother cooing into the hood. If she went ahead would she become like that, jeans-clad, full-breasted and full of the joy of living? She had seen friends who had had babies, watched their faces soften, their boobs droop, seen formerly immaculate career women wear baby sick on their shoulder as though it were an epaulette. She shuddered slightly, but even as she did so she was smiling.

As she drove out of Middlesbrough the gentle mounds of the hills were shrouded in a grey haze. She was in open country now, a far cry from the industrial landscape she had left behind. She could see houses and sometimes a farm tucked into the fork of the hills. The hotel loomed up, grey and reassuring, and she realised she was hungry and looking forward to a meal.

Last night she had dined in the bistro, dark and intimate in spite of every table being occupied. She had had scallops and chargrilled chicken, chosen from a menu that was a kaleidoscope of flavour, ginger and dill and basil and coriander, above her a ceiling like an old linen bedspread, embroidered with trails of strawberries and leaves.

Today she ate smoked-salmon fishcakes in a delicious sauce and smiled to herself as the man at the next table fell over himself to impress his glamorous companion. She felt relaxed now that the check-out time had passed. She would have to pay for another day, might as well use it. She was on to pudding before she realised that it was not a desire to follow the Middlesbrough trail that had kept her here but a reluctance to return to London.

She went back to her room then and took the telephone directory from the bedside table. There was a slim chance that her birth mother had been on the telephone and might still be listed in the phone book. I want to resolve this now, Rachel thought. I want it out of the way. But there was no F. Fielding in the directory and, anyway, who could say if Fielding was still her mother's name?

She tried to watch television, but there was murder on one channel, racing on two more and on the fourth a chat-show, whose purpose seemed to be to embarrass as many people as possible. Rachel tried to concentrate on the screen, but a picture of Keeler Street kept intruding. The pathetic steps that might once have been scrubbed each morning, or not, depending on how houseproud you were. Had her mother been a step-scrubber?

The unfortunate choice of words made her laugh out loud. And yet it was too easy to see the woman as a person of easy virtue. What about her father, who caused such havoc in people's lives without even a qualm? Despite his apologies she had seen no real evidence of contrition in his behaviour. Damn him, she thought, and then was submerged in childhood memories, her father laughing, swinging her up in the air. His face on Christmas morning as he waited to see if she liked her presents. The times he had taken them skiing on crisp mountain slopes. Why was life so difficult, so devoid of clear lines? She ought to ring Leigh now and let him know she was in Cleveland but she decided against it. Let him wonder. If he cared enough, he would ring her mother and then he would find out.

Suddenly she saw Keeler Street again, the moment she had turned into it from Newton Street, with its boarded windows and seedy corner shop. She had felt a surge of pity for a shop owner hanging on as an area died around him. Or her. There had been something on the fascia. She saw it in her mind's eye, a proprietor's name and then a logo, a newspaper. The *Sun*? The *Mirror*?

The next moment she was on her feet and reaching for her car keys. Newsagents delivered, kept records, might even have forwarded final bills. As she drove towards the shop her heart was pounding and no exhortations to calm herself served to quiet it. If she solved this, if she dealt with this sensibly, however it turned out, she could cope with the rest. Make decisions, tell the truth, sort out the rest of her life.

The name above the shop was A. Singh, the logo was indeed the *Sun*. There was an Asian woman behind the till, almost obliterated by the piles of goods that filled every square inch of floor space.

"I wonder if you could help me," she began.

The woman's beautiful eyes were wary. "Yes," she said.

"I'm trying to find someone, a relative, who lived in Keeler Street."

"Keeler Street? It's gone." The woman was already turning away

"Did you sell papers to Keeler Street — number eleven Keeler Street? Please, it's very important."

"But Keeler Street is gone — no papers."

"Excuse me." The boy was about twelve, bright-eyed and handsome. His mother — the resemblance was unmistakable — was looking at him with pride but a degree of exasperation. Suddenly she gave forth in her native tongue. He listened, then turned back to Rachel. "My mother says to tell you Keeler Street is demolished. No one lives there."

"I know." Rachel tried to keep her voice even. "But I

wonder if you had a register — a book — if you could tell me if my — if my friend was still living in number eleven. That would help me."

When he smiled, his teeth gleamed. "Easy," he said proudly, and dived under the counter. He turned the pages in a bedraggled ledger, then ran his finger down a column. "King," he said triumphantly. "W. King. Mr W. King."

"So it wasn't Fielding?" Rachel said, disappointed.

"No, it was Mr King. He's in the bungalows now."

"The bungalows?"

"For old people. He is there, still getting the *Sun* and the *Evening Gazette*."

He took her to the corner and pointed out the bungalows, half hidden by the building site. "Thank you," she said, and would have fumbled in her purse but he stilled her with a flash of his eyes.

"No, thank you," he said. "It's part of the service." Around his neck his striped muffler bore the logo of Middlesbrough Football Club.

"Is that your club?" she asked, pointing.

He nodded, proudly. "Ravenelli is the best in the world." Her agreement brought another smile to his face and he went on his way.

She found Mr King in the doorway of his bungalow. He was a small man and frail, but his eyes twinkled. "I'm sorry to disturb you," she began, "but I'm looking for a relative, a Miss Fielding. I know she lived in Keeler Street, at number eleven. I'm wondering if you have any idea where she might be?"

"Can't help you, love. It was Carter I took over from.

She got rehoused nearer the hospital. Poor old sod, she was. She's in a home now."

"When did you move in?"

"'Ninety-four. They were doing up my street so I went there temporary. She was only there a year or eighteen months – her legs were a sight. With veins. She's in Park View up by the Catholic church. Wait on, I mind she said there was a woman in there before her, lived on her own. I don't remember the name but it was English. That's something nowadays."

She left him muttering imprecations against incomers and drove to the nursing home.

"I'm afraid you won't get much out of Miss Carter." The nurse who was leading her through numerous pine doors sounded weary. "She can be quite lucid sometimes, but only about food. She can tell Stork from butter before it's left the kitchen. Let her hear the *Coronation Street* introduction and she comes alive. But for anything sensible, I'm afraid she's a no-no. Still, you can but try."

"Have you brought any biscuits?" Miss Carter's request came as Rachel inched gingerly into a seat beside her.

"Now, Norah." The nurse's voice was sharp. "You know you're not allowed biscuits. You're carrying too much weight." To Rachel's eyes Miss Carter looked slim, almost fragile in her wheelchair. But the nurse defended the prohibition as if she had read her thoughts. "You should try lifting her into the bath. Doctor says she should lose a stone."

"They starve you here." Miss Carter put out a hand

and clutched Rachel's arm. "Tell someone. Tell my mother. She used to rock me, you know. Loola, loola, loola, loola bye-bye. That's what she sang. And I got a palm leaf on Sundays. Cream. Proper cream." She leaned closer. "Are you sure you've got no biscuits?" Her white hair was scraped back into a bun and her chin was bewhiskered above a blouse stained with some previous meal.

"It's no use." The nurse was impatient to go. "I told you, didn't I?"

"Thanks anyway," Rachel said. She turned back to look at the frail figure, absorbed now in her television. "If, by any chance, there's an improvement, would you let me know?"

"Leave your name. They do come round sometimes but I wouldn't build your hopes up." Rachel left her home number and address. "I'm at the Cleveland Tontine till tomorrow," she said, "just in case."

This time, as she drove back to the hotel, she was quite sure of her feelings. She felt disappointed. The trail had petered out and although she would still write the letter she wouldn't hold her breath for an answer. Her mother had left the area too long ago for that and the house had been occupied at least twice since then. When she got back to her room she dialled Leigh's number. He was not in his office, nor was he at the flat. She dialled Jago's number and was relieved to hear his voice at the other end.

"Jago, have you seen anything of Leigh?" His voice, as he detailed the comings and goings from her flat, was warm and comforting. "I'm in Cleveland," she said, "trying to find my mother, but the trail's gone cold."

"Come home," he urged. "I've got something for you, actually — or I will have by the time you get back. We'll have a toddy, a good cry and a bit of a curse, and you'll feel heaps better. Come home now."

"I can't, Jago. Not tonight. But thanks for being such a friend." It was the thought of him waiting for her, with his friendly monkey face and his kindness, that helped her through the rest of the night and eventually to bed. Tomorrow she would pack and go home, and together she and Jago would sort out the mess that her life had become.

It was only after she had put out the light that she realised she was not looking to Leigh to help her sort out her problems.

21

Cleveland, Friday, 18 April 1997

When she awoke Rachel switched on the radio. It was full of reports about the bombs the IRA had placed at Leeds and Doncaster and on the M6. "It's chaos," the commentator said. They'll screw up the election, Rachel thought. They've probably got Semtex under every polling station in the country.

Indeed, London did seem chaotic, if the pictures shown when she switched on the television were a true representation. A mighty city and it could be thrown into disarray by a small, tight-knit group of fanatics.

She had almost finished packing when the phone rang. She picked it up but no one was there. She was still wrestling with her morning nausea, and she stood for a moment till it subsided.

She had checked the bathroom and retrieved her forgotten deodorant when the phone rang again. "Hello." She had expected it to be an offer to bring down her bags but the voice on the other end was unprofessional and hesitant.

"Miss Trewhitt?"

"Yes." As she spoke, Rachel's eyes flitted around the room in search of something unpacked.

"You were at Park View yesterday?"

"Yes." Suddenly Rachel was alert. Had the old lady had a flash of clarity?

"I'm Norah Carter's niece. The nurse said you were after someone's address. I used to look out for my auntie. I just thought I might know what you wanted."

"It's very kind of you to bother." Rachel tried to contain her mounting excitement. "I was hoping to find out about Miss Fielding. She lived in number eleven. Well, she was living there in nineteen ninety."

"Freda Fielding? I remember her all right. There was another woman living there with her and then she went to live with her son."

"What happened to Freda?" She wanted to get to the nub of the thing, but she tried hard to keep the impatience out of her voice.

"She went off to be a housekeeper. Did nicely for herself, Auntie Norah said."

"Where?" This time she snapped out the question.

"I don't know the address . . ." Rachel's mouth opened on a silent O of anguish. ". . . but I could show you the house. I went there with a parcel for her. It's out towards Stokesley. My brother drove me there but I could find it again."

Rachel checked out of the hotel and drove to the corner

of Keeler Street where the woman was waiting. She was small and bright-eyed, and very appreciative of the twenty-pound note Rachel pressed into her hand. "That's it," she said, indicating the road that led to Stokesley.

They were passing a church with a statue and then a flower-shop. Would flowers be appropriate? More important, would they be welcome? In the distance the Cleveland Hills were low and brooding. The house, when it was pointed out, was equally dark and imposing.

"How will you get back?" Rachel said, as the woman alighted.

"Don't worry about me." She went off down the road with such alacrity that Rachel wondered if the whole thing was a con, a cynical attempt to get money out of someone. But, con or not, she was here. She locked up the car and trudged up the gravel drive to the front door.

The bell rang when she pressed it. If there was anyone at home they couldn't fail to hear. And not only the bell. In Rachel's ears her heart boomed out a rapid, irregular beat. Someone was approaching the door, she could see them through the distorting plate glass. When they opened the door she could always give another name, say she had come to the wrong house.

The door was beginning to open when Rachel spotted the doll's pram, rusted and leaning because a wheel was missing. There must be children in the house. She made an instant calculation. Her mother was forty-eight. Lots of women gave birth in their forties. She might have a sister or a brother or both. She felt her heartbeat quicken until it caught at her breath. And then the door was held wide and she was looking into the face of a girl hardly as old as she was.

"Hello." The girl was smiling, putting up a paint-flecked hand to tuck hair under the striped bandana that held it back.

Rachel smiled too. "This may sound crazy — and I'm sorry to trouble you — especially when I can see you're busy." From within the house came the sound of a crash.

"Oh, God," the girl said. "What's he done now? Look, whatever it is, come in. I was going to stop for coffee anyway." She turned and rushed along the hallway, leaving Rachel no option but to follow her through to a room where a wall had been demolished to take in another, smaller room. A baby of about a year was standing up in a lobster-pot playpen, the telephone he had pulled from a nearby table in there beside him.

"No harm done," the girl said, restoring it to its place and smiling indulgently at her child. "He's a handful. Not like his big sister. She's as good as gold. Now, tell me what I can do for you while I put the kettle on."

"I hope I'm not wasting your time," Rachel said.

The girl waved a hand. "Not a bit — glad of the company. I don't see a soul most days till it's time to collect Tilly from school." She was spooning coffee into mugs. "Only instant, I'm afraid. We're doing up the house, as you can probably see. We've been here two years but we couldn't afford it before and I was pregnant with Freddy." She looked round the room. "Sorry, I should have said, 'Sit down' . . . if you can find somewhere, that is. Just shift something."

Rachel moved a pile of magazines and sat. "Thank you," she said, and accepted the proffered mug. "As I said, I hope I'm not wasting your time. I'm looking for someone – a relative – who might have lived here . . . well, worked here. Her name was Fielding, Freda Fielding."

The girl pursed her lips. "We bought from someone called Ancaster. They didn't live in the house. They lived in Cheshire. The house had been their father's, I think, his or hers. They were selling it as part of his estate. He'd lived in it for ages, practically since it was built, and he'd done very little except basic repairs. We got it cheaply because of that but it's been an uphill struggle and there's years of work to do yet."

"I think she was a housekeeper – at least, that's what I was told."

"That could figure," the girl said. "He was very old, ninety, I think, so there must have been someone."

The baby had flopped down on his bottom and was making grunting noises. "Oh, Freddy," the girl said. "Not another nappy!" The baby smiled, a seraphic, satisfied smile. "Sorry about this," the girl said, "but if I don't get it off him he'll get into a horrendous mess."

She seized a plastic roll and spread it on the floor alongside a hold-all in the same Disney character pattern. "Come on, then!" The baby was lifted out of the lobster-pot and laid on his back.

Rachel watched, fascinated, as the girl peeled off the soiled nappy and dropped it into a plastic bag. The baby's round pink backside was cleaned with wet-wipes and patted dry. "There," the mother said. "A nice, clean boy."

Freddy smiled again and cooed and Rachel felt her heart lurch. Could she cope as the girl was coping? Or could she snuff out a smile like that before it was even born? Before she had known she was pregnant she had seldom noticed babies. Now they seemed to be everywhere.

"I'll tell you what," the girl said, when the new nappy was in place and the baby back among his toys, "we'll have the details of the house purchaser somewhere, addresses and everything. If the Ancasters are still in Cheshire they might know about a housekeeper. They might have kept in touch. Maybe she was mentioned in the will. You never know."

She was scrambling to her feet when the baby began to cry. "Poor Freddy," she said. "Wants his din-dins, does he?" She looked at the clock. "He shouldn't eat until twelve," she said, "but once he gets hunger pangs he's lethal. Could you hang on to him while I heat his tins?" Without waiting for agreement she deposited Freddy on Rachel's knee and bustled over to the split-level cooker. "Tell you what," she said, "if you give him this – he's no trouble as long as you keep it coming – I'll go through David's bureau. He's pretty systematic. I think I know where it'll be."

In no time Freddy was in his high chair and Rachel, having put aside her untouched coffee cup, was holding a spoon in one hand and a saucer in another, on which was balanced a tin of something puréed and pungent. "Lamb stew," the girl said apologetically. "Pongs, doesn't it?"

Feeding a baby was quite easy, easier than Rachel had feared. She spooned it in, occasionally catching stray dribbles on the tiny chin, all the time marvelling at the ease with which the girl had left her child alone with a stranger. I wouldn't do that, she thought. Not with my baby.

She was murmuring approval at Freddy's appetite when the girl came back waving a paper. "Here it is," she said. "I've copied the Ancasters' address and the estate agent's number, just in case. Has he nearly finished? Good boy!"

A few moments later, Rachel was back in the tree-lined street. She climbed into the car and turned on the engine but she didn't move off immediately. Had she found the key to her mother's whereabouts, or merely the directions to another dead end? She sat for a long while, thinking about Freddy's eager little mouth, his tiny fingers, the powdery smell of his peachskin head when she had kissed him goodbye.

I liked it, she thought. Her mother, her birth mother, must have held her, fed her, even if it was only in the hospital. How could she give me up? Suddenly Rachel was filled with impatience to find Freda Fielding and confront her with that question.

22

Cleveland, Saturday, 19 April 1997

Rachel had had breakfast and was back in her room when
the phone rang.

"Rachel?" It was Leigh. "Thank God," he said, when
she replied. "I've been chasing you all over."

Her reply was sharper than she intended it to be.
"Hardly all over. I expect you rang Mum and she told you
I was here."

"Yes, well . . . After you just disappeared I was
worried. You might have let me know. You could have rung
last night."

How could she tell him that she had relished being
"lost" for a little while? Easier to lie.

"I tried to get you last night," she said.

"Oh, sorry, darling, I was chasing an interview with
Will Self. Didn't get it. Still, I'm hoping for the Minister
of State for Northern Ireland later. They're putting out
feelers now. And the rumour is that Vanessa Redgrave's

coming out for the Lib-Dems. That'll be a turn-up for the books — for Paddy, come to that. He who grabs a tiger by the tail—"

"Not such a tiger now," Rachel said. "She's calmed down as she's got older. We all do."

"You sound gloomy." At the other end of the line he was trying hard to be placatory. "You're missing me, that's what's the matter. Come home."

"Why don't you ask me if I've found anything?" she asked. There was irritation in her voice and she saw that her knuckles were white where she was gripping the receiver.

"I assumed you'd've told me if you had," he said, oblivious of the fact that he had launched into election news almost as soon as he had heard her voice.

"I got an address — two, in fact, but she left the first one two years ago."

"And the second?"

"She was never there but the people who live there might know where she is. I rang them all last night but there was no answer. I'll try again today."

"You may have to give up in the end," Leigh said. "And, after all, parentage is not that important. Lots of children are adopted — or used to be — and never know their mothers. And hundreds of men father children and never know it. The kids never know who their father was but life goes on." Towards the end of the last sentence his voice shook a little as though he realised he was on shaky ground. "Are you all right?" he asked.

"I'm fine — but I'm still pregnant, if that's what's

worrying you." She couldn't resist the dig but once it was out she regretted it. "I'm coming back to London as soon as I can," she finished, "but I must see what I can find out first."

They were both uneasy as they said goodbye and when she put down the phone Rachel felt only relief.

She finished her packing and then sat down at the telephone. It was nine thirty. If there was again no reply from the Ancasters' number the estate agent would be sure to be open now. She tried the private number but it rang and rang without answer. She depressed the receiver rest then tried the second number, this time with success.

"I'm sorry to bother you," she said, then launched into her tale. From time to time the woman at the other end gave a weary sigh, and Rachel felt her heart sink. An estate agent would be quite within their rights to say, "Sorry, no can do," and what would she do then?

To her relief, after an even heavier sigh, the woman gave a long dissertation about the difficulties of looking things up and then relented. "I can't do it now but I'll see what I can find this afternoon. You can ring about four. No promises, but I'll do my best."

Rachel stammered out her thanks and put down the phone. It was still ephemeral but it was better than nothing. She could go home to Fenton Marske and ring from there.

She had a definite feeling of nostalgia as she left the Tontine. Rain was threatening and cloud hung low over the hills but the grey stone building exuded warmth. I was safe here, Rachel thought. Not happy but safe. She consoled herself with the thought that, one day, when life had settled down and she was happy once more, she would come back and enjoy all that this place had to offer.

One good reason for going home was the chance of seeing Tom again. He was the one person she could trust to give her objective advice. Jago was wise and kind, but he was too fond of her to be completely dispassionate. She could trust Tom as an old friend. After all, they might have been lovers if their schooldays friendship had lasted.

At first, as she drove through the awakening spring landscape she felt eager, almost euphoric, but as she neared Fenton Marske her mood changed. What if she was intruding upon a reconciliation between her parents? Perhaps they needed time alone if they were beginning again.

The trouble was that you never thought of parents as sexual beings although you yourself were proof that they were. If you were forced to acknowledge that they were, you felt an initial distaste. She had been brought face to face with her father's sexuality and it was not pleasant. As she swung on to the road that led home she resolved to try to give her father some of the liberality she had always extended to her friends.

But even as she half resolved one problem she acknowledged another, that she might be expecting too much of Tom Lattemore. Already she had unloaded most of her troubles on to his shoulders. Was she taking advantage of his good nature? As she drew up at her parents' door she put the dilemma to one side and prepared to face whatever was waiting for her inside.

What she found was an atmosphere prickling with tension although her unexpected appearance was greeted with delight.

"Darling!" Her mother was moving forward, arms outstretched. "How lovely — and just in time for lunch."

Over her mother's shoulder Rachel looked at the table. It was laid for three — and yet no one had known she was coming. As if she sensed Rachel's puzzlement, her mother spoke. "Vanessa's here. She came last night." There was that note in her voice that said, "Trouble!" and Rachel felt her throat constrict. Not Van, too. Soon there would be no family members intact.

"Sit down, dear, unless you want to wash your hands. Daddy is in the garden somewhere and Van should be down directly. And remind me to tell you about Liz. She rang last night. They're having a wonderful time — I've never heard her happier."

Thank God for Liz, Rachel thought as she tidied her hair and reapplied lipstick. The face that looked back at her from the cloakroom mirror was pale and strained, but not half as gaunt as Vanessa's face when at last she appeared.

Not even her father's unfailing bonhomie could lift the atmosphere around the dining-table. Her mother was determinedly bright, Vanessa almost silent. Rachel watched her sister push her food around her plate, and longed for someone, somewhere, to speak out instead of pretending they were all taking part in a Noël Coward play.

When the meal was over she followed Vanessa upstairs,

but hesitated at the closed door of her sister's bedroom. At last she raised a hand and knocked.

"Who is it?" Vanessa's voice was muffled. She was crying. Rachel turned the handle and opened the door.

Vanessa half lay on her bed, a handkerchief clutched in her hand, grey trails of mascara on her cheeks. "I've left him, Rachel," she said. "I've left him and I'm never going back."

"If that's what you want, OK," Rachel said firmly. "But let's talk about it first."

She listened as Vanessa poured out her garbled tale of woe. "I just want the children," she finished. "He can keep everything else." There was a little pause and then she added, "Except for the new furniture. I chose that. I'm not leaving it behind for him."

Rachel closed her eyes on a vivid picture of Vanessa fleeing down the A1 with her children under one arm and a three-piece suite under the other. She was desperately seeking something to say when she heard a splutter. To her relief, when she opened her eyes she saw that Vanessa was smiling. "I know," she said, wiping her eyes. "It's crazy, isn't it? Well, at least I haven't lost my sense of humour."

But she was not inclined to joke about her father. "He's swanning around as though it had never happened. At least Trevor has the grace to look hangdog."

"Are you determined not to go back?" Rachel asked, glad to divert Vanessa from the subject of her father's behaviour.

"I suppose not – maybe I will when he's really sorry.

When I'm very, very sure that it's over. And I don't want to worry the kids. I left them with him because of school and I thought, let him have the responsibility for a while. But I can't let it go on too long."

It was a quarter to four when Rachel came downstairs. Almost time to ring the estate agent. Better not ring too soon and risk annoying them. She picked up the phone and dialled Tom's number.

Again she felt that ambivalence, a desire to hear his voice, anxiety in case she did. The ringing tone went on, and she felt both relief and disappointment – until it ceased and she heard his voice.

"Tom? It's me, Rachel."

He sounded genuinely pleased to hear her. "Where are you?"

"I'm fine. I'm here – at Mum's. I'm leaving tomorrow—" Before she could say, "I was wondering . . ." he had interrupted.

"Dinner tonight? I'm free if you are." There was no ambivalence in her feelings now, only relief that she would have him to talk to.

When she put down the phone she dialled the estate agency. "Ah, yes," the receptionist said. "We've got something for you."

Rachel reached for the pen and pad that lay by the phone. "Yes," she said. "Fire away."

"The Ancasters have emigrated, but we did have a note about mail, a forwarding address for the housekeeper. Miss Fielding, that was who you were interested in?"

"Yes," Rachel said, gripping the pen until it bruised

her fingers. "Yes, it's Miss Fielding I want to find." She wrote down the address, a house in Northallerton, a mere thirty or forty miles from Fenton Marske. "Thank you," she said. "I can't tell you how grateful I am."

23

Fenton Marske, Sunday, 20 April 1997

Over dinner Tom had been as patient as ever. Now, as Rachel headed for Northallerton, she remembered his eyes, wise and kind, above the smoking candle in the pub last night. There had been lines of good humour about them but the gaze was steady. "Go easy," he had urged. "You have a lot on your plate just now. If it turns out to be tricky in Northallerton, back off. Retreat and take stock. Once you've found her you know where she is. You can go back. It's not worth forcing a showdown now."

"You think it might be like that?"

"Not necessarily, but it's always a possibility. If you were going through the proper channels I'd be happier. You'd have counselling, someone else would make the initial contact — you're doing it in the most dangerous way."

"I don't have time," Rachel said. "I know you're right but time is running out for me."

"So you still haven't decided whether or not to terminate?"

"I want to keep it," she said. "The more I think about it the more I want it. But it's not just me and a baby, it's me and Leigh and a baby. It's a baby's right to a father—"

"So you think he might go if you hold out for seeing the pregnancy through?"

She wanted to salvage her pride and say, "No, of course not," but it would be pointless. "I think he might. If he felt it might snarl up his life. He'd support me financially, but for the rest I'm not sure."

Tom put out his hand then and squeezed hers where it lay on the table. "Well, you can't be sure of that. Once it was a certainty he might feel differently. Now, when there's still an element of doubt, he's opting for the easy way out. He could change. Take things one at a time. First stop Northallerton. And remember I'm here whenever you want to talk." He smiled and withdrew his hand. "Actually, I'm coming to London soon, to a seminar. We could meet up if you'd like."

"I'd like it very much," she said, and the vehemence of her tone surprised her.

She was thinking of Tom as she turned into a side-road and saw the house she was seeking at its end. It was double-fronted and ivy-clad, but there was something sad about it, an air of disuse. She parked on the driveway, then picked her way around flower-beds where no flowers grew to the solid but blistered front door. It had glass panels but there was no sign of light or activity inside.

While she waited for an answer to her ring on the bell

she tried to marshal her thoughts. What should she say? Should she be formal or informal, forthcoming or cautious?

She was about to ring again when the door opened suddenly. A woman stood there, dressed in a short-sleeved grey sweater above a pinstripe skirt, fluffy slippers on the end of bare legs, a cigarette held aloft in nicotine-stained fingers. She had large and rather luminous eyes, but there were deep furrows between her brows as though she often frowned.

Panic engulfed Rachel at first. This couldn't be her mother. This woman was old, too old . . . and much too unattractive to have caught her father's eye. And then, with the woman looking at her expectantly, fear drained away and only curiosity remained.

"Miss Fielding?"

"Yes." The voice was faintly accented. Not Middlesbrough. Scottish, perhaps. No one had mentioned Scotland. But, then, no one had said anything much about the woman who had given her birth.

"I wonder if I could talk to you for a few minutes."

"You'd be wasting your time, pet. I won't buy anything."

"I'm not selling." The door was beginning to close, the woman's face had hardened. "Please, if we could just speak for a moment—"

"I'm sorry. I'll have to go."

"My name is Trewhitt. Rachel Trewhitt."

The door began to close again but faster this time. It was almost shut when it opened again. The woman's face was deadpan. "Come in," she said, "but I can't be too long. He needs his lunch on time."

Rachel followed her down a carpeted corridor to what had obviously been a morning room. "Sit down." There were two armchairs either side of a plopping gas fire. Beside one a cup of cold, yellowing tea stood on a side table, beside a full ash-tray.

The woman gestured to the other chair as she stubbed out her cigarette, and Rachel subsided into it. The woman turned to the mantelpiece and took up cigarettes and lighter. "Do you?" Rachel shook her head and the woman lit a cigarette for herself then sat down.

"I suppose I've always known you'd turn up some time," she said, as she exhaled a column of smoke. She smiled then. "You're not like me."

"I'm supposed to resemble my father."

The woman's eyes narrowed. "Yes," she said. "Well, are they both all right?"

"My mother and father?" It was out and she wondered if it would cause offence but the woman was smiling again.

"Oh, don't worry. I didn't know girls could still blush. You've gone red. No, she's been far more of a mother to you than me. Besides," she exhaled smoke, "I've never been that anxious to be someone's mam, let alone a grandma." She looked at Rachel's hand now and seemed relieved to see no ring. At her temples and parting, the hair was grey but her short wavy bob was a burnished maroon.

"I didn't know about you – about anything – until this week."

"Didn't they tell you? I wondered." She blew a small ring and studied it for a second. "I wouldn't have let you go, you know, if they hadn't been there. I'm not that bad. But she was keen – desperate. I could never make that out when she had two kids of her own. Still, like I said, she was keen. I was young – young for me age, even – and I knew you'd have a good life. Those kids had everything, ponies, music lessons, the lot. Why not? I thought. So I said I'd let you go. I was five months then. If I'd seen you I might not have agreed but even once I did there was no going back. Did they tell you how we did it? About the hospital and the false name?"

"They didn't tell me – well, not both of them. My sister hinted at it and then Mum told me."

"Was it Vanessa? She was a little cow in Germany. So your dad didn't tell you. Typical that – he could always slide out of things."

I don't believe this conversation, Rachel thought. So matter-of-fact. She doesn't even seem surprised. Aloud, she said, "Would you tell me – from your point of view?"

The woman – impossible to call her Mother, Rachel thought – hesitated, then stubbed out her cigarette and reached for another. It was the only sign that she was disconcerted, this rapid abandoning of one cigarette only to light another. She blew the first column of smoke skywards and smiled again. "It's weird this, isn't it? Of all the times I've thought about how it would be, I never thought it would be like this. The two of us sitting here . . ." She stood up. "Would you like a drink?"

It was too early for spirits, and gin was the only alcohol

visible, but somehow it seemed wrong to refuse. The glass was thick, the gin plentiful, the tonic merely a suggestion.

"I'll have to be quick," the woman said. "He's a diabetic, you see, or I'd let him wait." Around them the house was silent, not even a suggestion of "him". She drew on the cigarette and took a determined breath. "I was in the services too. Did they tell you that? Other ranks. That's why they had to keep it quiet. He'd've been out on his ear otherwise. When she first said about me taking her name I thought, ha-ha, destroy the evidence. In the end, though, I knew she meant what she said. She was good to me that last week. I was shouting for me mother, God, anyone in the end. And she was there. She has been good to you, hasn't she?" Briefly she looked genuinely concerned.

"Yes," Rachel said firmly. "She's been wonderful. I couldn't have asked for a better childhood."

"And him?"

"Yes." Rachel sought the right words. "Yes, he's been a good father." She purposely left out any mention of his philandering but it was in vain.

"And a lousy husband, I'll bet." Now the woman was really smiling. "Don't bother denying it. I wasn't the first so I'm quite sure I wasn't the last."

"What happened to you afterwards?" Rachel said, anxious to move on.

"I was invalided out – bundled out. Being up the duff was a hanging offence, in those days. After you were born I went back to Ashington. In Northumberland. I come from there. Me dad was a miner, God-fearing, hard-

working. They'd've taken you, if they'd known, and
never mind the gossip. I never told them. There didn't
seem much point. I said I'd got fed up and chucked it.
They tut-tutted a bit but that was all. I got a job in a hotel
in Newcastle, then I did bar work. What came to hand,
really."

"And you never married?"

"No. I lived with someone once. Eleven years, but it
didn't work out."

She would have said more but suddenly there was an
angry buzz and Rachel saw that an electric bell on the
wall was vibrating. "I'll have to get on — he's a devil for his
Sunday lunch." The woman had risen to her feet and, for
one horrific moment, Rachel wondered whether or not
she should embrace her when they parted. You couldn't
merely hold out your hand to the woman who had given
you life.

"I'm glad you came." The dilemma was resolved for
Rachel by her birth mother preceding her to the door,
patently anxious now to get rid of her. "But I wouldn't
come back here again. Not at the moment. If you drop me
a line we could meet up. Do you live with them? Wherever
they are now."

"No," Rachel said. "I'm in London."

"Ooh." The woman was impressed. "What do you do?
I often wondered if you'd make something of yourself."

"I'm in television — a floor manager."

"Floor manager?" The sallow face drooped, as though
disappointed.

"It's quite an important job," Rachel said hastily. "I'm

in charge of the studio, under the director."

Freda's face brightened again and she moved closer. "I'm glad you've done well. I've often wondered . . ."

Should I tell her about the baby? But even as the thought came, Rachel decided against it. Much too soon to confide anything but the essentials.

"I'll let you know when my next programme is on," she said instead. "I'm on leave now."

"Yes, that'd be nice." They were on the step, and already she was withdrawing. "I'm glad things turned out for you," she said, but her words were almost obliterated by another angry buzz upon the bell. And then the door was shut, her shadow moved from the glass of the door and there was nothing for Rachel to do but move towards the car. She looked at her watch. The whole thing had taken less than half an hour.

When she got back into the car she sat still, her legs shaking. I have just met my mother, she thought. I have just uncovered the reality of my life, the truth and not the sham, and I don't know what I feel, if I feel anything at all.

She closed her eyes, recalling the scene, wondering what the woman was doing now. Was she, too, sitting somewhere, shell-shocked, wondering if it had really happened or if it had been a dream? What if I had reached out, she thought, if I had taken her in my arms, poor unloved Freda Fielding who has wound up at the beck and call of an electric bell? As she turned on the ignition and let out the clutch, she was crying.

24

London, Monday, 21 April 1997

In the background the radio crackled and popped as John Humphries tore into yet another hapless Tory. Yesterday John Major had professed himself happy at the way the campaign was going but his confidence was looking a little misplaced, to say the least.

Leigh had been listening to the radio since six thirty. Now his arm snaked behind her head. "All right?" he said, and then, when she didn't answer, "Did you sleep?"

She had been awake since five but had lain feigning sleep because that was easier than having to talk and she could tell from his restlessness that he was ready, even anxious, to talk.

She had been too tired for discussion last night, after the long drive home through weekend traffic, all the time mulling over the meeting with her birth mother and finding only dissatisfaction there.

"You're back!" he had said, and folded her into his

231

arms. But she had been unable to respond, partly through fatigue, partly through fear that he would want to discuss the baby. "Did you find her?" he asked, and when she nodded, "Well?"

She outlined the visit and turned for the kitchen. "I'm having some hot milk," she said. "I'm bushed. Do you want some?" She hoped he would get the message and it seemed he did. He kissed her cheek gently before he put out the light and they turned back to back. They had been apart for days but desire had left them. Truly a baby changed things from the moment of conception. Now they lay there, the radio burbling away, each waiting for the other to speak. But there was too much to be said to begin now, with a working day looming up.

At last he said, "We'll talk tonight. Try to get some rest." He slid out of bed then, and twenty minutes later he had left the flat.

Rachel got up at eight and looked out over the roof-tops. Usually she loved the sight and sounds of London waking up. The rattle of the occasional milk-float, cars starting up below, the woman across the way who practised deep breathing for two minutes precisely as soon as she opened her curtains.

Today she looked out with unseeing eyes, obsessed with mental pictures. Yesterday she had met her mother. In a De Mille movie there would have been trumpets, a roll of thunder, a shaft of heavenly light. But it had not been De Mille, it had been real life, a curious, flat little occasion that had evoked little or no emotion on either side, as far as she could see.

They had sat and talked like two people who had met up on a train. "She's your mother," Rachel told herself, and felt nothing but a sense of unreality. I wanted more, she thought. I wanted to hold her, hit her, shake her till her teeth rattled. I wanted her to love me.

She padded to the kitchen, feeling the tiled floor cold to her bare feet, and stood, shifting from one foot to another, while the kettle boiled. What should she do today? She tried to prioritise but it was impossible to tie things down. She ought to phone her mother. Her real mother – her adoptive mother – who must be wondering about the result of her trip to Middlesbrough.

Perhaps she should send a note to her birth mother. Even flowers. But what would she put on the card? She felt a sudden stirring in the belly. Wind undoubtedly. Babies didn't move before sixteen weeks, even she knew that much. She felt a terrible desire to rid herself of this intrusion, this alien object that had invaded her unaware and was at once dear and fearsome.

"I'm not a child," she told herself, as she stirred and sweetened. "I should have known this might happen."

It was a relief when she heard Jago's radio below and could dress herself for the journey downstairs. "Get you!" he said, when the door opened. "I don't have to ask how it went. You look shagged out."

She told him the details of her trip and he let her talk without interrupting. With each minute she felt the load lifting from her. "Oh, Jago," she said, when she had finished. "What would I do without you?"

"Cope," he said.

They were discussing what she should do next when she heard her phone ringing upstairs. She flew up the stairs two at a time but the ringing ended as she put out her hand. Was it her mother or Leigh? She dialled 1471 and winced as she heard the robotic voice intone the number. It had been Nick, not at the office but at home.

She decided to shower and dress before she called him. It was not yet nine o'clock, which meant she had been top of Nick's agenda for the day, not a good sign. When at last she got through to him he said, "I hope you've had a good rest."

"Not really," she said. "It's only been three weeks."

"That's a lifetime. Can you get in here today? I've got a job for you."

She agreed to be at his office at twelve and then went back downstairs.

"They want me at the studios," she said. "Which means they've got a job lined up. What will I tell them?"

Jago grimaced. "Until you've made a decision, what can you tell them? I'd play for time."

He sounded uncharacteristically downbeat and Rachel frowned. "That's not like you."

"What do you mean?" He was half turned from her and he did not meet her eye.

"Well, you're usually so cheerful. You sound down."

"It's not that." He turned now and faced her. "It's just that it's so important that you make the right decision."

"Which is?"

"I don't know. That's up to you." He shrugged. "I'll tell you. I was fifteen when my mam told me I wasn't wanted.

In the beginning, that is. What she was saying was that she loved me *now*, but if she'd had the opportunity in the beginning she would've done away with me."

"Oh, Jago."

He was smiling now, but it wasn't reaching his eyes. "It hurt. It still does. That I wouldn't be here if there'd been an alternative. That's why it's important to get it right. Sod Leigh! You have to want this baby. Really want it. If you don't, let it go!"

His words were still ringing in her ears as a cab carried her towards the studios and Nick's office.

She walked through the lower floor, seeing around her the paraphernalia of programme-making, here an antique desk, there a cobbled street that looked sturdy but was made of paper, everywhere dead flowers, discarded once they had served their purpose.

As the lift carried her up towards the office floor she thought of what a make-believe world she worked in, except that life outside was proving to be even more of a sham.

"How do you feel about drama?" Nick said, when she was seated on the opposite side of his desk. "There's thirteen weeks' filming on *Richmond and Son* coming up. That should carry you nicely to autumn and then you can go back to the show."

Should she tell him she was pregnant? She knew how his mood would change then, from affability to caution. And when she had gone he would call for her contract to make sure it left United TV in the clear as far as maternity leave was concerned. "I'm not sure, Nick. You know I like live shows — there's a buzz to them . . ."

". . . and actors are temperamental sods to work with," he finished for her. He put his well-manicured hands together and touched them to his lips. "Tell you what, how would you like to go to *Eleventh Hour*?"

Rachel's heart leaped. *Eleventh Hour* was the new ratings leader, the show everyone wanted.

"I'd like that," she said, "but could I have a few days to decide?"

"Not longer. Annie Murray's been with it since it started. She wants out at the end of May. I want her replacement up and ready by the end of this month. No later."

"Give me a week, Nick." It would have to be decided by then. For better or worse. She emerged into the sunshine, half elated by the offer, which she knew was a compliment, half horrified that a job could even weigh in the balance with a baby.

"There'll be other babies." That was what Leigh would say when — if — she told him about *Eleventh Hour*. "There'll be other babies. You'd be mad to turn it down." But this baby was unique. Once lost it would never come again. And it wasn't up to Leigh. As Jago had said, she must decide for herself and for the baby. No one else.

She got into a cab and sat back to watch London flit by, trying to focus on the everyday things that must be done because that was easier than thinking of the real imperatives.

The phone was ringing as she unlocked the door of the flat. She put down her bag and lifted the receiver to hear her mother's voice.

"I hoped you'd ring, darling. Did you find her?"

"Yes. She was in Northallerton."

"How was it?"

For some reason her mother's need to know was annoying and Rachel had to curb a desire to say so. "We had a very reasonable conversation — well, reasonable in the circumstances."

"She would be surprised, I expect?"

"No," Rachel said. "I think she'd always known it would come. She just accepted it. She was neither glad nor disappointed. She said you'd been good to her. That was why she . . . why she let me go."

"What is she like now?"

"Old," Rachel said slowly. "She was so much older than I expected . . . and a bit sad."

"She was pretty once." Her mother's voice had softened, almost as if she was talking to herself.

"Well, she isn't now — and she probably drinks too much."

"Is there anything we can do? I mean, are you seeing her again?"

"Maybe," Rachel said shortly. "We didn't arrange anything."

There was a pause before her mother spoke again. "Did she ever marry?"

"No," Rachel said evenly. "No, I think you could say my father quite effectively screwed up her life." It was cruel and she had meant it to be. It had the desired effect. A few seconds later they said goodbye.

Rachel collected a shopping bag and went in search of food. She felt an overwhelming urge to create warm, filling food, casseroles for the freezer, cakes and pies and crisp golden biscuits. In the end she prepared only *coq au vin* and an apple tart before her enthusiasm departed. It was four thirty. Leigh wouldn't be home for at least two hours, probably more.

She went through to the bedroom with the intention of tidying her makeup drawer. She was there when she heard the phone ring, but somehow she couldn't be bothered to lift the receiver. It rang four times and then the answerphone clicked into action. "Rachel, I won't be home until late. Sorry. Don't wait up — it's seven kinds of hell here, I'll tell you later." There was a pause before he spoke again. "About the other thing . . . Well, I'm sorry. I was a bit hyper. We'll talk tonight — or tomorrow."

At least he was willing to discuss it, Rachel thought. That was something . . . except that a note in his voice had told her that he had not changed his mind. She sat down on the bed and lifted the telephone directory. She found a pregnancy help-line without much difficulty and dialled the number.

"Hello." The voice was sympathetic and calm. "Can I help you?"

"I'm pregnant." To her surprise, Rachel found it was surprisingly easy to say.

"Do you want to go ahead with the pregnancy?"

"I'm not sure. Probably not."

"Well, you have several options. Don't worry, we'll

help you whatever you decide but the decision must be yours."

"I know." Her voice was so low that she wondered if the woman on the other end had heard but obviously it was par for the course.

"It's difficult for you, I know. Don't worry. How far gone are you?"

"I'm not sure . . . About seven weeks, I think."

"Are your periods usually regular?"

"Usually. I'm on the pill."

"Are you sure you're pregnant? Have you had a test?"

"The test was positive. I was sick a few weeks ago — that interfered with the pill apparently."

"So you've seen a doctor?"

"No — yes — well, not really." Was that a sigh at the other end of the line? Impossible to tell, but the woman was talking about coming in to a clinic. Rachel listened for a moment and then gently replaced the receiver, thanking her lucky stars that Leigh had made sure that their number did not respond to 1471. She knew they never rang back but crises made you paranoid.

It grew dark as she lay on the bed, thinking over the phone call. At last she undressed, letting her clothes lie where they fell, and crawled naked between the sheets because she couldn't be bothered to do anything else. She was half asleep when she remembered the chicken in the oven on a low light.

She dragged herself from the bed and went to turn it out but she left it where it was. If Leigh was hungry he would root it out. It took only a minute, but by the time she returned to bed the desire to sleep had left her. She tried making her mind a blank, planning next summer's holiday, dreaming her favourite daydream of saving refugees in Africa. Thinking of what it would be like to manage *Eleventh Hour*.

She was still awake when Leigh returned. She heard him enter the flat, check the kitchen and then cross to the bedroom door. "Rachel?" She kept her breathing even and did not answer. She couldn't face him now. It was a relief when she heard the TV start up in the living room. *Newsnight*, of course.

25

London, Tuesday, 22 April 1997

Leigh left at the crack of dawn. "The only time
Mandelson can spare to be interviewed," he said, in
explanation. He insisted on getting ready in the dark "so
as not to wake you darling", but the muttered curses
when he couldn't find his shoes, tie, socks meant that, for
Rachel, sleep was out of the question.

When he was ready to leave he sat down on the bed.
"We'll talk tonight. I'll get back somehow. I want to hear
about your trip, your mother, and we'll talk about the
rest. I promise you."

She wanted to say, "By the rest, do you mean our
baby?" But she didn't. She felt strangely flat, as though it
didn't really matter any more. As though nothing much
mattered.

She lay for a while after he had gone, watching light
dapple the ceiling, hearing the world wake up outside,
knowing that today she must decide. She couldn't face

another night of indecision.

There was a card from Liz in the post that morning. It began with a eulogy about the honeymoon and ended, "Nice seeing you, sis. Hope the next get-together is more tranquil. Take care. Lizzie and Hugh." Rachel smiled at Liz's attempt to smooth things over. There was a PS on the side of the card, a thank-you for the china she had sent to them from the shop that held their wedding list. Rachel felt strangely warmed by the card. Liz knew that she was not completely a member of the family but she cared about her just the same. And there had been no mistaking Vanessa's affection: she had been exasperated by her father's misdeed but not against its end product.

As she drank her tea, she tried to analyse her feelings about the child within her. She couldn't visualise it. Was it a boy or a girl? If she squeezed her imagination she could conjure up images — bathtime, playtime, putting to bed — but the baby in those pictures was no more real than a doll and the mother was not her. If she had the termination everything would go back to normal, to the time before Paris when they had been happy.

The phone rang and she forced herself to answer it. "Rachel? It's me, Liz."

"Where are you?" Rachel was confused. "You're in Turkey. I got your card."

"We got back last night. I've just phoned Mum. She's worried about you." There was a pause. "She told me what happened — about telling you and everything. I'm sorry . . . although perhaps you're glad to know?"

"Yes. It was a shock but I think it's better to know."

"Look, Rach, I don't go back to work until tomorrow. Can we meet this afternoon?"

"What about Hugh?"

"What about him? He's gorgeous but he's going into the office to sort things out. I can easily come up."

They arranged to meet in the Dôme café near Selfridges. "I'm mad about olives," Liz said. "Can't get enough of them. Do you think it's a craving?" She was laughing and Rachel tried to laugh, too, but it wasn't easy.

When Liz rang off she replaced the receiver, then picked it up again. The helpline number had stuck in her mind and she punched it out. "I'm pregnant," she told the sympathetic voice, "and I've thought it through. All I need is an address."

An hour later she was dressed and ready to leave for a nine o'clock appointment in Earl's Court. "It's a private clinic," the voice said, "but you'll find them helpful. You'll need counselling but they'll arrange everything for you."

She waited in a green-painted anteroom. There were copies of *Private Eye* on a table and two women working in a glass-fronted cubicle in a corner. They had ticked off her name from a list and smiled an uninvolved and uninvolving smile as they directed her to sit down.

Then, ten minutes later, she was shown into a consulting room. The woman doctor was small and stout, dressed in a well-cut brown wool crêpe suit with a cameo brooch at her neck.

"You know you're pregnant?" she asked, looking down at a case-sheet. "Did you do a test yourself?"

"No." Rachel hesitated. "A friend, a doctor, had it done for me. It was positive."

"Is he the father?"

"No!" The genuine shock in Rachel's voice brought a smile to the doctor's face.

"All right, I only asked. Does the father know?"

"Yes. He doesn't want me to go ahead with pregnancy."

"Is it your first?" Rachel nodded. "And you're sure you want to terminate? Well, my colleague will need to agree but we can do it tomorrow." She pressed a bell and began to tap on the desk with her finger-nails.

Rachel felt a shaft of fear. Tomorrow! It was too soon. Except that she couldn't muck them about. If she asked for more time they might think she was undecided and send her away.

She was wrestling to remain calm when a door opened and a small, exquisitely pretty Chinese woman wearing a white coat entered the room. She moved to the desk and looked down at the case-sheet, then up at Rachel. "You've made up your mind?" she said.

"Yes." It came out as a gasp and the Chinese doctor frowned. "You're sure?"

"Yes," Rachel said firmly. "I'm sure." The doctor nodded and bent to sign the case-sheet. She straightened up and, with a nod to her colleague, left the room.

"This is the address," the first doctor said. And then, more kindly, "It doesn't take long. You'll be able to go home after a few hours. You'll get a thorough examination beforehand and we'll talk about contraception afterwards."

"I was on the pill," Rachel said. "I was sick — gastritis or food poisoning, that was how it happened."

The doctor nodded but there was disbelief in her eyes. "Thank you," Rachel said, and scuttled for the door.

She was seated in the open front of the restaurant when Liz arrived. "There you are," she said. "I ordered them in advance." The olives were huge and succulent and Liz fell on them with whoops of delight.

"I expect they're horribly fattening," she said, but her face was glowing as she chewed.

She's happy, Rachel thought, and felt a pang of envy. Aloud she said, "The green ones are only about eight calories, the black ones are more."

Liz licked her lips and then, serious, put out a hand to touch Rachel's arm. "Are you all right? Vanessa is a bitch sometimes. Still, she's got her own troubles."

"Is she still at Mum's?"

"She was last night but Mum thinks — hopes — she's going back soon."

"I hope Mum's not pushing her. Do you know anything about what Trevor's done — or is supposed to have done?"

"There was a woman." Liz had lifted another olive and held it ready to bite. "But I'm not even sure they went to bed with one another. I think he was flattered at getting some attention so he played up to it."

"And Vanessa immediately assumed it was history repeating itself," Rachel said.

"Probably." Around them the café hummed with laughter and conversation but they sat in gloomy contemplation of their family history.

"Anyway," Liz said at last, pushing the remaining olives out of reach, "tell me about you. Mum says you traced your birth mother."

"Yes. I found her in Northallerton, of all places. Practically a stone's throw."

"And?"

"She was . . ." Rachel paused. "She was older than I expected, a bit seedy. It wasn't in the least what novels lead you to believe. I'd say the meeting was unemotional. It was certainly unproductive. She confirmed what Mum had told me, was fairly unflattering about Dad and said she was glad I'd done well. And then she practically shooed me out because she had to make lunch for the elderly gentleman she cares for."

"What a swizzle! Still, it could've been worse." Liz's face was screwed up in sympathy. "She might have been some dreadful harpy who'd batten on to you. Or she might have shut the door in your face. You hear tales. And, anyway, we're your family, me and Van and Mum. You do know that, don't you? All for one through thick and thin."

Rachel felt tears prick her eyes. "I do know but it's still nice to hear it." It would have been so comforting to confide in Liz but some instinct held her back. If there was to be no baby it was better that no one knew — or as few as possible. And yet Liz could tell her what the abortion process was like. The moment that thought entered her head all inclination to confide left her. She didn't want to know what it was like. If she knew, she couldn't face it. Odd words from her conversation with

Tom flitted into her mind and none of them was comforting.

"Well," she said. "If we're going to eat we ought to order."

As they ate, they talked about *Eleventh Hour*, about Liz's new home and her plans for the future. "I want a baby soon," Liz said. "Hugh does, too, so we're not waiting." Her brow clouded. "You know what I told you the other night, about what I did, it won't affect my chances, will it?"

"No," Rachel said firmly. "A properly performed termination has no effect on future conception." She couldn't say Tom had told her. Instead she said, "I read it in *Marie Claire*."

They parted with hugs outside Selfridges, Liz to a taxi that would take her to the station, Rachel to the tube. "We'll meet soon," Liz said, as the door closed. "Remember what I said, one for all and all for one."

She was watching the news when Leigh came home. "See?" he said. "I made it, just as I promised. It's comparatively quiet today. They say Channel Four is refusing to show the National Front broadcast. Good for them, if it's true. But tell me about Yorkshire."

"Later," she said. "I went to a clinic today. I'm having a termination tomorrow. I thought you'd like to know."

If his face had showed relief she would have smacked it but it registered only concern. "Are you sure? Why didn't you tell me? I'd've come with you. Tomorrow? So soon? But if you're sure . . ." She let him take her in his arms and draw her down on to the sofa. His cheek was cold when he laid it against her brow and she closed her eyes. By this time tomorrow it would be over. They could start again and it would probably be all right.

"What made you decide?" he asked, but when she shook her head to display lack of an answer he let it go.

26

London, Wednesday, 23 April 1997

They were both awake in the early hours. "Are you sure?" Leigh said. He put out his arm and slid it beneath her head. "You have to be sure. I mean, it's up to you. It's not something I can decide for you."

She contemplated saying, "Why have you been pushing me, then?" but she hadn't the energy. Instead, she said, "Yes, I'm sure," and felt his body relax.

He brought her a cup of tea and sat on the edge of the bed as she drank it. "What time are you due there?"

"Nine thirty. If it all goes according to plan I'll be home tonight."

"Nine thirty." She could see him making calculations, trying to shuffle his schedule.

"It's OK," she said. "I'd rather go on my own, if you don't mind." It was true. She couldn't bear the thought of having to make conversation. The thought of the "counselling" that had been promised was daunting enough.

He took her in his arms before he left. "This'll work out. You'll see." He kissed the top of her head. "I love you. I'll be in the office most of the afternoon. Ring me when — when you're ready and I'll come and collect you."

She could smell the familiar odours of his skin, soap and aftershave. Her face pressed into the softness of his neck. She raised her head a little, feeling his newly shaved chin against her forehead. "OK," she said. "I don't know when so don't worry." He hugged her once more and then he was gone.

Jago arrived as she was drinking her breakfast tea. It was ten to seven and she savoured every mouthful, wondering when her next would come.

"Well," Jago said. She had told him the day before and he had nodded solemnly. "As long as it's your decision." Now he accepted a cup and stood with both hands wrapped around it and his back to the sink. "How are you getting there? Is Leigh—"

"No. I wouldn't let him," she cut in, because she couldn't bear to see disapproval of Leigh in his eyes.

She must have looked downcast for he put down his cup and reached for her. "There's time to change your mind, you know. God knows I'm not an expert on the parenthood stakes but I know you don't push abortion. Have it by all means if you want it, poppet, but don't touch it if you're not sure. God! It's not something to do under duress." And then, because he could never resist a joke, "Duress? Where did I get that from? It's got six letters in it. I didn't know I knew more than five. And I thought Duress was a contraceptive."

She clung to Jago for a moment, then distanced herself. "I am sure. And the sooner it's over, the better, now."

"Do you want me to come with you?"

"No, thanks!" Her voice was so fervent that she turned to make sure she had not hurt him. "If I did want company I can't think of anyone I'd rather have than you — but somehow it seems easier to do it on my own. If I change my mind I'll ring you . . ."

"Just shout," he said. "I'll hear you." His brow clouded. "Are you taking your mobile?"

"I wasn't — I can't imagine wanting to make calls while I'm in there."

"Take it," he said firmly. "Take it for my sake. If you need someone to come over and keen with you, I'll be there like a shot."

An hour later she left the flat, a sports bag on one shoulder, her handbag on the other. She looked at the clock. In twelve hours — less, with luck — she would be back here and everything would be as normal.

Her induction into the clinic took only a few moments. Her file was already on the receptionist's desk. She had only to sign and it was done.

"Try to relax," the receptionist said, as she ushered her into an anteroom. "Someone will be with you soon. You'll find it's all quite straightforward." She didn't say, "We do it all the time," but it was obvious that that was what she meant.

Rachel sat erect on the edge of a chair until she realised that her knees, pressed together, were trembling. She sank back in her chair and made a conscious effort to let go of tension. There was a sound far-off and she strained to catch it. Someone was crying, not the healthy sobs of anger or frustration. This was the soft, regular sobbing of despair.

At that moment the door opened and a woman entered. She wore a white uniform coat over a blue jumper. A string of pearls lay on her ample bosom and the shoes at the end of her stumpy legs were misshapen like the feet beneath them.

"Rachel? I'm Molly Strong. I'm the counsellor here. Oh, don't look alarmed. I'm just here to answer any questions you might have. And to make sure you really want a termination. Have you talked with your partner?"

"Yes," Rachel said. "It's what he wants too."

"Good." The woman ticked a box and then licked her lips. "Now, if you go home tonight is there someone there?"

"Yes," Rachel said. "My partner."

"Does he work?"

"Yes." Another tick.

"This is your first termination?"

"Yes," Rachel said, and even to her own ears she sounded resentful.

"I'm sorry. I have to ask these questions. You'd be surprised. Well, do you wish to pay by cheque?"

A moment or two later Molly had laid a consoling hand on Rachel's shoulder and was gone. A uniformed nurse appeared. "Rachel? We're ready for you now."

There were two of them in the room, one recording, one performing. They checked urine, pricked her finger for blood, sounded chest and heart, bound her arm tightly and recorded her blood pressure. Dressed in a skimpy gown tied at the back she was led to a small room containing two beds.

"Someone will be along shortly to see to you," one nurse said.

"Try not to worry," said the other. "It'll be over soon."

Rachel lay in the quiet room, hearing her heart thunder in her ears. She tried to fix on pleasant things. In Paris the irises would be in bloom now. Purple or yellow? There would still be horse chestnut blossom and hot crêpes in the market and sun on the steps of the Sacre Coeur.

As she thought of the white-domed building there was a crash and the door opened. A man dressed in green theatre clothes was wheeling in a trolley bearing a girl who, judging by her stature, was hardly more than a child. There was a mask across his mouth and a smear of blood on his white clogs. He lifted the girl from the trolley and laid her on the empty bed, throwing aside the pillow as he did so. He pulled up the sheet to cover her, lifted an eyelid to check and then, with a swift reversal of the trolley, was gone.

A nurse entered and took the girl's flaccid hand in hers. "Come on, Margaret. You can have a nice cup of tea in a minute." But the girl's eyes remained stubbornly shut. The nurse sighed, checked her patient's pulses and then, with a half-smile at Rachel, left the room.

In a moment they will come for me, Rachel thought. Across the room the girl's eyes were open, staring into space. "Are you all right?" Rachel said. There was no answer, at least not a spoken one. The girl raised herself on one elbow, turned to face the wall and lay down again.

Terror engulfed Rachel, but only for a moment. Her handbag was by the bed and she reached into it for her phone. "Jago? Can you come and get me? I want to come home."

They sat together in the flat, speaking now and then of nothing of much significance, mainly letting the minutes slip away. At one o'clock Jago heated soup and made toast. At four o'clock Rachel telephoned Leigh.

"Where are you?" He sounded startled.

"I'm back home."

"Is it – did you—?"

"It's over," she interrupted. "It's over and I'm home. No need to rush back. I'll be fine on my own."

London, Thursday, 24 April 1997

Rachel had not intended to deceive Leigh but she had.
Now, for the moment, she must live with the lie. I'm not
up to a showdown, she thought, in the early morning
hours, watching light dapple the ceiling, hearing London
awakening outside, sensing Leigh's careful movements
beside her.

He had been so solicitous last night, waiting on her
hand and foot. Because he thinks he has got what he
wanted, she thought. She wanted to feel bitter, to arouse
herself to anger. Anything, any emotion, would be better
than the way she felt. I am in limbo, she thought, and felt
suspended in time and place so that nothing seemed to
matter because she was not part of it.

"Do you think you should?" Leigh had asked, when she
said she was going to have a bath. And when she insisted,
"Well, leave the door. Don't lock it." For a second she had
felt almost glee. Let him worry! Serve him right! But then

apathy reasserted itself. She lay in the scented water, hearing the television beyond the open door, seeing her body still marked by the life within. How long could she wait before confessing? And should she confess? She was not even sure that she wanted the pregnancy to continue. She had fled that particular clinic rather than the concept of termination. I want it to go away, she thought. I want it to cease invasion and leave me free once more. But had she the courage? When the water grew cold she pulled the plug with her toes and let the water ebb away until cold drove her from the bath.

She was roused from her memory of the night before by Leigh slipping from the bed. She heard him shuffle into slippers, knew he was reaching for his robe, which meant he was making for the kitchen. "I'm awake," she said. "You can open the curtains."

He pulled on the cord and light flooded the room. "It's a lovely day." He turned back to the bed. "Is there anything you'd like for breakfast? What about a poached egg?"

She struggled up on her pillows. "I'm getting up. I don't really fancy anything — tea and toast, perhaps."

"You should eat something." He was moving to the bed. In a moment he would sit down, reach for her, look into her face and she couldn't meet his eyes. She felt panic overwhelming her. Why hadn't she told him yesterday? She threw aside the bedclothes and swung her feet to the ground.

"I'm OK. I'll have something later on. Don't worry about me."

"But I do." Now he was reaching out, holding her close, his breath in her hair. "I do care, Rachel. I'm sorry these past few weeks have been so awful but, you'll see, we'll be fine in a week or two. Let's get away, as soon as the election's over. I've got leave—"

"I'll be back at work then. I'm going to *Eleventh Hour*." It was a lie but she wanted to seem unavailable.

"*Eleventh Hour*! You'll like that. Still, we could get away for a few days. Think about it – where you'd like to go. What about Venice? We could be there on a Friday night, come back Monday morning. You wouldn't miss the show that way. I'll check out flights, you concentrate on getting pulled up."

His solicitousness was irritating, especially because it was misplaced and compounded her guilt. "I'm not down, Leigh, so I don't need pulling up. Just go to work." But he was too concerned for her to be offended by her brusqueness.

"I'll put the kettle on," he said soothingly. "You come when you're ready, I'll see to the toast."

It was a relief when he left the flat, still engulfing her in TLC. How different it would be if he knew the truth! She showered, with one ear cocked for the sound of Jago at the door. He was sure to come up to see how she was. He would ask about Leigh's reaction and she would have to confess that she hadn't told him. She dried herself hurriedly, put on trousers, a warm coat and hurried down the stairs to the street. If she could find the courage to go back, not to that clinic but to another, more humane, she could have the termination and Leigh need never know.

She walked then until she saw a taxi, stepped in without giving a destination. "Where to?" the cabbie said, without turning his head.

"Anywhere." It was not enough. "St James's Park," she finished, and sank back as he started the engine.

They drove between the parks, St James's on one side, Green Park on the other. There were swans on the lake, sliding serenely under the trailing trees like white wraiths on the dark water. London is beautiful, she thought. And yet I would rather be anywhere else than here.

"Can you take me home?" she said at last. "Back to where you picked me up." The driver shook an incredulous head and turned at the next opening but his obvious contempt for her vagaries seemed not to matter. She let herself back into the house, but before she could take off her coat the phone rang and the sound filled her with panic. It might be Leigh, checking, and she didn't want to speak to him. Not now, when she was still vulnerable in her indecision.

She stood as though rooted to the floor while the phone rang on and on. When at last it ceased she felt sweat, cold and prickly, trickle down her back to be lost between her buttocks.

Who could it have been? She squeezed her eyelids together, trying to guess, then she reached out and dialled Vanessa's number.

"Oh, Rachel, I was just ringing you. Where are you?"

"I'm here. I've just come in. How are you?"

"I'm fine." The tone was brisk. "I'm back here, as

you'll have gathered, and we've talked it through. It wasn't all Trevor's fault. I see that now. It was getting away that helped me. Thank God for home. All the same . . ." The voice changed now, became resolute. "I'm not going to be like Mummy. Life is too short, Rach, too precious to throw it away. I know what Mummy thinks, that anything is worth it just to keep Dad. Well, I'm not like that and now Trevor knows it."

"Do you think Mum and Dad are all right now?" Rachel asked. "You were there for a few days."

"As right as they'll ever be. And he'll be good for a while. He always is after a showdown. I know now that I'll never change her, though. And in a funny way that's helped me. She knows what she wants and she takes it. Well, so do I. What I want is different but the principle's the same. I know what I want and I mean to take it."

These words lingered in Rachel's mind long after the phone-call was ended. "I know what I want." A state of bliss that for her seemed unattainable. She put on a CD and let the glory of Vittoria de los Angeles wash over her as she glided through *Songs from the Auvergne*, but suddenly the haunting notes meant to travel from mountain-top to mountain-top were sad. Unbearably sad. Rachel switched off the stereo and looked at the clock. It was a quarter to twelve and Leigh could arrive at any time, on the pretext of getting lunch.

I don't want to see him, she thought, and that thought was decisive. But where could she go? She thought longingly of the Tontine. Tonight they would light the myriad lamps and play the evocative music, and the harsh reality of life would melt away. If she went there she could drink wine with lilting names — Sangiovese, Rippoli, Sassicaia — see the gold-flecked grey-striped cat wind its selective way between chairs, bestowing friendship on one guest, ignoring another. She could forget.

But Leigh would know to look for her there. And when he learned the truth he would step up the pressure for a termination.

The phone rang again. If it was Leigh and she didn't answer he might panic and come over to check. She picked it up and felt relief overcome her as she recognised the voice at the other end. "Tom! No, you're not interrupting a thing. I'm glad to hear from you." He was coming to London tomorrow, to his seminar. He wanted to meet. "Oh, yes," she said. "I have so much to tell you."

When she put down the phone she wrapped her arms around herself in an ecstasy of pleasure. Tom would understand, help, sort it out. "Tom." She whispered his name aloud, remembering his lips on her cheek. A voice in her head reminded her of the child in her belly. Leigh's child. But nothing mattered except that if she could make it to tomorrow everything would be all right.

28

Knowing that she was seeing Tom that night made it easier to keep up the pretence. It gave her a deadline. When she got to Tom all would be plain. But even as she took reassurance from that she despaired at the muddle her life had become. She was carrying one man's baby and turning to another man for comfort.

It helped her to understand one thing, however. Why the young Freda Fielding had allowed another woman, a comparative stranger, to take over her life, to make decisions about her future and eventually to deprive her of her child. And Mum is formidable, Rachel thought. The word "implacable" popped into her mind, but it was inappropriate. Her mother was too gentle, too co-operative ever to be called that — except when it came to something she wanted. She has hung on to Dad when many another woman would have let go, Rachel thought. Admirable or foolish? She gave up the struggle to decide and turned her thoughts to the evening ahead.

She was choosing something to wear to dinner with Tom when Jago arrived. "Well," he said, "what did he say?"

"I haven't told him." She said it baldly because there was no way of wrapping it up.

"You're mad," Jago said, after a moment of stunned silence. "You're mad and he has to have a PhD in non-observance. What are you going to do? Pretend you've taken to stuffing éclairs?" He mimed a burgeoning stomach and then looked at her, awaiting an answer.

"I may not have to tell him." Rachel reached for the kettle and filled it. "I ran away yesterday because that place was wrong. It was a conveyor-belt. I'm not sure about what I'm going to do. I need more time."

"And you need to talk to the person most intimately concerned," Jago said. "He should help you decide."

"I *can't* talk to Leigh. He's got so much on his mind—"

"And you haven't?" The interruption was sharp. Now Jago advanced on her, taking her by the shoulders to emphasise his words. "Think what you're saying, Rachel. You were close enough to Leigh to fuck and conceive and yet you can't talk to him. You're crazy."

She spooned coffee into a cup for Jago. "I will. Tonight or tomorrow." For some reason she didn't want to tell Jago about Tom. How could you explain that you could talk to one man and not another more intimately concerned?

Leigh telephoned at twelve thirty. She assured him that she was fine, promised to eat a nutritious lunch and hung up. She had not told him about her date with Tom.

If he came home in time she would explain that a dear friend had turned up unexpectedly. If he didn't, she would leave a note.

She spent the afternoon flicking from channel to channel on TV, trying to find something that was worth watching and not in black and white, all the time telling herself that she must get up and do something constructive.

Jago came up again at three bearing a steaming bowl. "Chicken broth," he said. "I bet you haven't eaten, and before you fret, it's free range – or it was."

She ate to please him and then discovered she was hungry. "Lovely," she said, "but I'm eating out tonight." She saw his brows rise in curiosity. "With an old friend – from Yorkshire. No one you know." She didn't enjoy keeping Jago in the dark but it had to be. Tomorrow, next week, she would have regained a hold on her life. As she showered she wondered if she was expecting too much of Tom in hoping that he would make sense of her jumbled thoughts. But it was all she had at the moment.

As she was dressing Leigh came in. "Are we going out?" he asked, looking confused.

"No," she said gently. "*I'm* going out – with an old friend from Yorkshire." She meant him to think that the friend was female and she could see that he did.

"Are you sure you're up to it?"

She nodded. "Yes," she said. "I'm fine."

His face cleared. "Well, if you're sure. I really shouldn't've left the office. I might go back for an hour – we're really pushed. Stuff's coming in every minute on the minute."

They shared a cab as far as Horseferry road. "You look lovely," he said, as the cab slowed to allow him to alight. "I'm so glad you're, well, coming to terms with it. It was for the best, wasn't it? And I'll make up to you for it, see if I don't."

As the cab drew away Rachel put up a hand. Her cheeks were hot, as she had suspected. I'm getting in deeper and deeper, she thought. Lies breeding lies, to Leigh, to Jago, to everyone.

As Tom rose from the table to greet her she had to resist the impulse to lean her head against his chest and let it stay there. Instead she said, "How did your day go? Good meeting?"

"As meetings go. I kept thinking of all the other things I could be doing – when I wasn't thinking of meeting you."

"Flatterer. Still, I'm very glad to see you."

He filled her glass. "Bring me up to date."

She told him everything that had happened up to her retreat – she almost said escape – from the clinic. "I don't know. Maybe it wasn't as bad as I've painted it, maybe I just chickened out . . ."

"It sounds pretty gruesome." Tom pursed his lips, then continued. "Perfunctory counselling, minimum nursing care, get you in, get the cheque, get you out. They're not all like that." He looked down at his glass. "How did Leigh take it?"

"I haven't told him. You'll say I'm mad but I just couldn't face a showdown. Not then. Not with all that horror so fresh in my mind. Can you understand that?"

"Yes." His eyes were kind and fixed on hers. "Yes, I can understand it. But I think it's a pity that you couldn't turn to Leigh for comfort. You've had to bear it on your own and that's rough."

"There was another reason why I didn't tell him." She had his attention now. "I'm still not sure about the pregnancy. I keep trying to make up my mind. I'm ashamed at the way I oscillate, one minute this way, the next minute that."

He was nodding. "I know. But you have to accept that you've been through a hell of a lot in a very short space of time. The upset between your parents, the facts about your birth — in fact the complete reversal of everything you knew about your place in the family — and an unplanned pregnancy. That would make anyone oscillate, wouldn't it?"

Around them the restaurant hummed with activity, but they seemed to be held in a small, dark womb, its centre the candle lamp glowing on the table. "You're such a comfort, Tom. I'd forgotten how nice you are."

"Nice!" He pretended to wince. "I'd rather be dashing, or handsome — even rakish would do — but nice! There, I've brought a smile to your face . . ."

"I keep thinking about my birth mother, you know. Freda Fielding. Lance Corporal Freda Fielding. Wondering if she felt like I feel. Was she uncertain? Did she waffle?" His hand on hers was warm and then, suddenly, he raised it to his lips and kissed it. Rachel was bemused by the gesture but only for a moment. "I have to see her again, Tom. I have to know more about her — about everything!"

She was glad that he didn't answer immediately, that he gave her words due consideration. "Yes," he said eventually, "I can see that you do. Would she be willing?"

"I think so. Well, I don't think she'll be keen but she'll agree."

"There's a determined note in your voice. Agree or else! When will you go? You're still well within the limit but—"

"I haven't unlimited time," she finished for him. "I know. I'm going to go tomorrow."

"We could travel up together," he said, but she shook her head.

"No. It's kind of you to offer but I know you want to get away early. You only stayed tonight because of me – and I need to sort things out."

"OK. But if you change your mind . . ."

"I won't, but thanks anyway and thank you for tonight."

"Not at all." His eyes were not smiling but his voice was kind. "You're doing me a favour. My social life is not exactly glittering, so a meal out with an—" He hesitated and she threw back her head in the first genuine burst of mirth she had known for days.

"A what, Tom? Neurotic, self-obsessed, dithering . . . what am I?"

"You're a rather nice woman – I daren't say girl nowadays, it's not PC. And, yes, you have problems, but you're still good company and I mean to enjoy tonight."

"Good," she said. "So do I. Anyway, that's enough of me. You'll never know how grateful I am, although one day I'll try to tell you. But for now, let's talk about you."

"What would you like to know?" His eyes were twinkling and she was in the mood to be light-hearted, even flirt a little.

"Well, what's a personable man of your age, and a doctor to boot, doing as a bachelor?"

"I've never found the right woman, is the flip answer. The truth is that I did find the right woman a long time ago but it didn't work out." He paused. "She died quite suddenly — an aneurysm."

"I'm sorry."

"It was a long time ago. I survived. And, given the rate of failure, I could well have been alone now even if I'd married."

"True," she said. "It doesn't inspire you to settle down, does it? How many weddings now are second-time around?"

"A huge number, but I have the feeling marriage is here to stay."

"You must see a lot of things in your surgery — human relationships, I mean. They often end up in a doctor's lap, don't they?"

As the words left her lips she realised how apt they were to her own situation but he seemed not to notice. "Marital discord is the single greatest cause of indigestion," he said. "But don't quote me on that. I just made it up. Tell me about your job."

They talked about television then, and the possibility of her job with *Eleventh Hour*. Over coffee they reminisced once more about their student days, and, whether it was the good food or his company, she found herself at last relaxing.

"Before you go off to Cleveland," he said suddenly, "I have to say this. Are you sure you know what you may be getting into? I tried to say it last time, but I was too vague. I ask because this crops up again and again at the surgery – the urge to trace the birth mother, a meeting and then, well, sometimes it can go wrong."

Rachel smiled at him. "I know, I can see the risks but I'm grateful to you for bringing it up. At the beginning I did wonder if my – my birth mother might latch on to me. Now that I've met her I think she's really quite indifferent to me."

"Well . . ." He sounded doubtful. "It helps that she doesn't have other children – that can complicate things. But be careful."

"I will," she promised, and put out a hand. "Anyway, let's get back to you. Are you still mad on sport?"

"I suppose so. I play five-a-side football quite well and cricket not so well. Which is odd, because I'm not bothered about soccer but mad about cricket."

"I know that," Rachel said. "You've got a wall of *Wisden* in your dining room. You must have been collecting for ever."

"Since I was ten, which is almost for ever but not quite."

"Where do you play?"

"Village cricket, there's a ground in Martlesham, but the bones are beginning to creak a bit. I belong to a squash club, play about twice a week. I play bridge, I read . . . I suppose I'm a bit of an old fogey now."

"You sound contented."

"Pretty contented. Lonely sometimes."

As they left the restaurant, he said, "I'm interested in seeing you resolve this situation. Call me any time." In the street-lights his hair glowed like a golden aureole.

"I hope you know what you're saying. I could become a nuisance."

"Not you." He put up a hand and touched her hair, her temple, her mouth. "You're a funny kid still, aren't you?"

She felt her throat constrict. "Was I always a funny kid, then?"

"Yes," he said firmly. "Funny but unforgettable."

A cab appeared and he flagged it down, giving her address and then his hotel. They didn't speak much on the way and his parting kiss was brief. "Remember," he said. "Anytime. And be careful what you do."

29

"I need to get away," she told Leigh, as soon as he woke."I'm fine, but I'd like to go home for a couple of days. And I expect you'll be working through the weekend."

"Probably . . . Definitely, with less than a week to go. If that's what you want, darling . . ."

As soon as Leigh left the flat she rang her mother. "I'm coming home, Mum. I've got to get out of London for a few days. I feel — I feel a bit down at the moment."

"I know it's difficult, darling. I'm so sorry, but things will settle, you'll see." As the train rattled north, Rachel damned her mother for her complacency. If she had been firmer, years ago . . . I might never have been born, Rachel thought, and was startled by the idea.

When the train got in her father was waiting for her. "Rachel," he said, bending to kiss her cheek and removing her bag from her hand in one easy movement.

Despite the resentment she felt towards him she

271

couldn't help admiring his grace. "Daddy," she said, acknowledging his greeting. It was formal and stilted, and totally unlike their old, exuberant form of salute.

As they drove towards the village they talked of Leigh and the election. "He must have a lot on his plate," her father said, "but you're the right kind of girl for a high-flyer."

Her mother was in the kitchen when she entered the house. "I'm coming, darling. Sherry's out in the living room." They sipped Tio Pepe and made careful conversation, her mother popping out to baste and check in between.

Why did I come? Rachel thought despairingly. There were no answers here. When her father made his excuses and left, a silence fell upon them. At last Rachel put down her glass and cleared her throat. "I need to talk, Mum." She felt her eyes prick at the sight of her mother's hunted expression but this was no time for showing mercy.

"Shall we leave it until after lunch?"

"No!" Rachel felt a new strength. For too long her mother had lived inside a safe framework of meal-times and fresh linen. It had to change. "I want to know why you did what you did. I need to know why she gave me up. I'm pregnant, with a baby that Leigh doesn't want and I'm not sure about. Do you understand why I have to make sense of my own existence? It's so that I can decide whether or not this child has an existence. That's how important it is."

"Oh, darling, I would say that I'm glad for you but if Leigh . . . What is it? If it's money I'm sure Daddy and I could help."

"It's not money. And let's not waste time on our motives, mine or Leigh's. I want to understand *your* motives. Why did you let Dad get away with it? You made it easy for him, no scandal, no guilt, no need to lift a finger. You and she made the sacrifices, he got off scot-free. Why?"

For a moment she thought there was to be no answer but at last her mother spoke. "I don't know if I can make you understand. I was sixteen when I first saw your father. It was New Year's Eve and my father — he was Daddy's CO — was giving a party. Daddy looked so handsome in his blues. He was a second lieutenant then and he was laughing and talking with some of his fellow officers. I was coming down the stairs. He looked up and smiled, and I fell in love. Simple as that. I don't know how to describe the way I felt. He delighted me. That's the nearest I can come. He always has. Even when I've hated him — and I have sometimes — he's still lit up my life. Does that make sense?"

"In a way." But Rachel could not comprehend the intensity of the love her mother had so vividly portrayed. Was that what she felt for Leigh?

"And I've never regretted it. Especially not his affair with Freda, because I got you and you've been such a joy."

"Was she the first?"

Again a pause. "No. There was someone before that, the nanny I had for Vanessa and Liz. I thought that was just proximity — but of course it wasn't."

"What was it, then? What *is* it? I know he loves you but

he keeps on hurting you. Why?"

"Because he's unsure of himself."

Rachel's howl of disbelief was loud and instant. "Daddy? Unsure?"

"He always has been." Her mother spoke with such quiet certainty that Rachel was convinced. "He's never sure that he's good enough. When promotion didn't come quickly enough – full lieutenant, major, colonel – he was always going to resign his commission."

"But he did so well?"

"I know . . . and he's so attractive to women. You can see it, I can. He has to keep proving it. It's worse now that he's getting older. 'Do I have it?' has become 'Am I losing it?'"

"So he'll go on like this?"

"I expect so." There was calm resignation in the tone.

"How will you bear it?"

"More easily than you think, Rachel. As long as I have him, that's all that counts. The occasional humiliation, the pity of my children, our friends, that's the price I pay. There's a price for everything. You're finding that out now. You want the baby, I can tell that, but if Leigh leaves you because of it, can you live without him?"

There was no more to say after that. Afterwards Rachel walked Sally, the Labrador, and tried to let the beauty of the springtime countryside calm her thoughts but not even the budding hedgerows and drifts of daffodils in the lanes could soothe her.

She was turning for home when she saw her father in the distance. He whistled and Sally froze for a second, then flew towards him in a paroxysm of joyful tail-wagging. He's the Pied Piper, Rachel thought, but her anger had left her, for now she knew that the piper was uncertain of his tune and much to be pitied.

They walked home together, making polite remarks until the house came into view. She heard him clear his throat and knew he was struggling for words. "Your mother tells me there may be a baby on the way."

"I'm not quite sure," she said. No need to mention termination here.

"No, of course not. Well, I just wanted you to know Mummy and I are here for you, whatever. Now, how about a nice cup of Earl Grey?" She was glad of the change of subject, even if it did demonstrate even further her father's inadequacy. I must try to love him, she thought, as they entered the house. After all, I am flesh of his flesh.

The sun was shining outside as they ate lunch, filling the kitchen with pools of light and shadow. Rachel felt a sense of unreality sitting with her mother on one side, her father on the other. They passed condiments and remarked on the excellence of their lamb, chatted of this and that. In truth, they were — what was the modern phrase? — a dysfunctional family. She counted them off: two betrayed wives, three if you counted Liz's first marriage, one serial adulterer and one who had a terminal inability to make up her mind about anything. But that must change.

Her father went off as soon as lunch was over pleading a need to "get the car seen to".

Rachel moved to the sink and began to fill it with sudsy

water. "Just leave them, dear." But Rachel ignored her mother's suggestion.

"I'm going in a while, Mum."

"Oh, that's a pity. I was going to do moussaka tonight. You love moussaka."

Rachel subdued the urge to thwack about in the foaming dishwater, and replied politely, "I do. Can we have it next time? But I really do want to get off. I've got to see her again, Mum. Last time was too brief. Almost casual. I have to know more about her."

Her mother stopped brushing crumbs from the table and subsided into a chair. "If you're sure . . ." she said doubtfully. "It was all such a long time ago, darling. I'm not afraid for my sake. I don't think anything could alter the bond between us. But what will she be like, after all these years? If you get to know her better what will she want of you?"

"I don't know." Rachel turned at the sink, feeling the tiny bubbles pop on the surface of her skin, reaching for a towel to dry hands that shook slightly, as if she were afraid. But she was not afraid. "I don't know what I'll find. I just know I have to look. Especially now." She slipped into a chair next to her mother and propped her elbows on the table. "What did you feel when you were carrying Van and Liz? I feel . . . very strange. But I can't work out how much of the strangeness is simply being pregnant, hormonal, and how much is shock. Two weeks ago I had a firm idea of who I was. Now I'm not sure. Can you understand that?"

"Of course I can. And I bitterly regret that we weren't

more honest with you, now that I see how hurt you are. But I did it to protect you. I hope you realise that. And . . ." she sighed and reached out a tentative hand ". . . I came to love you so much, so quickly. As soon as you were mine, in my arms, needing me. Can you forgive me?"

"Don't be silly!" Inside Rachel's arms her mother seemed smaller, weaker, less a protector than a dependant. "There's nothing to forgive."

Before she left she went up to her bedroom. How safe she had felt in the days when those drawers and cupboards had been crammed with the paraphernalia of childhood and adolescence. How insecure she felt now. Was she capable of mastering her problems? Certainly she did not possess her mother's single-mindedness. When they had talked today about her pregnancy her mother's attitude had been clear: if it threatens your relationship, it must go. But it was not that easy.

Her father took her to the station, his disapproval of her trip to Cleveland visible in every line of his body.

"Tell me something, Dad." They were turning into the station car park. "Do you mean to hurt Mum?"

"Of course not!" His tone was vehement. "I love your mother. If I lost her I think it would kill me. But . . ." He shrugged and Rachel let it go at that. But she couldn't return his goodbye kiss. That was asking too much.

She had meant to read on the journey, even do *The Times* crossword, but as York fell away a great inertia overcame her. She closed her eyes and soon she was in a state of half sleep, half waking. It was not unpleasant. Her worries seemed to slip away, her fear of the future dissolved and instead she thought of Paris. It seemed not to matter why that city preoccupied her.

When she woke, she could see the hills from the train window, running parallel to the railway line and then the white horse emblazoned on one particular hillside. Time to collect her bags.

She alighted at Northallerton and took a cab to the Tontine. The grey stone buildings sparkled in the sunshine but she was in haste to settle into her room. It was four thirty. Would there be time to meet tonight?

The phone rang for several minutes. She persevered because she knew there must be someone in the house and at last she heard a woman's voice on the other end. "Miss Fielding?" Or "Freda?" Or "Mother?"

"It's me," she said. "Rachel," and heard a half-sigh at the other end. "I was wondering if we could meet. Perhaps I could take you out for a meal tonight?"

"Where are you?" Freda sounded surprised, as though she had believed her recently rediscovered daughter to be far away, on another continent.

"I'm quite near — in Middlesbrough. Well, just outside. I could be with you in half an hour."

"No." The refusal was at first sharp, then degenerated into waffle. "I couldn't — he needs — I'm not dressed — by the time—"

"What about tomorrow?" Rachel said.

"Not tomorrow!" This time she was emphatic. "He's got his appointment at the clinic tomorrow. I've got to go with him. There's no one else. Well, not up here."

"What time is his appointment?"

"Eleven fifteen. Not that that means anything. It was five to three when we got in last time."

"Could you get away for dinner?" Rachel said desperately.

"Dinner? You meant at night? Not a chance. It always shakes him up, the ambulance and everything. No, I couldn't make it tomorrow. I'm sorry but it's my job, you see."

And also a marvellous excuse, Rachel thought. She was not to be discouraged, however. She persisted, and at last Freda agreed to meet the following evening.

"I'll pick you up in a cab at seven thirty." It had to be late because the diabetic's dinner must be served at six thirty sharp.

"And I'll have to be back by nine."

"That'll be fine," Rachel assured her, and put down the phone. Outside, the sun was shining on a hillside green with trees. A few moments later she was out in the April air, striding towards the hills and the trees that clad their slopes.

She dined in the bistro again, baked lamb with a tarragon mousse and an excellent Chardonnay. The wine list was rich and spattered with comments. She particularly liked the note that said that Eugene, one of the proprietors "could live with this for a while". That was what made this place so special, the personal involvement of those who owned it. You didn't get that from a corporation.

She rang Leigh first and to her relief he answered immediately. "Where are you?"

"I'm in Middlesbrough – well, Cleveland."

"I thought you were going home."

"I've been home. I wanted to talk to her again, to Freda – I need to know more about her, darling. You must see that. There are so many questions, Leigh. I can't just meet her briefly and leave it at that."

"I suppose not." It was grudging but it was better than nothing. "When are you coming back?"

"I don't know. Maybe tomorrow, maybe later."

"Maybe next month?"

Rachel's patience snapped. "If you're going to be sarcastic there doesn't seem much point. I'll ring you tomorrow."

She had hardly put down the phone when it rang again. She picked it up, hoping to hear a penitent Leigh at the other end, but it was her mother.

"I'm fine. It's really nice here. I haven't seen Freda yet but we're meeting on Sunday." There was the same apprehensive note in her mother's voice as she had detected in Tom's. "Don't worry, Mum. If you could see her . . . I don't know what she was like twenty-eight years ago but she's rather pathetic now. I can cope."

She listened as her mother urged caution, longing for the call to cease so that she could ring Leigh. Why had she almost put the phone down on him? What if he went out? If she didn't catch him, anything could happen. At the back of her mind she felt contempt for her own insecurity but her fingers fumbled in their haste to press out his number.

She was about to push Recall when the phone rang.

"Darling?" It was Leigh and she almost wept with relief.

"I've just rung and you were engaged."

"I was ringing you. It's crazy our falling out like this."

"I didn't mean what I said——"

"Neither did I."

"I love you."

"Me too."

When at last the call was over she had promised to come home as soon as she could. "We'll work things out, darling. Just get back here." Euphoria carried her through the rest of the evening and into bed. It was only when she put out the light and settled on her pillows that doubt entered in. What would his reaction be if he learned that she was carrying a child that could be a millstone around his neck for the foreseeable future?

30

Cleveland, Sunday, 27 April 1997

Rachel had intended to spend a tranquil day, rising late, eating well, walking energetically, until it was time to meet her mother, but she was awakened at daybreak, thoughts going round and round in her mind like rats in a trap.

Freda had pleaded work as a reason for not meeting until later. What if it was simply an excuse? Even now she might be packing her bags, boarding a train . . . As she picked her way through an excellent breakfast, Rachel drifted between vivid imaginings and cool common sense.

In reality Freda Fielding could no more do a moonlight flit than she could fly. At a shrewd guess she had half a week's pay in hand and needed to keep her job, two good reasons for staying put.

She bumped into a fellow guest as she left for her walk. "It's lovely here, isn't it?" the woman said. "Are you enjoying your stay?"

"Very much," Rachel said. "I wouldn't've missed it for worlds."

"Have you seen the swimming-pool?" the woman asked. Rachel shook her head.

"Oh, you mustn't miss it. It's a scream." They walked round to the side of the house and there it was. A small sea of blue plastic in which two shop-window dummies, handsome and muscular in the male, pretty and lissome in the female disported themselves. It was crazy and anarchic and utterly right, even placed against mellow grey stone walls. The woman was turning away but Rachel's eyes had lighted upon a wrought-iron gate, which led into the garden containing sunlit trees. It was a wonderful gate, the iron swirling like some fairy tree, tinged here and there with gilt, looking like a doorway to enchantment.

I like this place, Rachel thought. I like it so much.

She had intended to walk in the afternoon too, but instead she slept, woke at five o'clock refreshed and, for the first time in weeks, mildly hungry. She lifted the phone and ordered a cab for seven o'clock.

As she replaced the receiver a faint tremor overcame her. She was spending money like water. But she put aside her worries with resolution. She had to do this. Afterwards, when life had returned to normal, she would work her fingers to the bone and recoup her fortunes.

As the cab bowled along the A19 she tried to work out how much her comings and goings in the last two weeks had cost her. Too much! Leigh was always telling her not to worry about money, her parents had always been generous, but now she felt a need to be self-sufficient. Taking money from her father after what she had discovered would be unbearable. She subsided into her seat, determined to be thrifty as soon as this was over.

On her left the Cleveland Hills ran like a bulwark between her and the sea. On her right, in the far distance, the Penines ranged as far as the eye could see.

Her mother was waiting in the porch as the cab drew up at the door. She wore a tailored suit, with sleeves that came too far down over her hands and made her look oddly vulnerable. There was a patterned cerise scarf tucked in at the neck, matching the cerise slash that was her mouth, and her hair was crimped and set. She's dressed up for me, Rachel thought, and had to blink to dispel her tears.

"Where shall we go?" she asked, when they were settled together on the back seat of the cab.

"Anywhere you like." Her mother's gloved hands were folded over her shiny plastic handbag, which was perched on knees clamped tightly together.

"Do you know anywhere we could get dinner?" Rachel asked the driver.

He took them to a pub half a mile away. "They do a nice roast and Yorkshire on a Sunday lunchtime," he said. "I don't know what you'll get tonight."

"Ooh." Her mother's eyes were wide. "It's posh, this. Very nice."

It was a relief to be settled in a wood-panelled booth, huge, brightly coloured menus in front of them, and an attendant waitress hovering, pencil poised. "Let's have a drink," Freda said. "It'll take ages to choose from this lot."

Rachel opted for a dry sherry, her mother a gin and tonic. "Nice," she said, smacking her lips over the ice-filled glass. They settled on a traditional meal, roast beef with Yorkshire pudding and vegetables.

"You can't beat it, can you?" Freda said.

She was more relaxed now and her cheeks were flushed: she looked more appealing. But old, Rachel thought. Twenty when I was born, so forty-eight now, but she looks ten years older than that. There were deep lines from nose to chin and the flaming lipstick had permeated a thousand tiny cracks along her upper lip.

"I was wondering," Rachel said, "could you tell me something about . . . my family? I don't mean Mum and Dad, I mean your family. My grandparents. And do you have sisters and brothers?"

"Eight," Freda said flatly. She had finished the gin, and now she turned the empty glass round and round in twitching hands. She had taken off the cotton gloves to reveal several rings. Only her thumbs and one middle finger were free of them. They were small and mostly silver, with here and there the gleam of gold or a red gem, but a sudden picture of her mother adorning herself for their meeting brought Rachel once more to the edge of tears.

"There were nine of us," Freda continued. "We lived in Ashington, Dad was a miner. There were four boys, five girls. The lads went into the forces, there wasn't much else they could do. That started me off in the services. I was the eldest girl, I wanted to get away."

"Where are they now?"

"God knows." It was said in a tone of flat indifference.

"You don't keep in touch?" Rachel spoke carefully to hide her shock. How could you lose track of eight siblings?

"We did for a while. Christmas, things like that. I went to a christening once. But people move on. One of the lads went to Australia, our Steve. Did all right for himself. He got a trade, though. In the Army."

"And your father?"

"Your grandpa? He was all right, I suppose. Liked his beer." She pushed her glass forward. "Could I . . .?"

Rachel ordered wine with the meal, a Cabernet Sauvignon. Her mother, who had finished the second gin, winced at the first dry sip, but bravely carried on drinking it as they talked of her childhood. It had been rough. Poverty, illness, a mother worn down by child-bearing. "So I was glad to get out. See the world, I thought, and never got further than sodding Germany. I was bonny then, you know. I always had nice hair."

She put up a beringed hand and fingered the crimped furrows. She was on to her third glass of wine and talking freely now. "Your dad was handsome." She leaned forward. "What's he like now? Grey?" She nodded as Rachel smiled in assent. "They used to call him Nigel 'cos he looked like Nigel Patrick." She saw Rachel's look of incomprehension and explained, "He was a film star. Ever so good-looking." She was maudlin now. "I believed every word he said, you know. Green! I'd know better today, lying sods the lot of them." She was reaching for the bottle, pouring wine so fast into her glass that one red drop sprang over the rim and made a rosy spot on the white cloth. "More?"

"No thank you."

Freda's eyes were brimming. "You've been all right, haven't you? You're happy, aren't you? He wanted me to get rid but I wouldn't. I was frightened but that wasn't the reason. I didn't believe in it. Besides, it was all back-street in those days. They said it was legal but you had to have reasons to get it done on the NHS. So it was still underhand." She shuddered. "You heard tales. Still, it turned out for the best. She was good, your mother. I couldn't say different. Always treated me like a lady." She drank deeply, wincing as she did so. "Could we have something else?" The bottle was empty by now.

"What would you like? Shall I order coffee?"

"Gin." Freda was looking at her almost fondly. "I can't get over how you've grown up. Rachel. I never liked that name. You wouldn't've got it from me. I would have picked something nice, something modern – Kim. I always liked Kim."

Rachel had attracted the waitress. "A gin and tonic and coffee please. A pot, if possible."

"Ta." Freda's voice was faintly slurred now, but her demeanour was still composed. "Tell me about yourself. You're not married? No kids, I hope."

"No kids. I have a partner. His name is Leigh and he works in television."

"TV!" Her mother's eyes widened in awe. "Fancy that." She shook her head in wonder. "TV, same as you.

Well, your father had talent. Doodling, he called it, but it was good. I might've known you'd be talented. Do you sing? He had a lovely voice, your father."

"Dad?" Rachel was incredulous. "He's got a voice like a corncrake."

"Ooh." Freda was suddenly agitated and a drop of gin dribbled down her chin. "Look at me. Messy faggot." She was rising to her feet and brushing feverishly at her jacket. "I'll have to go to the toilet. What goes in must come out, as they say."

The coffee came in her absence and, as she poured, Rachel thought over their conversation. Had she learned anything? Was she any further forward? She resolved to be more probing when the woman returned but her good intentions were in vain.

"I'll not have to linger over this," Freda said, as she raised her coffee cup.

"I thought you had till nine o'clock?"

"Did I say that? I meant now . . . well, in a minute or two. He gets edgy if I'm not back." She was drinking the gin and coffee alternately, in a fever to get away, and yet a moment ago she had looked as though she could spend all day there.

"You'd better ring for the cab," she said, and insisted on going out to the foyer to wait for it. There was a one-armed bandit there, and she fed it feverishly to no avail. "I hope you have better luck in life than me, chuck," she said, as they left the pub and, apart from a hurried thank-you for the meal as she fled to the cab, that was her last word.

Rachel called after her, "When can we meet again?" but she got no reply.

She did not look out at the moonlit hills as the cab took her back to the Tontine. All she wanted to do was make sense of her troubled thoughts. She had come all this way for what? To find out that her mother had a drink problem and her father had once possessed a vocal talent he had since lost? Apart from being tone deaf her father loathed pop music with a passion and, however hard she tried, she couldn't imagine him warbling Verdi to the young Freda.

The only moment at which she had felt in touch with any sort of maternal feeling in Freda was when her mother had asked her if she was happy. In that moment they had been close, and then somehow it had all gone wrong. She had asked about Leigh, been impressed that he worked in television. Surely it couldn't be that? She had been pleased about Leigh, her face had lit up. And then she had mentioned Dad singing . . . and choked on the gin, or pretended to choke on the gin, and the meeting had ground to a halt.

Rachel went to bed in the room with carnation-patterned wallpaper. But even as she tried to sleep, something was nibbling away at the edges of her mind. She kept seeing Freda Fielding's beringed hands, one reaching up to her chin to wipe an imaginary drop, the other brushing ineffectually at the lapels of her suit. Something threw her, Rachel thought. She didn't fumble her drink, something disconcerted her.

But what? What had they been talking about? Something had happened at that meeting, but what?

31

Rachel slept fitfully, dreaming of John Major, a clown's tear on his face as a grinning Tony Blair capered alongside and then she was looking at a document except that the words had melted into drawings, doodles, flowers, geometric shapes and faces . . . always faces.

At eight o'clock she rang the Northallerton number. "I have to see you," she said. "Today."

"I'm sorry, not today." Freda sounded fuddled and tired. Surely she didn't drink this early in the morning. Rachel was repeating her request for a meeting when she heard the click of a telephone extension.

"I'll have to go," Freda said. There was audible breathing on the line now, a third party.

"But I must see you. Today — now!"

"It's not her day off." The voice was faint but querulous. "Freda, it's not your day off. Tell them." There was a click as the receiver was replaced.

"See?" Freda was angry. "You'll get me sacked. You'll have to leave it. Next month. I get me holidays end of May—"

"I'm coming over." Rachel was resolute now. "I won't be long, but I'm coming over now." She cut off her mother's protestations by putting down the handset.

An hour and a taxi-ride later she was walking up the gravel drive. "Come in." Freda was composed now, or resigned. She led the way to the room they had used on Rachel's previous visit and they sat down. "I won't offer you a coffee. There won't be time." She didn't say "What do you want?" but her tone implied it.

"I need to know about you and Dad. Did you love him? How did you feel when you knew I was on the way? I need to know these things. I'm pregnant. I don't know whether or not I want this baby. Knowing how you felt is important to me."

Her mother was clicking her tongue against her teeth in a gesture of disgust. "Let yourself get caught, did you? I don't know why we always fall for it. Still, it's different now. No more back-streets. Will he pay for it?"

"It's not that easy. I haven't decided. And you haven't told me about you and Daddy."

Freda's gaze went to the clock on the mantelpiece. "There's no time to go into all that. His friends come today to play bridge. I don't want him giving them a tale about me neglecting him."

"Then tell me – tell me and I'll go."

Freda's eyes signalled rebellion, but then she gave way. "It was the old, old story. He had a roving eye, I was green.

I thought he'd marry me — he didn't say it, I just thought it. I went on leave. It was when I got back — but it's years ago now. Why don't you ask him?"

"Because my father is incapable of telling the truth," Rachel said bluntly. "He has this vision of himself as a decent chap. I need the truth, but even you have a fantasy view of him, saying he used to sing, that he could draw — doodle! My father's never doodled in his life and he can't sing for toffee!"

This time there was no mistaking Freda's agitation. "Don't keep on about your father. I worked in his office, I let him have it because he said he and your mam didn't get on. The old story but I swallowed it. I fell wrong, your mam stepped in and it's a great shame you ever found out." She stood up and crossed to the table where the gin stood.

"Why did you say he sang to you?" Rachel asked, as Freda poured.

"Don't go on about that. I was wrong. I got muddled up. For God's sake, it's thirty years, what the hell does it matter if he sang or not? I mixed them up, that's all."

"Mixed who up?" There was no answer and Rachel didn't need one. "There was someone else, wasn't there? Another man who sang — and you said — you thought—" She fell silent, horrified by her own thoughts.

Freda threw back the gin in one gulp and went to refill her glass. When she turned back to Rachel her shoulders drooped, then squared. "So I lied! I did all right for you, didn't I?"

There was a singing in Rachel's ears, a buzzing in her brain, that turned to total weakness. I will never be able

to get up from this chair, she thought, and realised it
didn't matter. She could stay there for ever, frozen in time
and space because that was better than thinking.

"Come on," Freda said, apologetic. "I did what I
thought was best. He might've been the father – he
couldn't argue – and I knew you'd be all right with them.
I did it for the best."

"Where is he?" Rachel asked, her voice seeming to
come from a long way off.

"Your dad – your real dad? He's dead. He died a long
time ago."

"Did he . . . did you . . ." Where did she begin?

"Did he know about you? I couldn't tell him. Well, it
wouldn't've been easy." She drained her glass again and
put it down. "Look, you'll have to go. He knows
something's up and he's got a nasty tongue on him when it
suits. There were things about your dad—"

"What was his name?"

"Billy. Billy Dixon. He was an ordinary serviceman."

"In my father's regiment?" Why did that matter? Why
was she asking pointless questions?

"No. I didn't meet him in Germany. He was the lad
next door, joined up same time as me. We met when we
were on leave, it was never . . . Well, it might have been
something one day."

She was opening a drawer, extracting a battered box
that had once held chocolates. The lid was padded and
beribboned with a picture of a kitten, ears a-prick. "It's
all in here. Take it."

She was holding out the box and, with the other hand,

taking Rachel's elbow to raise her from the chair.

"I don't know why I kept it all. It's matterless now and I wish to God you hadn't found out. But I did keep it and it's no use to me so you might as well have it. I'd get rid of it, if I was you, but that's not my business."

They were out in the hall now, and Rachel allowed herself to be led past the oak hallstand with its array of tweed hats and horn-handled walking-sticks. Freda indicated them with one hand. "He never uses them now but he won't have them moved. More than my job's worth to touch them."

She looked at the beribboned box. "That's as much as I know," she said, as she opened the door. "Everything's in there. There's nothing else." And then Rachel was over the step, the box clutched in both hands. "I hope everything goes all right," Freda said. "But don't come back. I've got expectations here. I can't afford to spoil them."

Rachel walked for a while, attempting neither to open the box nor to wipe away the tears that streamed down her face. She might have gone on walking if a phone-box had not loomed. Five minutes later she was in a taxi and speeding back to the hotel.

In her bedroom she opened the box. There was a card on top, lace-edged and bearing a red satin heart. "Guess who?" was written inside. She laid it aside and picked up a yellowing newspaper cutting. "Army Apologises for Fatal Accident." She looked at the date. September 1968. Six months before she was born. She read on.

*

An Army spokesman today apologised to villagers in Porling whose houses were evacuated after a petrol tanker crashed into an Army vehicle in the village's main street. Two Army personnel were killed in the vehicle, which Army sources say had been taken without permission. The dead soldiers were Private Anthony Head aged twenty-three and Private William Dixon, aged twenty-one.

There were other things in the box, letters, cuttings, a yellowing official paper, photographs, but Rachel sat holding the cutting. So Billy and Freda had conceived a child and Billy had died, joyriding in a stolen jeep. And Philip Trewhitt, who had reason to believe he might be the father, had been told he was. And the rest was history.

She started to laugh then, spluttering tears of hysteria that caused her mascara to run so that, when she wiped her eyes, her fingers grew black. She stood up and regarded herself in the mirror, seeing the face that had once been Rachel Trewhitt, daughter of Philip and Dodo, and was now Rachel, offspring of God knows whom.

32

London, Tuesday, 29 April 1997

The flat had a faintly musty smell. It reached Rachel's nostrils as soon as she opened the door. No one had opened the windows, dusted or vacuumed in the last few days. We're hardly living here now, Rachel thought. Both of us are ricocheting around like balls in a pin-ball machine.

The thought depressed her and she went into the bedroom. It was strewn with cast-off clothes and underwear, but she resisted the impulse to pick them up. Let him do his own tidying!

She lowered her bag to the floor and sat down on the edge of the bed, reviewing the way in which her life had disintegrated since that day in Paris. When had it been? Three weeks ago? Four? A short while in terms of a lifetime but long enough for a revolution.

She had believed herself of good family, certainly loved by that family and by her partner. Now, how could she be sure of anything? Had Vanessa and Liz really loved *her* all these years or simply accepted a cuckoo in the nest? As for the pair she had supposed to be her parents, how long would their affection last now that the truth was about to be revealed? But even as she thought it, she realised she was being unfair to Dodo – to her mother, whose loyalty was infinite.

As for Leigh, anger was replacing anxiety now. He wanted things to run smoothly. Nothing, not even a new life, must disrupt his routine. But this baby was all she had, the only relationship she could rely on now, for there was no rapport between her and Freda and she doubted it would grow with time.

But could you live without him? Dodo's words came back to haunt her. Could she exist in a lonely flat with only a baby for company?

Almost instinctively she reached into her bag and took out Freda's box. Was this what her making had come down to, a box of yellowing cuttings and photographs curling at the edges? She picked out a letter. "Dear Fred," it began. She turned it over and saw the signature "Yours, Billy". So Fred was Freda and this was a love-letter. She read on. "Dear Fred, hoping this finds you better than it finds me. I've had a spot of bother and am on jankers for a week. It was good last weekend, wasn't it? I told Mam about us before I left. She huffed and puffed a bit but she'll come round."

They were close, Rachel thought, unable to read on. One day she would explore the box, learn everything she could about her beginnings but it was too painful now. She longed to know but was afraid to find out.

Instead, she let herself out of the flat and tiptoed past Jago's door. At this moment she did not want to see even his dear, familiar face. She walked through the streets, seeing the burgeoning gardens, sensing spring all around her, trying to tell herself that by summer all would be well. A couple were sitting outside the pub on the corner, either side of the table, gazing into one another's eyes, oblivious of the nip in the air because they were in love. Rachel walked past them into the cool, empty interior and ordered a drink. But even as she began to sip she knew that this was not where she wanted to be.

She pushed away the spritzer and walked out into the sunshine. A news-stand caught her eye. "Major's Bitter Attack on Blair," said the poster. She felt a surge of sympathy for an embattled John Major. It was a pity the rest of his party had not measured up to him.

She took a cab back to the flat, but going home was the last thing she wanted to do. This had been Leigh's flat originally; now she felt an interloper there. When she was a child she had always run home. When the bee stung, the frost nipped, the best friend became the enemy. "You're home now," her mother would say, and draw her into the warm. But there was nowhere to run to now, nowhere where she belonged. She could go downstairs to Jago but what could he do? If she phoned Tom it would help, but it wasn't fair to foist her problems on him, and she couldn't phone her mother without the risk of letting slip something that might be better kept secret. She took off her jacket almost automatically, then pulled her sweater over her head. Her hair felt stiff with lacquer. That was what she could do, wash her hair.

She was about to step into the shower when she heard the door open and close. "Leigh?"

He heard her call and returned it. "Only me."

"I won't be long." She stepped into the shower and closed the door.

He came upon her in the shower, slipping behind her, holding his face to the flow and shaking it like a seal. "I love you, Rachel." His hands were on her breasts now, slipping on the soap, gripping, hurting. She moaned a little and his hands fell away.

She turned then, her face seeking his neck, feeling the tension in him and then the sudden withdrawal. "It's all right," she said. "I'm all right." Her back was against the smooth wall of the shower and then he was within her, urgent, thrusting. She put up her mouth, too late remembering her unbrushed teeth. It seemed not to matter, their mouths devouring one another.

"*Is* it all right?" She could sense the sudden hesitation as he remembered the abortion.

He doesn't like it, she thought. He doesn't like the idea. She urged him on, kneading and pummelling his back, arching her body until they were panting in unison and he was suddenly spent. He touched her then, fiercely and swiftly until she sagged against him and they were both sober and turned to the business of getting clean.

Later, they drank tea and coffee in the kitchen. The radio burbled away, drowning conversation. According to one report, the jail population had broken the sixty thousand barrier but Leigh's eyes were gleaming at a report of yet another outburst by Jimmy Goldsmith against the Tories. "He's really gunning for them now," he said. "He's doomed but he's magnificent."

He left the kitchen to get dressed, and returned complete with box-file and briefcase. "Don't wait up tonight," he said. "I know it's crazy but it's not for much longer. One more day to zero and two for the post-mortem and I'm off the hook."

"You've done well," she said.

"Yes," he said simply. "I've done myself no harm."

She would have kissed him then and let him go but he turned towards her.

"Don't think I'm not grateful," he said. "I know what it meant to you, doing that for me."

Rachel felt her shoulders sag. This was the Rubicon, the moment when the lying had to stop. "I didn't have the abortion, Leigh. I'm still pregnant."

She had a sudden crazy desire to laugh at the way his face seemed to disintegrate. His eyes widening, popping, his mouth opening and closing like a fish. "You're joking," he said, and moved like a drunk to ease himself into a chair at the table.

"I don't believe you've done this," he said. "I don't believe you could be so cruel. You mean you lied to me, deliberately set up a sordid little pretence of agreeing——"

"No," she interrupted. "It was never deliberate, not even a lie in the beginning. I did arrange it. I was admitted to the clinic. I couldn't go through with it. I ran away."

"But you lied to me!"

"I didn't. You came home, you assumed. I wanted to tell

you. It was just easier not to. Besides, I wasn't even sure I wouldn't go back — not to that place but there are others." She didn't mention Tom's offer to find somewhere more compassionate. That was better kept to herself. Besides, she had seen hope spring up in Leigh's eyes, and the iron had entered into her soul.

"So you will arrange something?"

"I don't know. I'm thinking about it."

"For God's sake . . ." He was trying to sound con-ciliatory. "What is there to think about, Rachel? Get it over!" And when she opened her mouth to protest. "It's no good, Rachel. I have to be strong for both of us. This is crazy. We're neither of us ready for parenthood. Soon, but not yet." And then, as she didn't speak, "Please, Rachel. Let's get it over and get on with our lives."

"Do you love me?" she asked.

"You know I do. Do you love me, that's the question?" She knew what he meant. If she loved him she would surely abort this baby that was causing him such concern.

"Oh, I love you," she said. "But I can't love you without hating you and I can't hate you without loving you. It's a mess, isn't it?"

"What do you mean by that?" he said irritably, standing up. "That's just meaningless mumbo-jumbo. You're giving way to emotion, Rachel, and it's interfering with rational thought. Look . . ." He moved forward and took her in his arms. "I love you. No caveat. I love you. I could never hate you."

She looked up into his face and smiled. "You're a shit, Leigh," she said.

He let her go. "We can't talk now. I'll try to get back tonight but I can't promise." He turned at the door. "It's up to you . . . but I hope you know you'll be on your own. I'll pay but I won't take responsibility. Children weren't part of the bargain. I thought you knew that."

He was looking at her, expecting an answer, but she was remembering something her mother had said about paying the price for love. What Leigh was suggesting was a straightforward transaction. If she wanted to keep him, there was a price to pay.

"Look . . ." He was moving away. "I wish you'd left this until the election is over. You know how important it is that I perform well. Let it go until the weekend – it's only two more days." And then, when she didn't answer, "I've got to go."

33

London, Wednesday, 30 April 1997

She had sat up all night in an empty flat, huddled in her chair, still in her dressing gown, incapable even of movement. Half of her felt there was no point in doing anything until Leigh came home, until she had his arms around her and could return to some semblance of now and reality. The other half doubted he would offer comfort even if he came, and she wasn't even sure that she wanted him.

At midnight, when her eyes burned in their sockets, she dragged herself out of the chair and went to bed, discarding her robe as she went, creeping between the sheets praying only for sleep.

It came at last, but it was fitful and filled with uneasy dreams. In one she dreamed of an England struck by some unmentionable disease that would only be eliminated by burning down every house, complete with contents. She stood with others on an open plain, watching everything

Denise Robertson

they cared for burn to the ground. When she woke in the early morning she was weeping.

She went to the shower then, hoping to feel the grime and despair of yesterday slip away. It was a relief to lather face and body, massage shampoo into her hair and then turn the shower to full force. She stood under it for a long time, hoping for a miracle. When she stepped out she was clean but still despairing.

She had made tea and buttered toast when she noticed the light on the answerphone. It had not been there yesterday and no one had rung today. Unless it had been while she was in the shower, giving herself up to the water. She pressed the button and heard Leigh's voice, a little weary but as confident as ever. "We were both overwrought earlier on. I'm sorry. I'll get home when I can. Edwina's shot her mouth off again — says there'll be a bloodbath in the Tory Party after May the first. She must be Labour's biggest asset at the moment, not that they need assets. The Conservatives seem to have a death-wish. I'll get home as soon as I can," he finished, and the message ended.

Her mother rang as she was dressing. "How did it go?"

"Fine." She must decide when to tell, but it wasn't now.

"You don't sound fine."

"It depressed me, Mum. If I'm truthful it was very depressing. She's sad and she drinks and that's about it. But we'll talk when I come home."

"All right." As usual, her mother was thinking more of her than herself. "Have you thought any more about the baby?"

306

"Not really. Not yet. But I will."

"Don't leave it too late. And remember, we're here for you."

"I know." Rachel said. "And I love you very much."

She was crying as she dialled Tom's number. It was eight thirty. He might not have left for the surgery yet. "Please let him be in," she prayed. And then he was there, at the other end of the line, and relief flooded over her.

He listened without interruption until she had finished her tale. "Look," he said, as her words dried up, "this is a mess but it's no more of a mess now than it ever was, last week, last year, last decade. You are now what you were then. Facts may be different, details, but you are what you always were. Hang on to that!"

"I'll try," she said, but her voice was woebegone and she heard him chuckle gently at the other end of the line.

"It'll pass, Rachel. I can't promise much but I can promise that. Everything passes, and people cope until it does. Look around you. The world is not littered with life's casualties." There was another, louder chuckle. "God, I sound like Patience Strong. But remember, I'm here, platitudes and all. I'll help you, whatever you decide. Or perhaps you have decided?"

She felt panic then, an overwhelming feeling of inadequacy. How could she argue with Leigh for her decision when she couldn't make one?

When the call was finished she curled up in a chair, the box Freda had given her on the coffee table in front of her. There was another cutting there, a report on the inquest into the two soldiers' deaths. The verdict was "misadventure", the coroner's summing up a savage indictment of service personnel who misbehaved.

There was a photo of William Dixon too, unbelievably young and earnest in uniform. Rachel looked at it for a long time. It was a pleasant enough face but still the face of a child. And that child had fathered her before his life was snuffed out in an overturned jeep in a village street. She might have shed a tear for William Dixon and his lost future, until she remembered Freda. She had been young and alive too but surviving had not brought her much in the way of fulfilment. Only me, she thought. I am all that is left of them.

She cried then, for both of them but mostly for herself and for the life within her that might, or might not, have a future. Perhaps the kindest thing she could do for it was consign it to eternity now, before anything had a chance to hurt it.

From there it was a short step to that other question. If Freda had aborted her, would it have been a waste or a solution? "I don't know," she said aloud. "God help me, I don't know."

There were other photos in the box, men and women, children, faces who might or might not be her kin. She turned them over, hoping for information, but there was nothing except a photographer's number.

One of them was of a girl in a polka-dot dress, sitting on a fence, her plump but well-shaped legs ending in high-heeled shoes of which she was obviously proud for she seemed to be thrusting them into view.

She was smiling up at the photographer from

underneath a wing of hair. Someone had said that Freda's hair fell like that — Vanessa or her mother. She peered closely at the laughing face. So this had been Freda Fielding before life, in the shape of Philip Trewhitt and William Dixon, had intervened.

A vision of Freda's agitated, work-roughened, beringed hands came into Rachel's mind. What carnage men caused in their passage through life! And women too! There was no difference.

Suddenly she saw her bag, only half unpacked, standing in the corner of the bedroom, her passport still in the outer pocket — she had forgotten to take it out when they got back from Paris.

It took only seconds to make up her mind. After that her actions were frenzied, driven by a terror that someone, anyone, might arrive and stop her escape. She needed to get away, to think, to make up her mind. After that she would face Leigh, for face him she must.

She didn't draw an easy breath until she was aboard a flight, fastening her seat-belt, hearing the engine rev as the plane began to taxi down the runway and darkness fell. She closed her eyes as they were airborne. She was safe from harassment now, at least for the next few hours.

When she opened her eyes the fairground lights of the runway were receding, red, blue and green, and then London was glittering down below like a brilliant piece of costume jewellery.

34

Paris, Thursday, 1 May 1997

Rachel was awake at dawn, sitting at the window to see and hear life filtering back into the Paris streets. The cab driver had found this hotel for her, set in a narrow street leading up from the boulevard de Clichy to Montmartre. It was the first day of May. In Britain people would be waking to the election, the result a foregone conclusion because what they wanted was anything but what they had.

Down below she saw a slender woman, bent almost double under the weight of a sleeping baby as she tottered up the street in high heels. A few moments later she reappeared, straight-backed now that she was free of her burden, intent on getting somewhere, probably to work.

If she went ahead with her pregnancy, and if Leigh carried out his threat, she, too, would be a single mother. If she took up Nick's offer she would have to work like a dog. What would she do with the baby then? Jago? The baby would adore him but he worked too. And would he want to care for a child? A small child. Rachel put a hand to her belly, imagining the tiny life beating there. No face as yet, no limbs even . . . It helped to think only of a single cell. And yet limbs came early, she knew that from somewhere.

She could always freelance, work when and where it was possible. Could she manage without Leigh? And, more important, could she live without him? Did she want a life if he was not part of it? She had a sudden sense of him there, with her, his hands in her hair, on her neck, cupping her breasts, sliding down to bring her alive. She let out a moan of arousal that turned into a whimper and brought her to her feet. The least she could do was tell him where she was and that she was safe.

There was no answer from the flat. She checked her watch. Seven thirty here, so it was six thirty in London. If he had slept at home last night he should still be there. Too early to ring Jago and there was no one else to call.

The sense of her own isolation swept over her. No one else could decide for her, no one else would have to take responsibility. She was alone. She took the key to the mini-bar and poured herself a whisky. She seldom if ever drank whisky and the raw spirit caught at her throat, made her gasp, but she went on drinking in spite of it, sitting on the side of the bed, drinking as though it was medicine she was taking and must be got down.

When the glass was empty she looked at it, wondering if it was a sign that she had reached a decision. Pregnant women should not drink. She was drinking. Therefore she had renounced pregnancy. She would get through today somehow and then go back to London. The election would be over, Leigh's working life would be back on an even keel, she would do what must be done and they could be happy again. All that would be lost was a cell and in the fullness of time there would be other children, to be loved and cherished and cement the bond between the two who gave them life.

She took the glass back to the window. She felt calmer, whether from decision or alcohol she could not tell. There were more people in the street now and most of them appeared to be carrying flowers, small white flowers in pots or carefully wrapped cones of paper. Stephanotis, perhaps, or freesia . . . but what for? They couldn't all be wedding guests.

Her breakfast came at eight o'clock, as ordered, redolent of fresh-brewed coffee and steaming croissants, she should have asked for tea, but strangely, now, the smell of coffee did not make her retch. "Excusez-moi," she began, summing up her schoolgirl French. "Les gens dans la rue, ils portent les fleurs, toutes les gens, ils ont les fleurs blanche. Pourquoi?"

The maid looked puzzled and then her face cleared. "Ah, le muguet. Le muguet de bois, n'est-ce pas? C'est la fête du travail . . ." She saw the look of incomprehension on Rachel's face and smiled.

"I'm sorry," Rachel said. "I know *muguet de bois* — that's lily-of-the-valley. Of course that's what they are — but why?"

To her relief the maid replied in slow but

understandable English. "In France the *muguet* is a good-luck charm, for spring, for new life, for the bad times of winter, which is over. It is — we give it for good luck. To friends, especially to parents. Everyone does it, even the children." Now her smile became a grin. "There is no law against street selling in *la rue publique* on the first day of May. It is *la fête du travail*, what you call Labour Day."

"Of course," Rachel said. "I'd forgotten that. We're having an election in Britain today. I'd forgotten it was Labour Day."

The maid's eyes rolled to heaven and she pulled a face. "Elections — *pouf!* No good. There is a big parade today, the FLN — the National Front—" She shook her head. "Pas bon."

"I know of your National Front," Rachel said. "And Jean-Marie Le Pen."

Again a rolling of the eyes. "Le Pen — that comedian!" She sighed. "Ah well, *bon appetit*, Madame," and she left. But not before she had wrinkled her nose, suddenly scenting whisky. Her expression said it all. "Les Anglais!"

The mention of Le Pen set Rachel counting. How long since she had lain in Leigh's arms in a different Paris hotel and talked of Le Pen? That day she had sat under the falling horse chestnut blossom and thought ahead to the wedding, to going home to be cosseted. And now . . .

She felt better when she had finished her breakfast and the thought of another drink was a temptation she put behind her. If she was staying here until tomorrow she couldn't sit and drink all day. She must get out.

She took a cab to Pigalle and walked up the rue Lepic to

the rue des Abbesses. She felt strangely tired, her legs weak and heavier with each step. She sat down outside a small, dark café and ordered coffee. "Et un Cognac, s'il vous plaît," she added on impulse. The coffee was sweet and strong, the brandy even stronger. When at last she got to her feet she did not feel refreshed, only determined. She kept on climbing, glimpsing the white dome of the basilica of the Sacre Coeur, losing it behind buildings, triumphant when once more it came into view.

As always, scores of others were making the pilgrimage, many of them carrying lily-of-the-valley or wearing it on their lapel. She reached the funicular, climbed aboard, and then she was out in the open air, the huge white bulk of the church behind her, Utrillo's Paris in front, falling away to the misty beauty of the city beyond.

Utrillo . . . Suddenly she remembered the picture she had seen in the gallery. The painting by Suzanne Valadon, mother of Utrillo, the most hopeless drunk in French art, bastard son of a mother herself a bastard. It would have been better if he had never been born . . . and yet he had created pictures so distinctive you did not need the signature to recognise the artist.

What was that poem about sperm? She struggled to remember. "A million million spermatazoa launched into the world alive . . ." then something about only one of them taking ark in the female egg. Conception was a one-in-a-million thing. Unique. And, as the poem had said, the one could be a Homer, a John Donne . . . or a latch-key kid, receiving only the fag end of a mother's attention. Rachel made a vow not to get sentimental and went into the dark cool of the church to sit and gather strength.

When she left, she caught the Métro at Abbesses and travelled to Concorde, emerging into the sunlight of the rue de Rivoli, intent on going to see the irises in the Tuileries gardens. They must have bloomed by now. Her head was aching and her mouth was dry.

It was then that she saw the National Front march coming towards her, stretching the width of the wide street, men and women carrying placards and shouting slogans, marshalled by sinister men with badges on their lapels. But what startled her was that several of the marchers were black and they were shouting as vociferously as the rest, "France for the French", if she had translated correctly.

She looked around her. Passers-by seemed indifferent. One or two tourists used their cameras and snapped away but they were the exception. Where were the protesters, the hecklers, the anti-Fascists? And yet the very absence of protest seemed to render the march impotent. Perhaps that was the way to deal with Fascism, treat it with indifference. "Dangerous, dangerous," said the voice in her head. "Remember Germany."

She stood as the long march wound past, then glimpsed a bistro across the road. When at last the marching column was gone the gendarmerie came, huddled in vehicles, laughing and joking, obviously seeing this as an easy shift. And after the police the street-cleaners, brushing and hosing as though to tidy away the last morsel of nationalism. Then the street was clear and clean, as though the march had never happened.

Rachel crossed over and walked along, past ordinary people peddling a half-dozen containers of *muguet de bois*. Ten francs seemed a popular price for a spray, more for a pot. She could smell it now, scenting the Parisian air. She smiled ruefully to herself as she ordered a coffee. Would she ever forget this strange day, marchers and *muguet* and misery all bound now into an alcoholic haze? She looked at her watch. Not yet noon. Where could she go? She had meant to sit in the gardens and contemplate the irises but that wouldn't occupy a whole day.

She contemplated turning tail and running for home, but that wouldn't do. She knew how Leigh would be once the election was over and he was left with an excess of adrenaline churning inside him. Better keep out of his way until he calmed down. She could go back to the hotel and sleep, but that would mean she wouldn't be able to sleep tonight in the long, dark, lonely hours that brought you to despair, if you faced them alone.

She had seen a cinema advertising *The English Patient*, which everyone said was wonderful but sad. Or she could go for a meal somewhere, the place in Montparnasse where they had eaten oysters, or somewhere even ritzier and more time-consuming. She had her plastic.

She was about to get to her feet and make a move somewhere, anywhere, when she remembered something Jago had suggested before they came to Paris on the Jean Le Pen assignment. "Don't miss the Musée Grevin," he had said. He had mentioned its whereabouts too but she couldn't remember what he had said. He had described it as an amazing place. "It'll curl your hair!"!

She sat down again, her legs shaky. A waiter hovered and she ordered a *café filtre* and a glass of wine. She would drink the wine as they brewed the coffee, which would sober her up. Then she could go.

When the waiter returned she let him slip the bill under the saucer and smiled at him. "Excusez-moi, Monsieur. La Musée Grevin?"

"Ah, oui, mademoiselle. English?"

She nodded and he burst forth in accented but impeccable English. "Musée Grevin is an incredible place – waxworks, the mirrors . . ." He sought for a word. "*Fantastique* . . . Big, slim—"

"Distorting?" she said, and smiled at his relief.

"*Oui*, distorting mirrors, magic, history, everything! Not cheap, you understand, but amazing."

"Where is it?"

"Boulevard Montmartre. Take the Métro to rue Montmartre."

When she paid, she left a handsome tip, then walked in search of the Métro. She felt giddy now. Too much alcohol, too little food. She saw a café selling crusty rolls crammed with different fillings, but her stomach churned at the sight and everywhere there was the scent of lily-of-the-valley.

On the train she tried to compose herself. She was only a little drunk. It took two hours for the body to deal with a unit of alcohol. How many units in a whisky, a cognac and a glass of wine? "Never mix your drinks." She should have remembered that.

She was sweating now and she felt a strange urge to giggle, to smile at strangers. And then her station loomed up. She negotiated the exit and the boulevard Montmartre lay before her.

She found the Musée Grevin with help from passers-by. Not a significant entrance but inside it was different. A sign: "Palais des Mirages. Au fond du couloir". Mirrors and red plush everywhere, so that her face appeared and reappeared ghost-like and pale. There were shiny green walls and lattices, balconies and stairways. She saw a seated figure, a middle-aged man soberly dressed opposite a group — she recognised Margaret Thatcher, François Mitterand, Helmut Kohl and Mikhail Gorbachev, lifelike and imposing, and then, with a shock, saw that the sober onlooker was wax too.

She looked around, suddenly anxious to see a real figure, a friendly face. There was a magnificent Negro woman, obviously wax, with a shaven head and one huge privateer's earring. And then the large mouth broke into a smile and Rachel realised she was not wax but flesh. Faces loomed, Raquel Welch, Rudolf Nureyev, looking like a man in the throes of crucifixion. Here Salvador Dali, there Yehudi Menuhin, wax all of them. So was the so-real man in the Homburg seated on a bench, and the fat man with a mobile phone should have been wax but was all at once alive.

What is real? she thought, and felt her senses slipping away. Was she drunk or was this place a vortex, sucking in unwary travellers? She felt tears on her cheeks and then she was descending a stair and there was sighing and groaning from barred cells. Gloating faces looking down at an imprisoned child. The Dauphin. And suddenly Michael Jackson, ten times larger than life.

Rachel turned, looking for the stairs. Must get up towards the light before it is too late. A voice was booming, urging *mesdames et messieurs* to go upstairs, and she was being carried along on a tidal wave of Spanish, American, Japanese humanity, up the marble balustraded staircase like guests ascending to a ball.

But it was not a ball to which they were going. They were moving, lemming-like, towards the Palais des Mirages, a polygonal room mirrored from floor to ceiling, accentuating the polyglot crowd. The lights went down and she screamed as she saw the door closing behind her. And then she was falling, falling through hands that were reaching out, down, down into infinity.

They took her from the mirrored room, into a corridor and then another, she all the while protesting that nothing was wrong. In the end they gave a Gallic shrug, took her down a staircase into an alley and abandoned her. "*Merci*," she said. "*Merci*," and held her breath until the door closed and she was alone.

She went forward then, stumbling, reeling, crying because she was drunk and alone and frightened and nothing was real any more, in this or any other part of her life.

An arcade opened up before her, deserted today, boutiques and stalls closed because it was Labour Day, only one café open and that devoid of patrons. She sat down on a flimsy chair and put her head in her hands, but her brain only whirled the faster and she felt bile in her throat.

"Madame." The proprietor was swarthy, heavily built and kind. Algerian probably or a Turk. He looked at her tearstained face, took in her disarray and turned on his heel. A moment later he was back with a small cup of black coffee, hot and sweet. She fumbled in her bag but he held up an admonitory hand and then, with a smile, he took the sprig of *muguet de bois* from his lapel and handed it to her. "*Bonne chance*, Madame," he said, and went back into the dark recesses of his establishment.

The little flowers were bell-like, fragile but perfect, and their perfume was overwhelming. She held them to her face and scented spring. What had the maid said? The coming of spring and the end of winter.

He came again with more coffee and she drank it gratefully, but it was his kindness that lent her strength rather than the coffee. This time she did not offer money. She held out her hand instead and let him raise it to his lips.

On the boulevard she flagged down a taxi and gave the address of her hotel. There was a flight out of Charles de Gaulle at seven fifteen. If she hurried she might make it, for now she knew that she wanted to go home.

She checked her bags at the airport and then went in search of a telephone. "Tom?" she said, when the ringing tone ceased. "Are you alone?"

"Yes," he said. "Where are you?"

"Never mind — I'm in Paris — just answer a question.

I've been stupid, selfish, I got drunk. Whisky, brandy, wine – will it have harmed the baby?" And then she knew that she had made up her mind, even before she heard Tom's chuckle.

"So you've decided," he said. "Good. I don't expect you've done any harm – foetal alcohol syndrome doesn't follow one binge – but get back here as quick as you can and we'll make sure."

She had pinned the *muguet* in her lapel in the Paris café. Now she unpinned it and wrapped the stems in wet tissue from the cloakroom. If she took care of it she might be able to keep it for a while, even preserve it. So many problems still to solve, not least when to tell the whole truth and to whom. If she told it all, and she felt she should, her father who-was-not-her-father might slide out from under a misplaced obligation. And Dodo, the mother who had never been her mother, would she be steadfast? Rachel was besieged with doubt, until she remembered that moment in the kitchen, the ticking of the clock and her mother's voice: "Nothing could come between us, Rachel. You are so dear to me I sometimes fear I love you more than the others." She picked up the receiver and dialled.

"Mum?"

"Rachel! Where are you? I've been ringing the flat – I was worried."

"I'm in Paris, Mum." Around her, the airport seethed and she put a finger in her ear to close out the noise.

"Paris? What are you doing there?"

"I'll tell you later. I'm OK. But, Mum, there's

something I must tell you." Get it out! Get it over before fear overtook her! "I talked to Freda – she told me – I don't know how to tell you, Mummy!" The old word came out, the childhood plea for help.

"What is it, darling? You can tell me."

And suddenly she could. "Dad isn't my father. Freda lied. She wanted you to have me so she blamed Dad. But my father was someone called Billy Dixon."

At the other end of the line there was a silence that seemed to go on for ever. And then the calm voice, unchanged. "I think I knew, darling. Somewhere inside. But it doesn't matter, Rachel. You are my dear, dear child."

"I'm keeping the baby, Mum. And I want to come home. To Yorkshire. Until I can see the way ahead." She didn't mention Tom but his face was there, in her thoughts.

"Where else would you go, silly? Come as quick as you can."

As she entered the departure lounge, Rachel was smiling.

They gave her a paper on the plane. A banner headline was proclaiming Tory doom and there was a quote from Jimmy Goldsmith to accompany it. "They are gone. They have committed suicide. The policies they adopted are abhorrent to those who normally vote for them."

By tomorrow the Tories would be gone and Labour would be finding out what it was like to be the tormented instead of the tormentors. But politics did not concern her. Not now. She thought of Leigh, rushing around drunk with election fever for all the world as though he was a candidate.

They had been happy once. Deliriously happy. Except that they had been in love rather than loving. That was the difference. She would always remember him, but it was passion she would remember rather than tenderness, excitement rather than fulfilment. For one second, no more, she wondered if she really wanted his baby. But it was only for a second. It was not Leigh's baby or hers. It was *a* baby, an individual, already growing, striving, struggling towards a life that would sometimes be good and sometimes bad but would never be boring. She slept then, only waking when the plane was about to land.

The taxi that was carrying her back to the flat stopped at traffic lights. There was an electrical store on the corner and Leigh was there, in the window, on a television screen, engaged in conversation with someone, presumably a politician.

He was urbane and smiling as he questioned, frowning in a charmingly intent way as he listened. He's good at his job, Rachel thought. He should do well. Just as she would do well without him . . . for her baby's sake.

POCKET
B O O K S

THE BELOVED PEOPLE

Denise Robertson

In the Durham mining village of Belgate, the legacy of World War I has far-reaching consequences for rich and poor, socialist and aristocracy, Jew and gentile alike.

HOWARD BRENTON, heir to the colliery, back from the trenches with a social conscience, but robbed of the confidence to implement it.
DIANA, his beautiful, aristocratic wife, afraid of her dour new world and fatally drawn to the jazzy gaiety of twenties London.
Miner FRANK MAGUIRE and his bitter wife ANNE, are fired by union fervour as they struggle to survive the slump.
ESTHER GULLIVER, to whom kindly Emmanuel Lansky shows new roads to prosperity beyond the pit.

PRICE £5.99

ISBN 0 671 01609 1

POCKET
B O O K S

TOWARDS JERUSALEM

Denise Robertson

Peace may have come to Britain, but for Frank
Maguire, his wife Anne and their family, poverty
and rationing are still making life hard.

To add to Anne's sorrow, her daughter, Stella is
taking Anne's grandchild to the United States,
leaving her with a grieving heart and a guilty
secret. Esther, Anne's sister, is to marry Howard
Brenton, former mine owner and Conservative
MP for Belgate. Looking towards the future,
Esther and her business partner Sammy Lansky
are about to change the face of the retail trade.

From the dawning of post-war optimism to the
peace, prosperity and political scandals of the
sixties, together the Brentons, Maguires and
Lanskys are building the future and heading
towards Jerusalem.

PRICE £5.99

ISBN 0 671 01610 5

POCKET
BOOKS

STRENGTH FOR THE MORNING

Denise Robertson

It is 1939 and the threat of war looms ever closer as Hitler unleashes terror across Europe. In the Durham mining village of Belgate the inhabitants brace themselves for the conflict ahead.

While Howard Brenton, conservative MP and colliery owner, attempts to pacify the miners, his beautiful wife Diana succumbs to the lover who once abandoned her. Meanwhile, Frank Maguire, chairman of the miners' union, and his wife Anne struggle to make ends meet. And, as the Lansky family copes with the arrival of two Jewish refugees from Germany, Sammy Lansky enlists, leaving the care of his thriving business to the increasingly sophisticated Esther Gulliver.

PRICE £5.99

ISBN 0 671 01611 3

POCKET
B O O K S

This book and other **Denise Robertson** titles are available from your
book shop or can be ordered direct from the publisher.

☐ 0 671 01609 1 **THE BELOVED PEOPLE**   £5.99
☐ 0 671 01611 3 **STRENGTH FOR THE MORNING**   £5.99
☐ 0 671 01610 5 **TOWARDS JERUSALEM**   £5.99
☐ 0 671 01018 2 **WAIT FOR THE DAY**   £5.99
☐ 0 671 85263 9 **DAYBREAK**   £5.99
☐ 0 671 85262 0 **ACT OF OBLIVION**   £5.99

Please send cheque or postal order for the value of the book, and add the
following for postage and packing: UK inc. BFPO 75p per book; OVER-
SEAS inc. EIRE £1 per book.
OR: Please debit this amount from my:

VISA/ACCESS/MASTERCARD ....
CARD NO...
EXPIRY DATE..
AMOUNT £..
NAME..
ADDRESS...
....

SIGNATURE...

Send orders to:
Simon & Schuster Cash Sales
PO Box 29, Douglas, Isle of Man, IM99 1BQ
Tel: 01624 675137, Fax 01624 670923
http://www.bookpost.co.uk
e-mail: bookshop@enterprise.net for details
Please allow 28 days for delivery.
Prices and availability subject to change without notice.